DIX

Elite 8 Studios Book 1

Emmy Sanders

Beta Reading by C.J. Banks, Georgia Johnson, Lauren, and Mary Ellen

Editing by LesCourt Author Services

Proofreading by Ky

Cover Design by Natasha Snow Designs

ISBN: 9781967130009

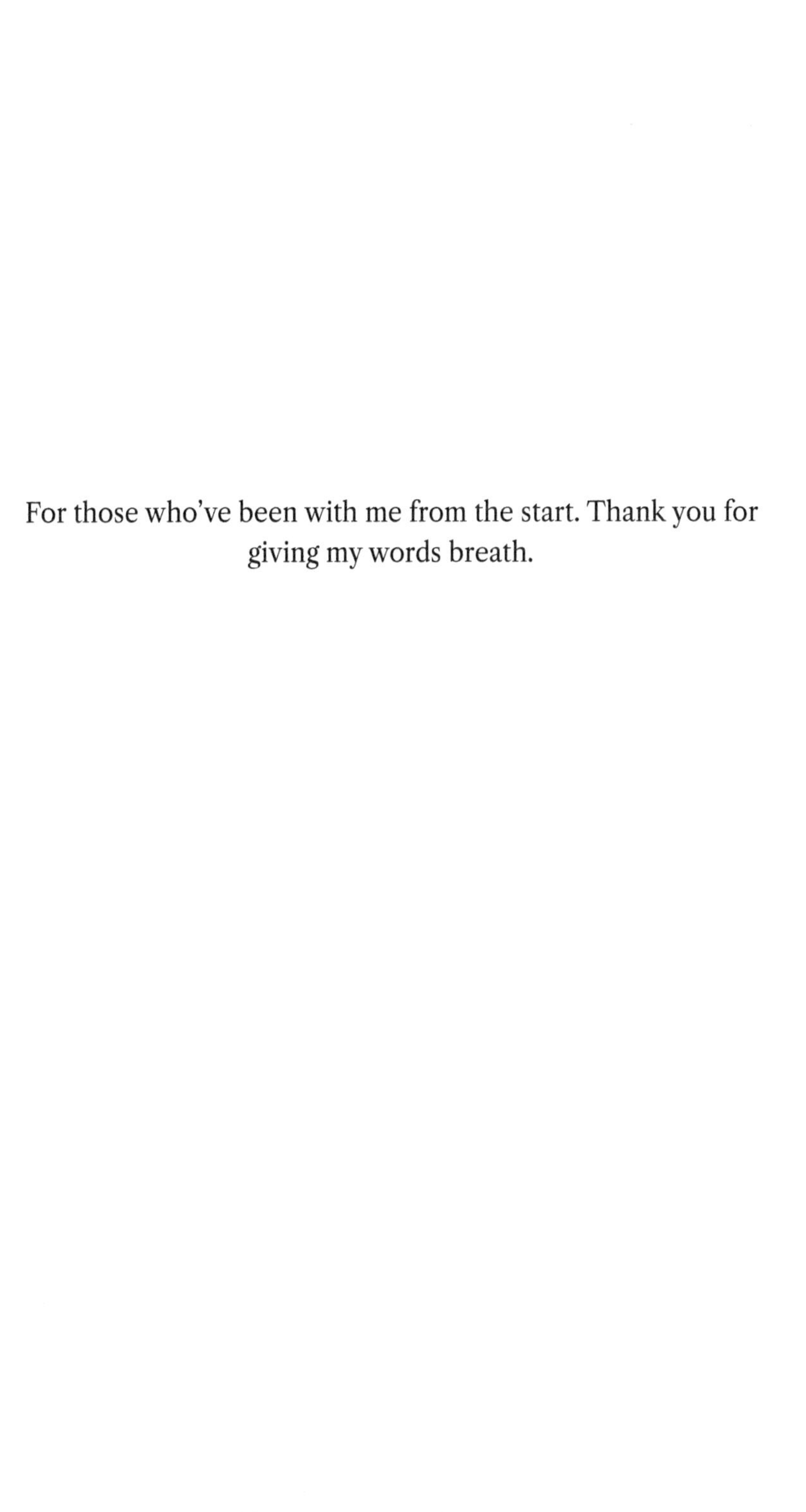

For those who've been with me from the start. Thank you for giving my words breath.

Contents

Chapter 1

DIXON

Do you believe in hate at first sight?

Neither did I, until Niko fucking Adamos strides into Studio 1 like he owns the goddamn place.

It's Monday morning, and things are already shit. Regina, my now *ex*-girlfriend, moved out over the weekend. My favorite coffee shop, Hyped, had a broken espresso machine—which means I'm down my typical morning hazelnut latte fix. And then Jerome informed me the minute I arrived on set that I'd be getting a new partner for a boyfriend arc. A goddamn *boyfriend* arc.

I don't *do* mushy love scenes. I'm one of Elite 8 Studios' most popular tops, and I fuck. Plain and simple.

And yet, when I reminded Jerome, our executive producer, of that fact, he rolled his eyes and said, "You need to change it up, Dix. Fans are getting bored of you."

As if I needed that blow to my ego at ten in the morning while under-caffeinated and dealing with a whole host of inconvenient, lingering *feelings* due to my girlfriend—excuse me, *ex*-girlfriend—dumping me for being "emotionally un-available."

Needless to say, I'm in a less-than-stellar mood when Niko Adamos struts into our monthly meeting ten minutes late, his hips swinging like the man thinks he's coming down a catwalk, a bigass smile plastered across his face. His shoulder-length mane of curly, dark hair is pushed back by sunglasses perched atop his head, but even so, the wild locks fly every which way, and I'm more than certain he spends a ridiculous amount of time perfecting that tousled look. Up top, he's wearing a white V-neck t-shirt one size too small that achieves the intended effect of showing off every single one of his stupidly perfect washboard abs, and down below, he has on designer jeans and caramel-colored lace-up boots that look like some sort of fashionable loafer and probably cost more than my entire wardrobe, shoes and clothing combined.

He looks like a modern day Greek god, and I hate him instantly.

"The fuck is this?" I growl, eyes narrowing as Niko takes an open seat at our team meeting, spreading his legs wide and smiling at the faces around the room.

Jerome sighs heavily but otherwise ignores me. "Everyone, this is Nikolas Adamos. Your new coworker."

The other performers and crew members perk up, chittering excitedly. Niko is new on the porn scene, but he's made waves with his self-made videos. I guess when you look that good, no one cares about poor video quality. I had no clue Jerome managed to sign him to Elite 8, but considering we have an exclusivity clause, that's quite the accomplishment. Begrudgingly, I admit it was a smart move for the company. Personally, I don't want a thing to do with the man.

Niko takes a moment to look around the room as a few of the other performers give him welcoming waves. When his gaze lands on me, I narrow my eyes, and Niko's smile becomes impossibly wider.

"All right," Jerome says, cutting off the excited chatter. "You know the drill. Introduce yourselves when the meeting is over. Make sure Mr. Adamos feels welcomed." He gives me and my glower a pointed look. "Now on to business."

Jerome spends fifteen minutes discussing this month's goals: what we'll be shooting, new ideas he's implementing, and last month's viewer trends and what that means for our performances. It's pretty typical stuff, but when he wraps up, he adds, "Dix, Mr. Adamos, come back to my office after introductions are done."

With that, Jerome walks out of the room, his assistant producer and second-in-command, Nathaniel, at his heels. The two men are barely out the door before Niko is swarmed. He positively preens under the attention, shaking Malibu's hand as the surfer-bro laughs at something Niko says. I scowl.

"Feeling a little jealous of the new guy, are we?" Alex asks, sliding into an open seat next to me.

I prop my ankle on my knee and cross my arms, raising a brow. "I don't do jealous."

Alex, who probably weighs 110 pounds soaking wet, cocks his head at me. For someone who looks perpetually eighteen and has a mop of blonde hair like an angel—or maybe a pixie, considering his moniker *is* Tink—Alex is surprisingly tough. The guy is a bulldog. He'll smile and flatter and kill you with kindness, but he's relentless when it comes to prying into his friends' lives. Or, as he calls it, *caring*.

He's also immune to my fuck-off attitude.

"*Oh*," he says, pink cupid lips tipping up at one corner.

"There's no *oh*. Cut that shit out," I reply, motioning to his face.

Alex bites the tip of his tongue, his eyes dancing mischievously as his gaze flicks to Niko. The man is still surrounded by our coworkers, his broad stubble-surrounded smile taking up half of his face.

"You like him," Alex whispers, his hair brushing the side of my head as he leans in close.

I let out a longsuffering sigh, closing my eyes for an extended moment. When I open them again, Alex is grinning, looking all too pleased about his *incorrect* assessment.

"No, I do not," I say flatly. "That man is a peacock. He's ridiculous."

"You don't even know him," Alex points out.

"Don't need to. Look at him." I wave my hand in Niko's general direction. "He's...smarmy," I settle on.

"Smarmy?" Alex asks, laughing once. "Oh, you've got it bad."

"Fuck off," I grumble.

"Your growling doesn't work on me," Alex says melodiously, popping up from his chair. "I know you're just a teddy bear under all that muscle-man posturing. All bark, no bite."

"I can bite," I defend, although the claim rings false, even to my own ears.

"Maybe you should take a bite out of Niko. He might like it," Alex says, bouncing his eyebrows and laughing when I shoot him an unimpressed glare. He swoops down to peck my cheek before I can stop him. "Don't forget to go make nice."

Alex flits away like the imp he is, and I watch as he introduces himself to our new coworker, popping up on his tiptoes to give Niko a welcoming hug. Niko grins at him, and I clench my jaw tight.

With a frustrated grumble, I heave myself out of my seat and approach the man. His admirers have dwindled, most of them having made their way over to the after-meeting brunch table.

I'm feeling the effects of hunger myself, not to mention I still need my morning coffee, but with Jerome's request to meet in his office hanging heavily over my head, I step in front of Niko Adamos to get this shit over with.

"Come on," I say. "Jerome wanted to talk to us."

Niko looks over from his conversation with Alex, his eyes widening in surprise at the blatant interruption. He blinks a couple times before recovering, that smile overtaking his face once more. "Hey, I'm Niko," he says politely, holding out his hand.

I look down at it. "Dixon," I grumble. "Let's go."

Alex sighs in exasperation and tugs my arm loose from where it was crossed in front of my chest. He opens my fist and slaps it into Niko's grip, keeping his hand over top of my own as he forcibly moves us in an approximation of a shake. I pointedly ignore how smooth and warm Niko's palm is.

"Nice to meet you, Niko," Alex says in a low voice I assume is meant to imitate me.

"You, too, Dixon," Niko replies, happily playing into Alex's little game.

"Jesus Christ." I pull my hand loose and turn on my heel, trudging toward Jerome's office. As I put the two behind me, I can hear Alex commenting that I'm "usually only sixty percent grumpy, not one hundred percent," but I ignore it and rap on Jerome's door.

When I hear his "Come in," I push inside, finding my boss and Nathaniel seated at Jerome's desk, both of their heads bowed over something on Jerome's tablet. For as much as Jerome looks like the categorical bad boy, with his distressed jeans, black combat boots, and leather jacket, Nathaniel is his nerdy counterpoint, always in khakis and a never-ending rotation of argyle sweaters. The two make for an odd pair of fifty-somethings, their only commonality the silver in their hair, but they work brilliantly together despite their differences.

I've wondered a time or two if they're shagging, but I've never dared to ask.

Jerome looks up as I step into the room, his gaze sweeping behind me. "Where's Mr. Adamos?" he asks.

I shrug. "He's a big boy. I'm sure he'll find his way," I say, plopping into one of the large, burgundy armchairs in front of Jerome's desk.

"I'm here."

I try not to tense as Niko's voice washes over my shoulder and the man himself takes the seat next to me, splaying his legs wide, his arms relaxed on the armrests to each side of him like a king waiting to be served, but it's no use. His simple presence puts me on edge.

Alex is right. I'm not usually quite this grumpy. But it's been a hell of a weekend, and my morning hasn't started off on the right foot. Can he really blame me for finding this pompous man-child annoying? The guy is barely starting out on the scene. He's practically a baby. And yet he walks around acting like his cock is a gift to queer mankind.

Well, fuck that. Niko still has to earn his dues, as far as I'm concerned. Anyone can set their phone on their dresser and video themselves fucking their flavor of the night. Consensually, of course. The guy isn't so much of an asshat that he put those guys online without their consent. But it takes talent and drive to make it in this business.

If Niko Adamos thinks he can walk in here, charm everyone with a flick of his wrist, and become the next big thing without putting in the work, he's got another think coming.

I cross my arms, focusing on Jerome. "What'd you need me for?"

"Charming as always, Dix," Jerome drawls. "I wanted you two to formally meet, seeing as you'll be working closely together."

My brows furrow with my confusion. "Well, yeah. We'll all be working together." Unfortunately.

Jerome cocks his head, looking at me like I'm an oblivious child. "Sure, but you and Mr. Adamos especially." When I don't respond, he adds, "As your partner."

Oh, fuck. Fuck no.

"This is the guy you want me to do that boyfriend crap with?" I bark, sitting upright.

Jerome nods, leaning back in his chair. "That's right."

"No way." I shake my head back and forth several times. "No. Nope."

Niko huffs a laugh from next to me.

"What?" I grit out.

"Nothing," he says, shrugging his shoulders nonchalantly. "I just can't imagine what you'd possibly have against the idea. You positively scream boyfriend material."

"What does that mean?" I ask through clenched teeth.

He runs his gaze up and down the length of my body once—*slowly*—before answering, "You know, you're so...warm and fuzzy."

He grins, and my eyes narrow.

"Like I told you, Dix, you need something new," Jerome interjects. "You've been on the scene for years, and you're getting less hits than you used to. Viewers are responding well to the boyfriend arcs, and I think it's your best chance for an increase in viewership right now."

"Why this guy?" I ask, flicking my hand toward Niko.

"Mr. Adamos will bring you a lot of viewers. He's new and flashy. He's your best option," Jerome says simply.

I rub the bridge of my nose, feeling a headache coming on. I really need that caffeine.

"And if I say no?" I ask.

Jerome shrugs. "You know I'll never force you into a scene you don't want to do. But I don't think you should dismiss this so quickly."

"How would it work?" I ask, much to my own annoyance. I can't believe I'm considering this.

"The pair of you would do a couple scenes a week, eight in total. If viewers like your story, we may keep going. If you don't mesh, we cut it off at eight videos and you go back to your usual scenes."

I mull it over, but when I glance at Niko, who's picking at his nail, looking like he couldn't care less one way or the other, my irritation flares.

"And you?" I ask.

"What about me?" Niko asks, tilting his head slightly as he appraises me.

"You're okay with this? Acting like my doting boyfriend?"

Niko lets out a sharp laugh. "Oh, sure, love," he says in a saccharine-sweet voice that instantly grates on my nerves. "I'm looking forward to waiting on you hand and foot. Sounds like a dream come true. Although I'll need to consult with one of your exes to find out what brand of oil you prefer having rubbed over that big head of yours."

He grins again, slowly, and I grind my teeth together so hard they squeak.

Inhaling through my nose, I forcibly quell the violent storm churning in my belly at the mention of my ex. Niko doesn't know about my recent breakup, but his words still chafe. The wound is fresh; it's only been two days since my relationship tanked. And Regina and I had been together for nearly *two years*. Not to mention she'd been living with me for the past six months, ever since my best friend and fellow porn star moved down to Texas, of all places, to follow his heart. Good for Mat, truly. I'm happy for him. Doesn't make me any less bitter that my own attempt at happiness crashed and burned.

And, possibly the hardest part of all, I didn't see it coming. I knew Regina wanted me to open up more, and I was *trying*—I was. Apparently, my efforts weren't good enough. Because all of a sudden, without so much as a warning, she was packing her bags, leaving me and my apartment painfully bereft. I didn't even get a say.

"You know what I mean," I snap at Niko, not in the mood to hear his assumption that I'm a crappy boyfriend. I'm *not*. "This isn't your bedroom with shoddy lighting, where you slap on a condom, fuck, and call it a day. You have to sell it here. You have to be a professional. Can you do that?"

"I can handle it, bud," he says, head cocked, hair spilling around his face in a stupid, artful mess. He's still lounging in his chair like a mansplaining alley cat—or maybe a brown-maned lion—and all I want is to reach over and tip him onto the floor. "But look, if you don't trust your own acting skills, feel free to bow out. It's no skin off my back. Tink is pretty cute. Maybe he'd work with me." He winks, *goading* me.

A muscle in my jaw pops. "Fine," I grit out, turning back to Jerome, who's watching the two of us curiously. Nathaniel, for his part, looks just as befuddled.

"Fine?" Jerome asks.

"I'll do it."

"Mr. Adamos?" Jerome asks the other man.

Niko shrugs. "Fine by me, boss."

Jerome looks dubious after our strained interaction, but he nods nonetheless. "All right. I'll have your first script out by the end of the afternoon, and I want the two of you to get together within the next couple days. Get comfortable because your first scene is Thursday, and this," he says, waving his hand between us, "doesn't look like two guys about to fall in love. Dismissed."

Niko claps his hands together once and rises fluidly, leaving the room without further ado. I linger a moment longer, wondering what in the hell I just agreed to.

Jerome raises a brow, looking up from his tablet. "Something you want to add?"

I shake my head, but then I ask, "Do you really think this is the best option for me? I'm not a *cutesy* guy, Jerome. I'm not like Tink." I try to articulate my main concern. "I'm worried this will throw off my fans."

Jerome leans forward, arms crossed on his desk as he gives me his best no-bullshit boss stare. "I'm not asking you to act like Tink. I'm not even asking for hearts and flowers, Dix. I'm just asking that you seem a little less unaffected. Act as if you like the guy, for Christ's sake. Act like you care about him. You can still be you—big and tough and even bossy, if you want. But use that in a way that makes you feel approachable. Be protective of him on camera. Let him soften you a little. If you allow your fans to see that side of you, even if it *is* fake, I think they'll eat it up. You don't exactly invite viewers in."

"No shit," I mumble.

Jerome shrugs. "And that works for heavy fuck scenes. But you've done hundreds of those. You need to adapt to stay relevant."

"Fuck," I mutter, rubbing a hand over my close-cropped hair. "Fine. I'll do my best."

Jerome nods, looking pleased. "That's all I ask."

I stand up, but before I can even take a step, I pause. "What moniker are you giving him?"

"We're going with a play on his last name. Adonis," Jerome says, looking back down and pointing something out to Nathaniel.

I hang my head back, staring up at the blackness behind my closed eyelids as I sigh heavily.

Adonis.

Fucking hell.

Chapter 2
Niko

I'm not used to people disliking me. *Everyone* likes me. I'm a likable guy.

I smile a lot. I listen. I *care*.

But Dixon? Wow, that man does not like me. And I'm almost positive it's me specifically and not that he dislikes everyone on behalf of his surly attitude. It makes me feel special, but not in a good way.

I probably shouldn't have poked the bear like I did in Jerome's office—I mean, I do have to work alongside this man for the foreseeable future—but something about that hard exterior of his makes me want to find his cracks and split them open wide. I do so love a challenge.

When Dixon comes back into Studio 1, which has been set up with chairs, a few tables, and a veritable buffet of brunch foods for the Elite 8 team meeting, he makes a beeline for the coffee carafe. I watch curiously as he fills up a paper cup with the bitter liquid, adds a large dollop of milk, drinks it down with a wince, and then fills it up again.

"So how'd you get into porn?" Malibu asks from beside me, drawing my attention away from Dixon.

I hum as I finish my bite of donut, brushing the excess sugar from my fingers onto my plate. "A good friend of mine told me people would pay to see me naked. I tried it, and here I am." I shrug, quirking a smile as I think about my bestie, Kipp.

Malibu nods. "Yeah, he's not wrong, man. You're smokin' hot. And your ass is a work of art."

I bark out a laugh. "Thanks. I'm particularly fond of your mouth."

Malibu grins. "It has many uses."

Malibu and I are a lot alike, I realize. Similar height and build, toned but not too bulky with muscle, long curly hair and versatile when it comes to fucking. He's like the blonde, blue-eyed, Cali version of me. Or perhaps I'm his dark-haired, dark-eyed Greek double. Either way, he's easy to talk to. I have a feeling we'll get along just fine.

Unlike me and a certain someone.

I glance over at Dixon again, who's now seated on a couch next to the cute little blonde, Alex, a piled-high plate of food on his lap. I'm not surprised the man eats a ton. He's a tank, built more like a linebacker than the surfer-toned Malibu standing next to me. Idly, I wonder how much he works out to maintain that body.

"Have you done the boyfriend thing?" I ask Malibu, curious about the whole concept Jerome's been testing out. I did a little recon, and it seems like the relationship angle is trending right now in porn. The most recent string of boyfriend videos on Elite 8's site involved Felix and Teddy, and they garnered a lot of attention.

Malibu shakes his head. "Not yet, but I'm guessing it's only a matter of time. Jerome is really pushing them lately. Can't argue with the numbers." I nod, and Malibu goes on. "You got thrown right into the deep end, though, huh?"

He cants his head toward Dixon, and I follow his gaze. Dixon looks up, perhaps able to sense he's being watched. His eyes narrow as soon as they land on me. Superb. I flash him a winning smile, and he looks away.

"Should be fun," I mutter.

Malibu laughs. "Dixon's a good guy, just a little bit of a hardass at times."

I'm not so sure about the *little bit* part, but I nod.

"I'm going to go play nice," I tell Malibu.

He chuckles. "Catch you later."

Malibu veers off toward a few of the other performers I met earlier, and I make my way over to the couch Alex and Dixon are on, dropping my paper plate in the trash on the way. Alex looks up as I approach, smiling widely, but Dixon's body tenses, like he can sense me coming even though he's dutifully avoiding looking my way.

"Hey, you two," I say cheerfully, plopping down in the space between them.

I'm pretty sure Dixon growls a little, but Alex is welcoming, angling his body toward me. "Hey, *Adonis*," he teases.

I huff a laugh. "Right. That's going to take some getting used to."

"Would've assumed you'd feel right at home with that name," Dixon mutters.

I turn toward him. "Is that because I'm Greek and look like a god?" I purse my lips and slap his arm lightly. "I guess you're right. It's pretty perfect."

Dixon glowers, popping a piece of gum in his mouth and chewing aggressively. *Okay, then.*

"How often does this happen?" I ask, gesturing around the room.

"Once a month," Alex replies. "The meetings are usually pretty short, but it tends to be the only time we're all in the same place at once. I think Jerome does it as much for the team-building as he does for updating us. You won't see me complaining either way. He orders the best bagels."

"Sure seems like these guys can put down a lot of food," I note, eyeing the mostly empty buffet table.

Alex titters a laugh. "Especially this one." He reaches over me to slap Dixon's shoulder.

Dixon just grunts. "Probably not the sort of spread you're used to," he says under his breath, leaning against the back of the couch and affecting a relaxed posture. Except the man looks like a slab of marble, tension lining his frame even in his reclined state.

"I mean, yeah, I was a little disappointed there aren't crab legs," I joke. "But it's not like they're worth getting anywhere other than the Bellagio, anyways."

Alex snickers from beside me, but Dixon barely reacts, his jaw working as he chews his gum. I'm pretty sure the man thinks I'm being serious.

I heave an internal sigh and turn back to Alex. "I have to ask—how old are you?"

Alex's eyes drag Heavenward with his exaggerated sigh. "Twenty-*five*, thank you very much. Perfectly legal, boo. Don't worry. You won't get into trouble for fucking me."

I laugh. I'm quickly learning that I love the bluntness of porn stars. "Good to know. It'll be a while, though. I'm stuck with this guy for the next month," I tease, motioning back toward Dixon.

Dixon makes a disgruntled noise, but Alex laughs along. "Don't worry about that, either," he says, patting my arm. "Dixon's got a great cock."

"Jesus," Dixon grits out, pushing upright and stalking away.

"A thank you would have been nice," Alex calls out after him.

Dixon swats his hand through the air before disappearing around the corner.

"Don't mind him," Alex says, crossing his legs and nudging me gently when he notices me watching Dixon's departure. "He's been extra sourpuss ever since his husband left."

I look over at him in surprise. "He was married?"

"Oh, no. Not for real," Alex responds, shaking his head. "He lived with Mateo...uh, Silver?" I nod to show I know who he's talking about. What queer man doesn't know of Silver? The guy is a ridiculously popular porn star. "Mateo and Dixon are really close," he explains, "but Mateo moved earlier this year, and it was pretty hard on Dixon."

"Were they more than friends?" I ask, curious about my new coworker.

Alex shakes his head and huffs out a laugh. "No, that's why it was easy for us to joke about them being husbands. They were tight, but never like that."

My mind pings back to something else Alex said. "So Silver doesn't work here anymore?"

"No, he's out of the scene now."

I didn't realize that, but now that I think about it, I haven't seen new videos of him for many months. I'm kind of bummed. I would have liked to meet him.

"I can't help but wonder if something else is going on, though," Alex adds contemplatively, drawing my attention back to our original point of discussion—Dixon. "This isn't normal for him, how he's been today."

"Maybe I've been gifted with the good fortune of having that effect on him," I say jokingly, even though I'm pretty sure that's the actual truth. The man can barely tolerate me, although Heaven knows why.

Alex shrugs, a mischievous little glint entering his eye. "Could be. But I have a feeling you're just the person he needs."

"For the boyfriend arc?" I ask.

"Sure," he replies. "Anyways, I have a scene to get ready for, and I need to visit Raylin first." He pops off the couch, scooping up his empty plate.

"Who's Raylin?" I ask, looking around for the one woman I noticed earlier but didn't get a chance to meet.

"Oh, you'll find out soon enough." He snickers to himself, the sound almost ominous, but I don't have a chance to question him further before he nudges my shoulder. "I'm glad you're here, Niko."

I smile widely in response. "Thanks, Alex. I'm glad to be here."

He sends me a wink before trashing his plate and walking out. The rest of the day passes in a bit of a whirlwind. The crew members and performers either get ready for work, same as Alex, or head home, and Studio 1 is cleaned up and changed into a hospital set. Nathaniel, who looks as if he'd be a golfer, not an adult film producer, spends the afternoon walking me through my employment paperwork and showing me around. There are three studios in the building, a huge break room that's more like a swanky lounge with a kitchenette and plenty of plush furniture, a large locker room that has shower stalls and an adjoining bathroom, and a few offices down a quiet hallway. There's even a small gym that I'll probably take advantage of so I can quit the one near home.

But I think my favorite part is the massive Elite 8 Studios sign near the entrance. It takes up most of one long wall, the characters joined together in bright yellow neon. I snap a picture in front of it to send to Kipp.

By the time I leave for the day, I have a lot to think about, but I'm cautiously optimistic. I think I'll enjoy working at Elite 8, even alongside one coworker who's determined to hate me, for whatever reason.

I'm not particularly worried about that. I'm confident I can win Dixon over one way or another.

The fact that everyone else was so warm and welcoming was a pleasant discovery. I'd heard of Elite 8 before. Of course I had. It's the gay porn mecca. I bet nearly every queer man knows about the site with a reputation for eight-inchers—hence the name—and even though it's subscription-only, their memberships are off the charts. Accepting a job with the company was a no-brainer and is bound to be much more lucrative than my self-publishing efforts. What I didn't expect was to feel immediately accepted and at ease.

So far, my experience in porn has been pretty singular. I've slept with several men who gave written and verbal consent to the videos, but I was working alone. That won't be the case anymore, and I was concerned it would be an adjustment. But based on the reception I received today, I don't think I have anything to worry about. Everyone was just so *nice*.

Well, everyone except for one particular grouch, that is.

"Ya," I call out in Greek when I get home. *'Hey.'*

"In here."

I untie my shoes, place them on the mat to the side of the door, and then follow my sister's voice and the alluring smell of simmering tomatoes and cumin to the kitchen.

"How was your first day?" Cassandra asks softly from in front of the stove. Her baby girl, Calliope, is strapped to her chest, sound asleep, her little curls visible over the top of the baby carrier.

"Interesting," I admit, nudging my sister aside and taking over dinner prep.

Cass squeezes my shoulder appreciatively and grabs a Pepsi from the fridge, unscrewing the top as she awkwardly lowers her weight onto a chair, doing her best not to unsettle her daughter.

"How so?" she asks.

I tilt my head back and forth, debating how much to tell my sister. We've always been close, as the two oldest Adamos siblings, and Cass knows about my work in the adult entertainment industry. Well, the whole family does, actually. Secrets don't keep in our household. But Cass is the person I've shared the most with, and she doesn't judge.

"Well, I got the tour and met the other guys. Most were really nice," I tell her.

"Most?" Cass asks, catching my unspoken *but*.

"The guy I'm going to be working with for the next month or more was less than thrilled with me," I explain, sampling the tomato sauce for the soutzoukakia. I add a pinch of sugar, gently mixing it in so as to not disturb the meatballs.

Cass rolls her eyes. "The sauce was fine. So what's up with this guy? Everyone likes you," she says.

I look back at her, my eyes wide. "Right? I don't get it. I've never had someone take an immediate dislike to me like Dixon has."

I turn off the heat and bring the dish over to the table, setting it on top of a trivet. I grab the rice next and two plates. Cass thanks me when I join her at the table, everything set to eat.

"What's he like?" she asks, dishing food onto her plate.

I think about it. *Hot* is the first word that comes to mind. He's tall, a bit taller than my six-foot frame. Beautiful, Black, muscles for days, thighs the size of tree trunks, sharp brown eyes.

"Grumpy," I answer instead. "Seems like a bit of a dick."

Cass raises an eyebrow, looking at me knowingly. "So you're attracted to him?"

I groan. "Maybe a smidge."

Cass chuckles, the sound quiet, seeing as Calli is still resting against her chest. "I've never understood your attraction to moody dickwads."

I shrug, taking a bite of my dinner to stall. *They're fun to unravel*, I think to myself. "Moody dickwads need love, too," I answer aloud.

My sister shakes her head, although there's an indulgent smile on her lips. "If you say so."

Cass turns her body to the side, moving Calli out of the way so she can eat without worrying about dropping hot food on her baby's head. She hums happily around her first bite.

"See? Needed the extra sugar," I tease.

"You're an ass," she says lightly. "So, like, is this Dixon guy the only one you're working with? I figured you fuckboys fuck around."

"Very nice, Cass. It *is* a job, you know. We're not just fucking for fun."

She raises an eyebrow. "Please. Enlighten me as to how hard your job is."

I huff through my nose, finishing my mouthful of food before I speak. "It's more complicated than just having sex."

"If you say so," she says again, clearly humoring me. Big sister knows best and all.

"To answer your question, Dixon and I are doing scenes exclusively with one another for several weeks as fake boyfriends."

"I'm sorry, what now?" she asks, looking at me in confusion. I thought I'd surprised Cass with every shocking porn-related revelation that existed. I guess not.

"Videos with a little more tenderness and connection have gotten more popular. Some viewers want to feel like it's real. So we act like it means something. They include short date scenes, more kissing, stuff like that," I explain. "It's almost like a miniseries, but, you know, still porn."

"Geez," Cass says, shaking her head. "I guess it makes sense, I just wouldn't have thought of that. And you have to sell it with the guy who hates your guts?"

I nod slowly. "Sure do. I'm not worried, though. I have a few tricks up my sleeve."

No one hates me. They just don't. I'll find a way to bring Dixon around.

"Well, good luck with that," Cass says.

"By the way, I shouldn't have mentioned his name. I'm not allowed to share details about videos before they're released, so just don't go blabbing that part to our sisters, yeah?"

Cass waves me off. "Whose name?"

I smile.

It isn't long before we finish eating, and I clean up while Cass feeds the now-awake baby Calliope a bottle of formula. Cass and I live here together, in a little house a half-hour outside of Las Vegas. We're the only two siblings who've moved out of our mama's large estate in Moapa Valley. Our other three sisters, Elina, Ioanna, and Sofia, are all still under twenty-one. Cass, on the other hand, is the oldest at twenty-nine. I'm not far behind her at twenty-seven.

We've always been thick as thieves, Cass and I, but we didn't start living together until this past year. When Cass's husband deployed, I made a sound argument for my moving in, and the fact Cass barely even fought me on it was telling. It weighs on my sister, doing this on her own. But she has me now, and I love being closer to my sister and niece.

"I need to do my homework," I tell Cass once the kitchen is clean.

She snorts, looking up at me. Calliope is draped against her shoulder as Cass bounces and burps her. "You have homework?"

"A script," I say, tugging the pages out of the messenger bag I'd dropped at the entrance to the kitchen.

"You're kidding," Cass says, looking amused.

"Nope. I told you it's more complicated than you think." I wave the pages as I make my way into the family room adjacent to the kitchen, separated only by a large, arching doorway. I plop onto our deep, gray couch and flip open the script, snorting when I see my lines next to the name "Adonis." God, my sisters are going to tease me mercilessly when they learn my alias.

In the script, Dix and I are at the end of our first date together. We're at my door, laughing about something that happened earlier that evening, when Dix leans in and kisses me. It lingers and heats up, and then I invite him in. The scene is pretty vanilla. Kissing against the inside of the door, touching tentatively. Then fucking face to face on the bed, slow and sweet.

Honestly, it sounds like a disaster waiting to happen. I can't see Dixon being *tender*. The man is like a giant block of granite, cold and unyielding. But he claims he can do it, so I guess we'll see what happens.

I, for one, hope I'm proved wrong.

Chapter 3
Dixon

"Marley, doll, please tell me the goddamn espresso machine is fixed," I plead, holding my phone down at my chest.

Marley raises one barbell-pierced eyebrow, fixing me with an expression part exasperation, part amusement. "Dixon, you're the only guy I'd ever allow to call me doll, 'cause I know you're not being a superior prick who wants in my pants. But watch that growl of yours. It's not polite."

"I'm not growling," I grumble before softening my tone a smidge. "Besides, I did say 'please.' I'm having withdrawals over here, Marls. It's been two days since I've had my Hyped latte."

"Don't you worry," Marley says, swinging the card reader in my direction. "Jason is already preparing your large hazelnut."

"Thank God," I mumble, tapping my card and adding a generous tip. "Thank you, Jason," I add, speaking up.

"You got it," he calls out from behind the espresso machine.

Marley chuckles. "What would you do without us?"

"I really don't know, and I don't want to ever find out," I tell the barista, moving down the counter to accept my piping-hot coffee. "You're a lifesaver, Jason."

The kid nods his beanie-covered head before sliding back behind the complicated machinery, already working on the next order.

When I bring my phone back up to my ear, my friend is chuckling. I take a sip of my latte—God, that's good—before addressing Mateo.

"What?" I ask.

"You're always more polite to people you don't know than your actual friends. You realize that, right?"

"Fuck off," I tell him, to which he laughs harder.

"Love you, too, Dixie-poo."

I sigh. "Mat, pumpkin, apple of my eye, little toaster strudel—"

"Toaster strudel?"

"—I called you for advice, not to hear your criticisms of my attitude," I say, taking a seat in the corner of the coffee shop. I have a few minutes before I need to head to work.

"Well, truth be told, I think it's your attitude that needs advising," Mat says, and even though I kind of want to punch him, I miss my friend and his stupid platinum-blonde head. "Why do you hate the new guy, anyway? That's not like you. As I so wisely noted, you usually get grumpier the *longer* you know someone. So, seeing as you just met this guy, you should be radiating sunshine from your pores. Spouting joy from your mouth-hole. Squeezing rainbows out of your tighter-than-a-clamshell behind."

I rub my eyes. "Why are we friends? Why do I put up with this crap?"

"You like him," Mat says, sounding so serious all of a sudden that it throws me.

"What?"

"I think you like this guy, which, you know, *terrifies* you. So you're overcompensating."

"No. No way," I tell him. What's with this nonsense? Alex said something similar.

I barely even know Adamos. Sure, I'd watched his videos before meeting him in person—for professional purposes, of course; it only makes sense to keep up with what's happening in the biz—but Niko rubs me the wrong way and has from the moment I set eyes on him.

I don't *like* him.

"I get it," Mat says, chomping down on something crunchy and then talking with a full mouth. "I was terrified, too. It's worth it, though, finding the right person."

"I thought I had that," I remind him sourly.

"I *am* sorry about Regina," he says after a moment. "But I'm going to be honest with you."

"Like you're ever anything but."

"You're always picking these good girls, Regina included, and I just don't get it. It's so not you," he says, startling me somewhat. Mat never gave any indication he thought Regina was wrong for me.

"What's wrong with good?" I ask a little defensively.

"Nothing," he says, and I can practically hear his shrug. "But you're a porn star. *Good* is for, like, Bible salesmen."

I scoff. "What about your Texan? Are you telling me he's not a good guy?"

Mat laughs somewhat darkly. "He's a nice guy. But he's not *good.*"

"Oh, Jesus. I don't need to know about the kinky shit you get up to."

"My point is," Mat says, as if I never said anything at all, "your relationships were boring. No offense."

"How can I not take offense to that?" I grumble.

He ignores me again. "I think you were playing it safe. You need someone to spice up your life. Like Adonis."

"Don't call him that. *Shit*. Drives me up a goddamn wall."

"Well, if the name fits," Mat responds.

"You don't even know him." I check the time and stand up, making my way toward my car. "How could you possibly think he'd be good for me?"

"*Because* he ruffles your feathers," Mat says confidently. "Think of the sex, man. It'll probably be explosive. You deserve passion in your life, Dixon. It's okay to let go a little."

"Easy for you to say," I mutter, even though I know that's not the truth. Mat had a really hard time opening himself up to something real. It wasn't easy for him to let go of his own protective barriers. "Anyways, I gotta go."

"Bye, love," Mat says.

I clutch the phone a little tighter. *Fuck*, I miss my friend.

"Pain in my ass," I mumble affectionately before ending the call.

When I get to work, I head straight for the showers. I came from an extended morning workout—figuring burning off some extra aggression might help me deal more level-headedly with the Niko situation—and I'm not about to go into today's scene sweaty. After dressing in my motorcycle club getup, I head to Studio 2.

I'm filming with Malibu today, my last scene before starting the boyfriend arc. We're doing one of those themed videos that's a little over the top, with cheesy dialogue and elaborate costumes and scenery. They're not all like this. In fact, the majority are considerably more subdued these days because that's what draws most of our viewers. Things like two average guys getting it on in the bedroom or shower or something a little more risqué, like a closet during a party. But we still do our fill of camp, too.

Like today's scene. With Malibu and I dressed in leather vests inside a fake clubhouse, an actual motorcycle nearby.

"Hey," Malibu says, coming up to me the moment he arrives on set. His blonde waves are tied back with a red bandana, and it looks like our cosmetologist recently spruced him up. But despite that, the guy looks tired. There are smudges under his eyes, and his expression looks unusually blank.

I cock my head. "Everything okay?"

He waves me off. "Yeah, of course. Just beat." He attempts a small smile, but it falls flat.

"If you're sure," I say tentatively.

"Positive," he says with a nod.

I flick his vest. "C'mon then, initiate. Let's get this show on the road."

Twenty minutes later, after some questionable dialogue about earning his badge, Malibu is spread over the clubhouse table with his jacket pushed halfway up his back, and I'm between his legs.

"That's it, initiate. Tell me who's in charge," I say, working off the script we were given.

Malibu doesn't respond, and when I bend to get a better visual of him, he looks a little...lost.

"Initiate," I bark out.

"Huh?" he finally asks.

I still and flick a quick glance over to Nathaniel, who's standing in the wings, overseeing our shoot. He furrows his brow. "Everything all right, Malibu?" he calls out.

Malibu turns his head, looking confused at the interruption. "What? Yeah, I'm fine."

"Mal…" I say quietly, thinking he doesn't seem so fine. I'm fully prepared to back off from our scene, but he looks over his shoulder and shakes his head.

"I'm fine, seriously. Just got lost in my head for a minute." He calls out to Nathaniel, "We're good."

"All right, continue rolling," Nathaniel says, stepping back.

After Malibu gives me another reassuring nod, I pick up where we left off. "Who's in charge?" I prompt again.

"You are," Malibu says, seeming a little more present now as we get back into the swing of things. "You're in charge."

"Damn straight," I say, threading my fingers through his hair and tugging. I get a wide enough grip that I know it won't hurt him, but it'll look like it to the camera.

Malibu plays into it, gasping and arching his back.

The rest of our scene plays out without incident, and when we separate, Malibu accepts his robe and walks away without a word. I check in with Nathaniel, who confirms we got everything we needed from the shoot, and then I follow Malibu to the locker room. He's already in the shower when I arrive, and I take the stall next to him.

I've worked with Malibu for years, but I've never seen him quite like that. Distant and withdrawn. Not fully *there* during a scene. It worries me. Not only because he's a coworker, but also because I consider him a friend.

"Mal?"

He hums.

"You sure you're okay?" I ask again.

"Of course," he says lightly over the sound of water pelting the tile floor. "I already told you I'm fine."

"O-kay," I say slowly. I've never been particularly great at the whole "supportive friend" thing, so I don't know whether or not I should push. "If there's anything you need to talk about, I'm here."

"Thanks, Dixon," he says simply.

Malibu makes it out of the shower before me, and by the time I'm wrapping a towel around myself and stepping out from behind the curtain, he's already gone. My concern doesn't disappear quite as quickly as the man himself, but hopefully, Malibu was simply having an off day.

Once I'm dressed, I don't linger around the studio. Some days I do. I'll spend some time in the break room and chat with the crew or fit in an extra workout in the small gym. But today, I'm not feeling either option. Instead, I head home, although the minute I open the door into my empty apartment, I wish I had somewhere else to be.

I've always liked this place. When I lived here with Mat, he let me decorate, and I bathed everything in soothing tones. Regina complained it wasn't enough color, but the cool grays, blues, whites, and occasional black have always made me feel at home. But now, without anyone else to occupy the space, it feels a little empty. There are bare nooks and crannies everywhere: on the bookshelf, in the bathroom, even in the kitchen.

I know I'm not the cuddliest person, or the warmest, but I do enjoy sharing my space and being in a relationship. I like the feeling of safety. I like knowing I have someone to come home to. And, contrary to what Niko may think, I do *not* expect my partner to wait on me.

I'm not a bad boyfriend. I know I'm not. I just have trouble talking about certain things. Mat would probably tell me that stems from my childhood and how my dad was very much a man's man. Reginald James didn't appreciate his only son showing emotion or being anything less than tough. Hell, the one time he found me playing with the neighbor's dolls, he reamed me out for a solid ten minutes. *"Boys don't play princesses, Dixon. That fairytale shit ain't even real. Stop crying and grow up."* But even knowing Mat's likely right, it doesn't make my communication barrier magically disappear. Everyone has faults, right? That's one of mine.

And sure, I could probably work on the whole grumpy attitude a bit. Except that's kind of who I am, too. I don't think I should have to change my personality for another person. There has to be someone out there who wouldn't mind it. Maybe even someone who'd appreciate it?

But that person wasn't Regina. Even after almost two years together, my longest relationship to date, I guess there were some things about me she didn't care for. I try not to let that hurt as much as it does, but it's a lost cause. It makes me feel...deficient.

And thinking about Regina brings back Mat's words from earlier today. Was my relationship really boring? I didn't think so. I thought we were stable, and sure, maybe there weren't fireworks, exactly, but there was a sense of comfort there. I thought that was a good thing, that lack of turbulence. I thought floating steadily down the stream meant we wouldn't capsize.

I guess I was wrong.

Mat might've been right about one thing, though. Maybe I need to try something new. None of the good girls, as he called them, have worked out. Maybe I need to go a different route.

Not a *Niko* route. That's never going to happen, despite what Alex and Mat may think. The man makes my blood boil. I'd rather throttle him than call him my boyfriend.

But maybe a few sparkler-level fireworks would be nice for a change. I just have to figure out how to break my pattern and play with fire.

Chapter 4

NIKO

When I get to work Wednesday morning, I'm immediately directed to Raylin, who I learned is the cosmetologist on set. With a mild amount of trepidation, I head to her workstation.

"Hey, sweet cheeks," the woman says as soon as I pop my head through the door. She's stirring a wooden stick through a warming bowl of wax, and I flash back to Alex telling me I'd find out who Raylin was *soon enough*, suddenly understanding what his little smirk and teasing tone were for.

"Oh, shit," I say.

Raylin laughs, sounding far too jovial for what's about to happen. She's a striking woman with expertly applied makeup and a wicked smile, but women have never been my jam, so I can't say it does a thing for me. "Ready for this?" she asks.

"Absolutely not," I tell her truthfully. I had no clue *this* was happening, so how could I possibly be ready? "What, exactly, are you about to wax?"

She lifts one perfectly manicured eyebrow. "Your asshole, honey."

"Oh, Jesus," I say, dropping my head and massaging my temples.

"Come on, hop on up and spread 'em," she says bluntly, patting the raised table next to her.

"I don't get a say in this, do I?"

I think back to the contract I signed under Nathaniel's watch, remembering the section about grooming that I skimmed. Not that I really have a problem being waxed. I simply wasn't prepared for it. Regardless, I know it's an unavoidable part of the job, so I tug off my pants and underwear and hike myself onto the table in front of Raylin, who's waiting expectantly.

"You sure don't get a say, but it's better this way. Those cameras will be right in your business. You don't want errant hairs showing up on the big screen," she says conversationally, nudging my legs until I get the hint and fold myself up for her perusal.

Christ, it feels weird to have someone of a female persuasion so close to my bits. Without warning, Raylin spreads the wax. I clench up tight, and she laughs.

"Please, have a good chuckle at my expense," I joke, looking to the side and focusing on the myriad of pink orchids lining the walls in an attempt to distract myself from whatever is about to happen.

It doesn't work. Raylin tugs, and then there's *burning*.

"*Maláka*," I hiss out. '*Wanker.*'

Raylin does, in fact, chuckle at my expense before laying a cold cloth over my asshole. "I'm going to neaten this up," she says, waving her hand in front of my crotch.

"By all means," I rasp out, dropping my legs wide and wondering why I didn't read the fine print in my contract more closely. "You're not going to mess with my head, right?"

Raylin looks up at me, her cat-like eyes swinging swiftly over my hair. "No way, sweets. That's your money."

I relax marginally. "Thank God for small mercies."

When Raylin sends me on my way, a few hairs lighter, I head to the locker room and drop my pants, curious what sort of difference she made. Looking myself over in the floor-to-ceiling mirror, I have to admit, I look good. I kept myself decently groomed before, but Raylin managed to manscape me in a way that makes me look neat and tidy while accentuating my dick.

I purse my lips, nodding, and that—of course—is how my new coworker finds me.

Dixon has a casual smile on his face as he enters the room, but as soon as he locks eyes with me, his lips pull down into a scowl. It's almost comical, the abrupt turnabout. Maybe I should take offense, but it only makes me more determined to win the man over.

"Should've figured I'd find you admiring yourself in a mirror," he says, heading to his locker and opening it much more firmly than necessary.

I hold in my eye roll. In all honesty, I don't know what Dixon's problem with me is. I pondered it all night, but I couldn't come to a conclusion. From the very little interaction we've had, it's clear he's pegged me as some sort of vain, self-important princess. Of course, finding me admiring my junk in the mirror certainly doesn't help matters. But it's also obvious he has no real desire to learn who I am, seeing as every word out of his mouth has been dismissive.

I could fight him on it. I could tell him I'm not the person he thinks I am...the person he seems to inherently hate. But I have a feeling that wouldn't work. The man seems too stubborn. Too headstrong. So instead, I roll with the punches and brush off his dig.

"Just wanted to look good for ya, honey," I reply with a wink before pulling up my pants and stepping away to peruse the room. Nathaniel mentioned my locker would be ready by today, and it doesn't take me long to find it. I almost snort when I see "Adonis" spelled out across the front in glittery gold block letters.

When I look back at Dixon, he's staring at me, unblinking.

"Are you ever serious?" he asks at last, turning toward his open locker and tugging out a small toiletries bag.

"When I need to be, sure. But I thought you wanted the doting boyfriend. Isn't that what you said?" I reply with a cloying smile and more snark than I intended. *Shit, so much for playing nice.*

Dixon exhales loudly, clearly exasperated. "You're gonna be a pain in my ass, aren't you?"

I raise my brows. "I think you're supposed to be the pain in *my* ass," I note, "but I'm happy to switch if you want." I waggle my eyebrows for emphasis.

Dixon gives me a *look*. "I don't bottom."

"Right," I say slowly, nodding my head. "Makes sense. No room up there with that stick firmly lodged in place."

Dixon slams his locker shut, brushing past me into the showers and flinging his curtain closed in a twirl of irate energy. I bite my lip as he tosses his clothes haphazardly over the veil.

"Don't be late, boyfriend," I call out. "We agreed to get comfortable with one another in ten minutes. Unless you'd rather me join you in there so we can start getting comfortable now?"

"Not a chance," he grits out, the sound dampened by the running water.

I huff a laugh, shaking my head as I make my way out of the locker room.

Maybe I shouldn't let Dixon get to me the way he does. And I definitely shouldn't enjoy it. But little does my new coworker know—the more he's determined to hate me, the harder I'll try to win him over. I don't like to lose, and there's a very fine line between *hate* and love. I just have to keep pressing, and Dixon will find himself on the other side of that line.

Mark my words. This time next month, Dixon won't know what hit him.

"Well, this is cozy," I remark, spreading my legs out in front of me on the couch.

Dixon and I are in one of the rooms I assumed was an office, except there's no desk in here. Just a couple plush couches, a coffee table, and a few decorations. Nowhere to run.

A freshly showered Dixon glares at me from the other end of the three-seater, blinking occasionally. I smile, and he snorts a breath out of his nose.

"Okay, then. So, I'll start. My name is Niko, or, if you prefer formality, Nikolas Adamos. You can just call me Adonis, though." I grin, but Dixon doesn't look pleased. "I have four sisters, one older and three younger, and one niece. Lots of cousins, but they're still back in Greece, so I never see them. Bampás—my dad—passed long ago, but my mamá lives nearby. My favorite food is fried cheese, I want a pet dog someday, I like reading mysteries, and I hate the desert. Your turn."

Dixon frowns. "You hate the desert," he says, matter-of-factly. "But you live in Nevada."

I nod. "That's right."

After a couple seconds of narrow-eyed perusal, Dixon makes a sound of frustration, like he can't believe he's allowing his curiosity to get the better of him. "*Why?*"

I shrug. "My family is here." It really is that simple. "So, tell me about yourself. Family?"

He crosses his arms and doesn't reply.

"Friends, then?" I ask hopefully. "Alex mentioned you and Silver are close. Although I suppose he doesn't go by that anymore?"

He blinks a couple times before grunting what I assume is an affirmative.

"All right, this is going well," I say, stretching my leg out until my toes bump his thigh. "Sharing. Getting to know you. The relationship is practically writing itself."

Dixon looks down at my toes pointedly before grabbing my foot and pushing it away. Christ, this guy is going to be hard to crack.

"I don't need to know what flavor of ice cream you like to fake it onscreen," he says.

"Pistachio," I answer.

"I didn't ask."

"I know, which is why I volunteered the information. One of us has to keep communication going in this relationship. What else do you want to know?" I ask, pulling my leg up and leaning my chin on my knee.

"Anything?" he asks, narrowing his eyes like he expects me to have some conditions.

"Anything," I answer. Little does he know I'm an open book.

He turns toward me slightly. "Okay, what do you like least about yourself?"

Ouch. Going right for the jugular.

"My hair," I answer on autopilot. Dixon looks surprised, but it's the truth. "It's utterly unruly. That's why I keep it long. Any shorter, and I can't pull it back." I demonstrate by tugging the strands back behind my head. As soon as I release them, they spring around my face, and I do my best to tuck them away.

Dixon frowns a little, his eyes pinging all over my head. He opens his mouth like he wants to say something, but then his jaw clamps shut, and his expression smooths to one of casual indifference. "You could shave it," he suggests.

I laugh, eyeing *his* hair. Although his head isn't shaved like it used to be—sue me, I watched his videos—his hair is still cut rather short and faded at the sides. It suits him. "I couldn't pull it off like you."

His eyes narrow again, like he doesn't know whether I'm complimenting him or messing with him. "Most embarrassing story," he says.

Clearly, he's trying to test the limits of my *anything goes* guarantee.

"Okay, let me think." I hug my leg as I contemplate what would rank as my most embarrassing moment. I think I have it. "When I was fifteen, I had the biggest crush on my sister's piano tutor. He wasn't very old. If I had to guess, he was probably in his mid-twenties. But, at the time, he was this hot older dude, right? And I was a horny gay kid. There was this one time...the *last* time he was at our house, where my mamá invited him to stay for tea and melópita. It's, like, this honey pie," I explain at Dixon's inquisitive gaze. "I brought the tray over to the coffee table, and when I set it in front of him, Christopher—that was the guy's name—leaned forward to grab the napkins that were about to fall off the tray. Only I didn't know that's what he was doing. I thought he was leaning in to kiss me, which makes *zero* sense, but, like I said...horny gay kid. Anyways, he jolted back the moment my lips touched his, and in a panic, he left."

I think back to that moment, to the stark surprise and possibly disgust on his face. To the way my gut simply dropped.

"He called later that night to explain to my mamá that he couldn't tutor my sister anymore, and she pressed me about it until I explained what happened. I felt so stupid," I admit.

When I chance a glance at Dixon, he's watching me with a troubled expression on his handsome face. "You shouldn't be embarrassed about that. It was an honest mistake."

I huff a laugh. "I don't know what I was thinking. Clearly, nothing was going to happen there."

"No," he agrees. "That would've been wildly inappropriate. But you were a kid, c'mon. That guy shouldn't have made you feel bad for it."

My lips twitch into a smile as Dixon's affirming words warm me. It doesn't erase the embarrassment of that rejection, but I can't deny it's nice to be on the receiving end of an emotion other than anger or irritation coming from the man beside me. It feels like progress.

"Thank you," I tell him honestly.

Dixon blinks, looking away, his brows scrunching together like he's frustrated with himself for being a human and treating me with kindness. I can practically see his walls going back up, so I aim to lighten the mood.

"I wouldn't have blamed the guy, though, you know? I mean, look at me," I tease, drawing my hand down my face.

Dixon immediately scowls, crossing his arms over his chest. But I swear—*I swear*—I can see a hint of a smile at the corner of his mouth.

"Now tell me something about yourself," I prompt, nudging him lightly. He doesn't even flinch this time.

"How about we talk about our scene?" he counters, clearly done with sharing hour.

"Okay," I agree. "So, we talk, we laugh, we kiss, we fuck. Done."

He tilts his head, one eyebrow raised. "That's not what I mean. Is there anything I need to know about you?"

"Like what?"

"I don't know," he huffs. "Are you ticklish anywhere, or is there anything you *don't* like?"

Huh. That sounds a lot like caring. I keep my smile to myself.

"To be honest, I'm not a fan of pain. I'm not one of those guys that can take a dick with zero prep. Jerome was very clear about the fact that prep and condom use are shown in the videos, so I'm not necessarily worried about it. But, since you're asking, there it is."

Dixon nods, rubbing his bottom lip absentmindedly. I can't help but drop my gaze there. He has really nice lips. Full and round. "Okay," he says simply.

"Anything I should know about you?" I ask, nudging him again with my toes.

He shrugs. "Not really."

I wait for more, but it doesn't come.

"Okay, then. Should we practice kissing?" I ask with a grin.

Dixon looks at me with a flat expression. "I don't think that's necessary."

"Oh, come on," I say, sitting upright and plopping myself beside the man.

To be frank, Dixon's brusque demeanor doesn't put me off at all. Yes, I want him to like me because there's no reason he shouldn't. I want him to judge me fairly, as the person I am and not whoever he's decided me to be. But his less-than-warm welcome doesn't negate the fact that the man is *hot*. Like, smoking hot.

His biceps are drool-worthy and look even better with his arms crossed. His chest is broad and strong and tapers down to a fit, yet still thick, waistline. His ass is firm and round and goddamn bitable, even though I might break a tooth if I tried. And his thighs. My God, those thighs look like they could crack me in half.

And don't even get me started on his face because that's quite possibly the biggest travesty of all. His face, even when he's scowling, is a work of art. Broad, strong features, plump lips framed by short stubble, and expressive eyes that I'm positive are capable of holding more humor than he's let me see. He's a sight.

So, yes, I'm attracted to him. Clearly. The grumpiness, like my sister said, draws me to him even more, however irrational that may be. It's a ridiculous trait of mine, that I like trying to cozy up to cold men. But it's *fun*. It keeps me on my toes, and it's oh-so-satisfying when they finally thaw.

When it comes to Dixon, I'm well aware he's not warmed to me yet, and, quite honestly, he might never be. But none of that stops me from *wanting*. Where that want will lead, I don't know. Maybe our physical relationship will only ever extend to what we do here for the cameras, for our job, and I'm okay with that. But it's going to be hard to even get that far when Dixon looks ready to bolt the moment I scoot closer to him on the couch.

"What're you doing?" he asks, watching me warily.

"Jerome told us to get comfortable with one another," I remind him, setting my hand gently on his arm. Dixon freezes. "It only makes sense to at least practice kissing before we start shooting tomorrow. If you tense up like this during our scene, no one's going to buy it." I rub his stiff-as-a-board bicep to express my point.

Dixon pulls out of my grasp, standing abruptly, and I flop back against the couch.

"We'll be fine," he says in a clipped tone. "I'll see you tomorrow." He doesn't give me a chance to respond before he's out the door.

I groan, letting my weight sink fully against the cushions under me as disappointment and a little bit of worry hits. I don't want my very first assignment here to be a flop, but I can only control my own actions, not Dixon's. How are we possibly supposed to develop chemistry and sell these boyfriend videos if my costar can't even stand to be around me?

"This is going to be a disaster."

Chapter 5
DIXON

When I get to work the next day, I'm surprised to see Niko already on set, looking like he's doing one more run-through of our script. I guess the guy is taking this seriously, after all. I pass by and head to the locker room, showering and changing into my clothes quickly before I begrudgingly make my way to Studio 3.

Niko beams when he sees me. He's wearing form-fitting jeans and a dark Henley, and his brown, curly hair is tied up, which showcases his sharp jawline. His stubble is shaved close to the skin, and his lips are shiny like he's wearing gloss.

I scowl.

"There's my boyfriend," Niko says, walking right up, a swagger in his step. He shoves me playfully.

I try not to let him get to me, I really do, but a sigh escapes my mouth as I take a step back. "Let's do this."

He grasps his chest. "Be still my heart. Keep talking to me like that and my pants are sure to melt right off."

"Jesus Christ," I grouse, heading over to the fake apartment door where we're starting off our scene.

Niko jogs lightly to catch up. "How are you today?" he asks, completely unperturbed by my attitude.

"Peachy."

"Wonderful," he says, that smile of his firmly in place.

I start to imagine various ways I could wipe it off—the possibilities are endless—but as Niko takes his place in front of me, I force myself to clear my thoughts and relax. I ignore the man's cocky smirk and the fact that he seems to delight in pissing me off, and I try to get into character for our scene. I try to embody the guy Jerome wants me to be. The guy who finds Niko attractive—okay, that part, I can admit to myself, is easy enough—and who wants to take him out on dates. I try to imagine that he's endearing and softly charming and that I'm taken with his gentle ways.

But then he winks at me, and the fantasy I've been building in my head dissipates like smoke.

This is never going to work. There's no way I can convince anyone I like this man standing in front of me, with his ridiculous irreverence and his stupid fucking man bun. And is he wearing eyeliner?

I squint, looking closer.

"Why, Dix," Niko says, fluttering his lashes. "Keep looking at me like that and we'll have to skip the kissing and go straight to screwing."

"You're ridiculous," I grumble, head snapping back.

"Are we ready?" Jerome calls out, standing in the wings of Studio 3. Nathaniel is next to him, tablet in hand.

I sigh. "Ready as I'll ever be."

"Yep," Niko calls back cheerfully.

"All right. Take one," Jerome yells.

Niko beams at me, but then he softens his grin to something less wild and much more...affectionate. He tilts his head slightly like he's paying close attention to me, and his body language becomes soft and languid as he reaches forward to brush his hand down my arm in a lingering caress.

I blink at his abrupt change of affect, utterly shocked, and promptly forget what I'm supposed to say.

Niko blinks at me, face never falling as he attempts to cover my blunder. "Did he really think you were the waiter?" he asks, prompting me.

I scramble for my line. "Uh, yeah. When I got to the table, he asked for a water with lemon."

Niko chuckles, the sound gentle and warm. "And he didn't even realize you were his blind date." He shakes his head affectionately, squeezing my arm before trailing his fingers away and leaning against the wall, like he's inviting me to chase after him.

I stand there, staring, completely thrown for a loop.

"Cut," Jerome yells. "The fuck was that, Dix? You couldn't imitate a statue better even if you were cut from stone. You're supposed to *like* this guy, not look like you're being paid to guard his body."

"Jesus," I mutter, scrubbing my hand over my face, trying to get myself in gear.

I was so stuck on my part in this duo, worrying about doing my job well and being convincing, that I never truly took Niko into consideration. Clearly, the guy is a decent actor because just then? I would've bet anything he was actually into me.

"Take it again," Jerome yells.

I shake myself off, and this time, I remember my lines without Niko's prompting. But we only make it as far as the moment I'm supposed to lean in and kiss him before Jerome calls cut again.

"Dix, you look like this is torture for you. C'mon, you've got a hot Adonis you're about to fuck. Look like you want it!" Jerome practically screams.

Niko raises a brow and leans in close. "Is he always like this?" he asks, soft enough that the boom won't pick up the sound. A hint of something spicy, like clove, hits my nose with his proximity.

I clear my throat. "Yeah, but only on set. Yelling is his love language. Don't take it personally."

Niko draws back, brows raised, a little smirk adorning his face. "Hmm. Sounds familiar."

"Huh?" I ask.

"Nothing," he says quickly.

"Take it again," Jerome calls out.

I let out a deep breath, and this time, we make it to the kiss. And it's...terrible. Truly. It's awkward and stiff, both of our lips unyielding, and I have no clue where to put my hands. Niko tries drawing me closer into his body, and I nearly trip over my own foot. It's quite possibly the worst kiss I've ever had.

"Je-sus," Jerome yells. "Cut! Everyone take five. When I come back, I want to see some goddamn chemistry."

With that, Jerome stalks off. Nathaniel stays on set, clicking something on his tablet, and Marco, our boom operator, sets down his heavy equipment, taking a seat and pulling out his phone.

Niko wings up one brow. "That was horrible."

"Uh-huh," I grunt, wiping my mouth.

"O-kay," he says, drawing out the word. "So, let's fix it."

"And how do you suggest we do that, Einstein?" I gripe.

"You need to loosen up."

"Me?" I ask. "And what about you?"

"I'm plenty loose," he says with a lopsided grin.

I scowl because damn it, he's right.

"Come on," Niko says, grabbing my hands and shaking them around. "You're too tense. Imagine your arms are spaghetti."

"That's the stupidest thing I've ever heard," I complain, feeling my muscles tense even more as Niko tries to loosen me up.

Niko drops my arms with a brief sigh. "Okay. New idea. Come here."

He grabs my hand and drags me around the set wall, into the fake living room where no one can see us.

"You suck at this," he says quietly, crossing his arms in front of him.

"Thanks for the pep talk. This was super helpful," I reply drolly, trying to take a step around him.

Niko doesn't let me. In a surprising move, he plants both hands on my chest and presses me against the wall, leaning in close. "Look, I know you don't like me, which is your choice, even though it's the *wrong* choice. But, you don't *have* to like me. I'm not even me right now. I'm Adonis," he says, rolling his eyes like he can't help himself. "He's nice and caring, and he likes you, and you like him back because he's simple and boring and easy on the eyes. Okay?"

I look at Niko, trying to imagine him as this uncomplicated person—the sort of person I'd normally go for—and I can't do it. He's much too complex. Too...frustrating.

Niko sighs, like he can tell I'm having trouble. "All right, next new plan." He grabs the back of my neck harshly and tugs me close, just inches in front of his face. I inhale sharply. "If you can't kiss me like you like me, kiss me like you *hate* me."

With that, he presses forward, dropping his hands to my chest and pushing again until my back thunks against the wall. He doesn't stop, either. He crowds me against the drywall, his body firm against my own as he leans in and bites my lower lip in challenge, practically growling.

Like a detonation, I snap.

I spin us around until *he's* the one pinned. He gasps, and I use it to my advantage, pouring all of my frustrations into the space where our lips and tongues and teeth meet. I want to teach him a lesson. I want to hear him fall apart. I want to show him I *can* do this, that I'm not this cold, hard person who's incapable of expressing emotions and feelings, that I'm not *unavailable*.

But as I cram my knee between his legs, forcing them apart, Niko's fingers spasm against my biceps, and he groans deep within his chest, and I realize...I've made a critical error. Because Niko fucking Adamos is shockingly addictive. And very quickly, I can feel myself spiraling out of control.

I back up in an instant, dropping him like a hot potato because I'm *not* the guy that loses control. I've always been careful, hyper-aware of my body, because I know my size can be intimidating. And the one thing Niko told me he doesn't like is pain. Yet here I am, shoving him against the wall like a brute and kissing him just like he goaded me into doing.

Like I hated him.

I may not like the guy, but that doesn't mean I'm going to be the asshole who doesn't respect his boundaries.

I take another step back, and then another, trying to outrun the lingering feel of Niko's lips against my own. "Shit, I'm sorry."

"You're sorry?" he asks, looking at me wide-eyed.

"For getting aggressive," I clarify.

Niko huffs a disbelieving laugh, but neither of us have time to say anything more before Jerome is shouting, "Where the fuck are the lovebirds?"

I give Niko one last glance before walking out from around the set wall, shaking out my hands as I go. "Here," I reply. Niko doesn't say a word, but his footsteps echo behind me.

"Let's try this again," Jerome says, not sounding all that optimistic. "Take it from the kiss."

I face Niko and take a deep breath.

I can do this. I can drop my fucking attitude and treat Niko with the courtesy he deserves as my coworker and bed partner.

I'm a goddamn professional.

As we're cued in, I lean forward slowly, and this time, when our mouths brush, it isn't awkward. It isn't hard and unyielding, nor is it filled with the bruising force of that hate-filled attack back behind the set wall. The kiss is soft and just the right amount of tender, and I sink against Niko's body as he tugs me in close. My weight presses him flush against the door, but there's no loss of control. No rush. There's only a languid, honey-sweet moment stretching out in front of us as our lips meet again and again.

It's good. Really fucking good, actually.

When I pull back, Niko's eyes are closed. He flutters them open after a moment and looks at me with a kind of lazy shock.

See? I can act like I give a damn. Like I care. I'm not always a fortress of ice and steel.

Niko continues watching me, blinking those brown eyes of his, and I realize I completely forgot what we were supposed to be doing now that the kiss is over. *Shit.*

"Cut," Jerome calls out, although he doesn't sound angry. When I look his way, his eyebrows are raised in surprise. "Okay, that was... We can work with that. Adonis, this is where you invite him in. Let's take it from there."

Niko and I reset, and as we gaze at each other, Niko smiles coyly and invites me inside. We make it through the doorway, and then I'm pressing back into his space as the cameramen move around us, getting the best shots. Niko's body weight nudges the door shut, and I cage him in, reclaiming his lips as Niko gasps happily. He moans against my mouth, snaking his hands up my arms and draping them behind my neck. His fingers stroke my nape gently, and I tug his hips, pulling him closer.

I don't even have to encourage myself to respond. I'm already hard inside my jeans, and based on what I can feel of Niko against my hip, he's hard as a rock, too. For some smug reason, that makes me glad. The fact I can make the man hard simply by kissing him, even though I'm a right asshole the rest of the time, feels like a goddamn accomplishment.

This time, when I break our kiss, Niko remembers his line. "Bed's right over there," he says, pointing over to where the queen-sized mattress sits along the wall. His lips are spit-slick, and my gaze hangs there a moment too long.

"This isn't too fast?" I ask as scripted.

He shrugs. "Maybe, but I really like you. Promise you'll take me on another date, and I'll let you fuck me," he says with a cheeky little grin.

I groan, shaking my head, before lifting my eyes back to Niko. "Promise."

Without overthinking the fact that the scene doesn't call for it, I scoop Niko up into my arms. He gasps, looking shocked, all wide-eyed and happy. But his arms and legs wrap around me instinctually.

Look, Niko is not a little dude. He's almost my height, but I'm bigger, and I have a lot more muscle mass. So while lifting him is not exactly *easy*, it is plenty doable. Niko, clearly, was not expecting the move, but he holds on tight. And as I spin us around to walk over to the bed, he hangs his head back and laughs, enjoying the moment.

The sound of that laugh, so bright and *joyful*, renders me momentarily stupefied. I almost stumble over my own feet—it's a near thing—but then I'm smiling, chuckling even, as I toss Niko onto the bed.

He bounces once and then falls lax, a few locks of his hair escaping the band and lying starkly over the white comforter. I tear off my shirt before following him down onto the mattress, kissing him again because I *need* to. No, not need to. Because I'm *supposed* to.

His lips, already becoming familiar to me, open immediately. The bottom is plumper than the top, and I suck on it, shivering when Niko's blunt nails rake over my bare back. I'm supposed to make my way lower now, sucking Niko's cock while I prep him with my fingers. But I don't want to, not yet. I'm not ready. Besides, we're playing up the boyfriend angle, right? Slow and sweet. I can be sweet.

I take my time at Niko's mouth, alternating heavy drags of my tongue against his own with shorter, nipping kisses. Surprisingly, I enjoy both equally. For as much as Niko's cockiness infuriates me the rest of the time, right now, it's infectious. He kisses in the same way, exuberantly and a little sure of himself, like he *knows* he's good at it.

When I catch Nathaniel holding up a cue to move along, I reluctantly pull myself back, straddling Niko lightly, making sure not to put my entire weight on him. I slip my fingers under the hem of his shirt, rucking it upwards until Niko bends forward, giving me the space I need to pull it off. I stay there for a moment, playing with the dark, flat discs on his chest, tweaking each nipple in turn. Niko watches me with a somewhat confused expression, his mouth parted gently, his chest rising and falling under my hands as his nipples pebble.

I remember I'm supposed to include some dialogue before we move forward.

"Do you have condoms?" I ask.

Niko blinks and then seems to catch up, nodding his head and reaching over to the end table. The move makes his upper body twist under my gaze, and I greedily soak in the sight of his abdominal muscles stretching taut. I can admit, at least in the security of my own mind, that the man has a fantastic body. He looks like he keeps to a rigid workout routine, much like myself.

When Niko comes back up with a condom and bottle of lube in hand, I accept the items and slide off his lap, crawling lower so I can divest him of his pants and underwear. I do it slowly, holding his gaze as I unbutton and unzip his jeans and drag them down his legs. I palm his cock—yep, definitely rock hard—through his briefs, before slipping those off, too.

I've seen Niko's dick secondhand from his videos. I knew what to expect when I unearthed what was under his briefs, but it doesn't make the moment any less satisfying.

Something about having a dick in front of me, standing at attention *because* of me, hard and leaking and just waiting for my touch, is heady. Intoxicating, really. It makes me feel powerful. Masculine and sexy. Wanted.

And when I finally bring my palm around the base of Niko's dick, stroking slowly and watching his gaze shutter, I feel like I come alive. Those thoughts I had earlier when we were hidden behind the set wall, wanting to make him fall apart, wanting to show him I'm not cold and uncaring, come roaring back to the surface. I dip my head, dragging my tongue over his slit, and when I close my lips over Niko's crown and hear his low, throaty moan, my chest hums in satisfaction.

I want to hear that sound again and again. I want to push this man to the brink, torture him with pleasure until he's exposed. Until I can see just who he is. I want him in my mouth, in my bed, under me, coming undone because of *me*.

And maybe next time, I'll...

My mind stutters to a halt. Because next time will be just like this: decided for us. Because that's what this is. Acting like boyfriends.

I am acting, right?

Chapter 6
NIKO

What in the ever-loving name of Baby Jesus is happening right now?

If I didn't know better, I would say Dixon actually liked me. *More* than liked me.

The way he's sucking me down his throat, worshiping my dick like I'm something he craves, is completely messing with my head. He must be a way better actor than I gave him credit for.

I mean, in most of his scenes as Dix, he's harder. Aloof, even. He's present, and yes, still very much hot and sexy, but it's like he's holding back behind a wall of ice. But the way he's looking up at me with those molten brown eyes is inspiring all sorts of feelings in me that are decidedly *un*-aloof. I feel very close to this man. Connected even.

It scares the crap out of me because I can honestly say I'm not even remotely aware of what my own face is doing right now. I'm supposed to be focusing on my scene, but I can't keep my thoughts off Dixon.

He snatches the lube up from beside my leg, never taking his mouth completely off of me, like he can't bear to be separated for even an instant. With expert ease, he slicks up his fingers as those lips move up and down my erection, making my spine tingle. When he presses against the back of my thigh, I gladly grab under my knees and open myself up, eager to feel what Dixon's thick fingers can do.

He takes his time, *slowly* loosening me, first with pressure and then a single digit. I lie back and go along for the ride because quite honestly, I'm not capable of anything else right now. I'm usually a little more of an active participant in bed, but the script did call for me basically *taking it*, and I've never been more grateful for an excuse to sink against the bedding and focus on the sensation of someone's warm, slick mouth and gentle fingers.

After a couple blissfully torturous minutes, he adds a second digit, carefully sinking into me and curling ever-so-gently against my prostate. A broken moan falls from my lips, and I let go of one of my legs to grab my hair in a grounding tug because *damn it*—this gentleness is killing me. It feels way too good.

Dixon's hand comes around my loose ankle, placing my foot on his shoulder, and I look down, my breath stuttering at the expression on his face as he slowly levers off my dick, dropping lower to lick alongside his fingers.

"*Fuuuck*," I hiss out. "You are way too good at this."

I know I'm going off script, but Jerome did assure me ad-libbing was okay. He said they'd stop and correct me if I went in a direction they didn't like.

Dixon simply chuckles against my skin, slipping a third finger in on his next slow thrust. He continues to flick his tongue around my hole, and suddenly, I can't be passive anymore. I start pushing my ass toward his face and fingers, chasing more of the unreal sensation he's bestowing upon me.

And I'd like to say it's entirely part of the act, what I say next, but that would be a blatant lie.

"Fuck me, please," I gasp out. "Need your dick."

Dixon's hand slows, and with one last pass over my sensitive prostate, he removes his fingers and sits back on his haunches. He's already shirtless, his mouthwatering chest on display, but he hasn't shed his jeans. And honestly, I don't know how, seeing as his massive erection is straining against the zipper in a way that looks downright painful.

He steps off the bed to remove his pants, and I watch the show, stroking myself slowly as Dixon drops the remainder of his clothes in one, smooth motion. His thick, cut dick springs upwards: dark, massive, and intimidating.

I've done my fair share of bottoming, even though for my independent videos, I only topped. But I've never bottomed for a monster cock like the one Dixon was graced with. It's...worrisome.

He crawls back up onto the bed, his erection hanging hard and heavy between his legs, and suddenly, I wish we'd done this before today, if only so I knew what to expect.

What if he's too big? What if I blow the scene because I can't enjoy it properly?

Dixon rolls on the condom and spreads more lube along his length before looking up at me. "Are you sure about this?"

And even though I know it's part of the scene and I answer with a shaky smile and, "Sure am. I need you *now*," it doesn't sound sincere, even to my own ears.

Dixon's expression flickers, a look of concern crossing over his face. And where I expect him to scoot closer and slide home, that's not what happens.

Instead, he says, "One more taste," and drops down. He laves his tongue over my hole again, and I gasp, moaning obscenely when he presses it inside my body, tongue-fucking me like it's his favorite pastime. When I feel another presence, I realize he's stretching me with his fingers again, four if I had to guess, and then his mouth descends on my dick like before.

"Oh God," I gasp out breathily. All right, the man is just being thorough. But goddamn does it feel amazing. "Okay," I add, squirming against his fingers. "I really do need you now."

Dixon pops off my dick, rubbing over my prostate one last time before he slides his fingers free. I barely have time to process before he's folding me in half and pressing his sheathed dick against my entrance. He doesn't give me any time to come back down from the high I'm riding. He simply notches against me and slides in slowly.

I open my mouth in shock when, after only the briefest resistance, he slips in. First his crown, and then all of him, filling me steadily. Inch by inch. There's none of that uncomfortable adjustment period I so dislike. There's only Dixon and the full feeling of his cock inside me as he comes to a stop, his balls resting against my ass.

Dixon's whole body shivers, and I blow out a breath, feeling so overwhelmed—but not in a bad way—that I'm not sure what to think. After a beat passes with Dixon holding eye contact, he retreats halfway and snaps his hips forward, dragging that thick length against my inner walls, lighting up a billion pleasure centers. Dixon's large hands keep my legs in place, spread wide for him, so I grab for something to hold onto as Dixon starts fucking me in earnest. I find the headboard above me and cling tightly, biting my bottom lip to keep from saying something embarrassing about how fucking good this feels, how mind-numbingly blissful. Dixon keeps up a perfect rhythm, his eyes dancing between my face and where he's repeatedly entering my body. I bet it looks amazing, the way his big dick is stretching me.

"*God*," I moan, my own thoughts overriding my goal to keep quiet. The script didn't call for lots of dirty talk or anything, after all.

Right, that's the only reason I'm trying to keep my mouth shut. It has nothing to do with the fact that I'm afraid of what truths I'll spew.

As Dixon leans back slightly, he pegs my prostate, and I squeeze my eyes shut, doing everything in my power not to come. I'm not supposed to come yet. But he keeps hitting me just right, and *fuck*, it feels unreal.

A sound, half-sob, half-laugh, breaks free, and then, suddenly, I'm *giggling* almost hysterically. I can't even help it, but at least my mortification helps keep my orgasm at bay.

"Why are you laughing?" Dixon asks, his face falling into somewhat of a scowl, even though I can tell he's trying to roll with it. He doesn't stop fucking me, but he does slow down, and that helps some, too, giving me time to come down.

I have to play this off. I'm *working*, for fuck's sake. This is the job. So what if it's quite possibly the most mind-blowing fuck I've ever had, without it even being over yet? It doesn't mean anything.

I scrub my hand over my face, doing my best to wipe away my remaining incredulous laughter, before saying, "I just...it's so *good*. I've never had a hookup half this good." I try to make my gaze open and affectionate, if not a little embarrassed—which I am—and hope that sounds convincing. If it's maybe also the truth, well, Dixon doesn't need to know that.

Dixon's face recovers, and he looks at me warmly. "I thought I was more than a hookup," he says, dropping his weight over my body and pressing me solidly into the mattress. *Fuck, that's nice.*

"Yeah, you are," I say with a little gasp and a nod. *Christ.* "I really like you."

He blinks a few times, not smiling, but looking serious and a little tender. "Yeah, I really like you, too." His voice is gruff, and I can't help but wonder if this is hard for him, acting like he feels affection for me when I know that's very much not the case. Just because this is, well, off the charts—at least for *me*; this could just be an average experience for him—that doesn't erase the fact that I know Dixon doesn't care for me. At least not yet. Maybe the sex will help bring him around. "I can't wait for our second date," he adds, dropping his head to nuzzle my neck.

Second date, right.

"Hold up," Jerome calls out, making me freeze. I'd almost forgotten there was an entire crew surrounding us. My cheeks start to flame. "Dixon, you're blocking Niko's face."

"Right," Dixon says, pulling his head up. His body is tense, like he, too, was thrown off by the interruption.

"Keep going. We'll pick it right back up," Jerome adds.

Dixon blinks at me a couple times before he starts pumping his hips again, making me gasp lightly. He drops his head to the other side of my face, pressing his lips below my ear. His movements feel a little more stilted now, and wanting to set him at ease—for the cameras, of course—I run my hands over his back soothingly. He lifts his head, an expression I'm unsure how to decode passing over his face, and then he leans down and kisses me.

I don't know why I'm surprised, but it does take me off guard. And yet, instantly, we're back where we were before Jerome's interruption. Dixon becomes more fluid, and I wrap my legs around him, pressing my heels against his ass and urging his movements on. My dick is trapped between our bodies, and the friction of Dixon's steel stomach against my aching flesh is almost too much. But he pulls back after a moment. Not far, just enough to look into my eyes as he angles himself to hit me like he did before, like he needs to see the moment he starts undoing me.

I can't even think about the scene at this point. I'm just praying Jerome doesn't need to interrupt again as Dixon fucks into me faster and harder. I wish I could see him. Not just his face, but all of him: the way his body is coiled over me, the tension in his ass cheeks, the way his dick passes in and out of my body.

And then I realize I *can*. Not right now, but later, I can watch this moment.

"*Fuck*," I moan out. "I'm really close."

Dixon drags his hand down my chest until it's wrapping around my shaft. The next thing I know, I'm gasping a breath and groaning like a porn star, my release coating Dixon's fist and landing in a hot, sticky trail over my abdomen. Dixon grunts, his pelvis grinding against me as he thrusts shallowly, coming into the condom.

For a long moment, I just breathe. My body is completely boneless, my toes are still tingling, and Dixon's heavy, warm presence on top of me feels better than it probably should. But I soak it up while I can.

Eventually, he lifts his head, and even though I know the words are coming, it doesn't make them any less shocking to my system.

"I, uh..." he says, tripping over his lines in an endearing manner. "I know we just agreed to start dating, but would you be my boyfriend? I don't want this with anyone else. I just want you."

"Yeah," I say, smiling. "I'd really like to be your boyfriend."

"This is a disaster," I tell my friend Kipp through my car's Bluetooth speaker.

"It was that bad?" he asks.

I told Kipp about my planned scenes with Dixon. Well, to a certain degree. I didn't give him details like I accidentally did with Cass, but I told him I'd be doing several scenes with the same performer. And I mentioned how the guy didn't like me, which Kipp thought was hilarious.

And okay, maybe the scene itself wasn't a disaster. Far from it. It was… Actually, I don't know *what* it was. Once Dixon got over his initial frostiness, he was downright convincing in his aim to be tender and sweet.

"It was too good," I tell my friend.

Kipp's one person I've always been completely honest with. We've had an easy friendship since high school, but we didn't start fooling around with one another until college. Even that felt easy with Kipp. There would be periods of time where we didn't have sex with one another, like when one or the other of us was in a relationship. But when we were both free, we'd inevitably end up in bed together.

Sex with Kipp was always great, and maybe that's what kept us both coming back for more, even though neither of us has an inclination for anything past the bounds of our friends-with-benefits relationship. I mean, he's the one who encouraged me to try porn in the first place. But even with our long history, sex with Kipp was never like what happened today with Dixon. I don't know that it's ever been like that.

"*Too* good?" Kipp asks.

"Yeah, like…" I make an explosion sound.

Kipp laughs. "Maybe because he's in the biz? It's bound to be good with people who are pros, right?"

"Maybe," I say with a frown. I hadn't thought of that.

"You still can't tell me who it was?" he asks.

"Nope, but you'll find out in a couple days when the video posts."

"Right. That's going to be a trip."

"Why's that?" I ask around a laugh. "Nothing you haven't seen before."

"No, I know. But this time it'll be, like, professional, you know? With closeups of your asshole."

I laugh harder, thinking back to Raylin's comment about errant hairs. "I got waxed," I tell him.

He makes a sound like he's choking. "Shit."

"Yeah, that was my reaction," I say, parking my car but leaving it running so I can continue my conversation.

"Do you like it there, though?" he asks. "I got the picture you sent."

"I really do. I think it's going to be a great fit, even though I'm working with my grumpiest coworker. At least I know he fucks like a god," I say wistfully.

Kipp laughs. "Which is a little ironic, you have to admit, considering you got the name Adonis."

I chuckle. "You have a point."

"Well, you fuck like a god, too, bro-friend," Kipp says.

I roll my eyes at the ridiculous term of endearment he refuses to give up. "I'm home now. Talk later?"

"Yeah, keep me updated. Can't wait to jerk off to you in a couple days," he says nonchalantly.

I huff a laugh. "Thanks. See ya."

"Bye."

When I get inside, I can smell dinner underway. Calliope is inside her portable crib, lying on her back and blinking up at the ceiling with a pacifier in her mouth. I wiggle my fingers in a hello.

"That better be you, Nikolas, and not some child-napper," my sister calls softly.

I round the corner into the kitchen and find Cassandra sitting at the table, her ereader in hand and a glass of wine in front of her.

"Just me," I confirm, swooping down to kiss her cheek. "Your daughter is awake."

"As long as she isn't screaming, she can stay right where she is. How was your day?" she asks, setting down her device.

I peek into the oven, smiling at the stew I see warming. It smells richly of cinnamon and red wine, and I wonder if it's our mamá's recipe.

"Good," I tell her. "Had my first scene." I waggle my eyebrows.

Cass rolls her eyes. "No wonder you're in such a good mood. Must be nice getting constant action."

A frown pulls at my lips as I take a seat across from my sister, who's sipping her wine. "Cass, I'm sorry. We don't have to talk about this stuff. I know it's hard for you with Carlos gone."

Cass's husband has been deployed in the armed forces for nine months now. He wasn't even here for Calli's birth, which I know was hard for both of them.

Cass shakes her head, though, setting down her wine glass and swallowing. "It *is* hard, but I didn't mean it like that, Niko.

I wasn't trying to make you feel bad. I like hearing about your life. Just, like, not in too much detail, okay?"

I chuckle lightly. "Got it."

"Any improvement on the grumpy coworker front?" she asks, getting up to grab us bowls and pull the stew from the oven.

I pause, thinking about that one blinding smile I saw on Dixon's face before he dropped me onto the bed in Studio 3. "Getting there."

Chapter 7
DIXON

Since I don't have another scene with Niko until Monday, my Friday is free. I'll need to familiarize myself with the next script once it comes through, but until then, my plans are working out and coffee. Or, in other words, my typical morning routine.

I start out on the treadmill at my gym of choice, and that's when my mind wanders.

Sex with Niko was...different. I don't know how else to explain it. I want to be pissed off at the guy for making me get so lost in the moment that I had trouble focusing on my *work*, but he's not to blame. I know that. It's not his fault he's a good actor, and it's not his fault that his body feels like Heaven.

Christ. I shake my head. Ridiculous thoughts.

I have a whole weekend before I need to worry about seeing him again. Hopefully, in that amount of time, I can get my head wrapped around continuing to work with Niko and approaching him with professionalism. Because the last time I saw him, I was pulling out of his body and hightailing it out of there before either of us could say a word.

Next time, I'll do better. Maybe I can even be courteous. Or, I don't know, just not scamper off like a complete jackass.

When I'm done on the treadmill, I hit the weights, but I can't keep my mind on my routine, and I keep losing count of my reps. I finally call it a day, wipe off as much of my sweat as I can, and walk out of there, down the street to Hyped. Marley looks up when I enter, nodding her head in greeting. I take my place in line and peruse the menu, even though I know exactly what I'll be ordering.

"Dixon, what a lovely surprise," Marley says when it's my turn in line. She calls my order back without me having to say a word.

I chuckle. "If I ever *don't* show up, send out a search party, please."

"I know you're joking, but I might do just that. You're our most loyal customer," she says, punching in my order and swiveling the card reader my way.

"I like my routine," I note idly as I pay for my drink.

"Workout, then coffee," she recites, nodding. "You know, one of these days, you're going to tell me where you go after this. I assume you have a day job like the rest of us plebeians?"

She's asked before, in a friendly manner, but I didn't reply. I don't make a point of telling people I work in the adult entertainment industry. It invites in too many invasive questions.

But, for whatever reason, today I'm feeling a little more relaxed than normal. So I find myself saying, "I'm a porn star," as I slip my card back into my wallet.

Marley laughs, shaking her head. Jason, who emerged to hand off a drink to another customer, peeks up at me with wide, startled eyes. He drops his gaze quickly, shuffling back behind the counter.

"Fine," Marley says, clearly thinking I'm joking. "Keep your secrets. See you tomorrow, Dixon."

"Have a good day, Marley," I say with a little smile.

I wait at the counter as Jason prepares my drink, and a moment later, he hands it to me, his cheeks pink. I peer at him, trying to figure out if he's being *more* shy than normal or his usual amount.

"Thanks, Jason," I tell the kid, who's probably not that much of a kid. But he looks young. Twenty, if I had to guess. I'm likely a decade older than him.

He mumbles, "Mhm," before going back to work.

Shrugging it off, I take a sip of my hazelnut latte—*fucking delicious*—and head for home. By the time I get there, Monday's script is waiting in my inbox.

I just about spit out my coffee when I start reading it.

Look, I've worked in porn for years. I've done a *lot* of things. *Racy* things, including group sex and double penetration. Not BDSM because we don't dabble in that at Elite 8. But when it comes to everything else, I've probably seen or done it.

But I've never, not even in my personal life, taken a goddamn bath with someone.

"Jesus fuck, Jerome," I groan.

I have to *bathe* with Niko, and then... Oh, well, that's not so bad. Then we blow each other. That's promising. I wouldn't mind shutting up that mouth of his.

Although how are we going to fit in a tub together? My ringing phone distracts me from that concerning question.

With a wry smile and soft sigh, I answer. "You again?"

"I need the deets!" my friend demands. "You never called me back."

"It's only been a few days since we last spoke," I point out.

"Exactly," Mat says with a huff. "*Days.*"

"Mat, you are like an impatient puppy. You have no chill."

"That's not true," he claims. "One time, I tied Hawthorne to the bed, and I decided to make him sweat it out a bit to heighten the anticipation, you know?"

"Oh, dear God," I mutter.

"I waited an entire thirty minutes for my treat. But then," he pauses, his words dissolving into soft giggles, "then, when I got back to the bedroom, Hawthorne was asleep."

He sounds fond, and I shake my head in disbelief.

"So cute," he goes on. "I took a nap next to him. Then I woke him up by stuffing his dick in my mouth."

I sigh heavily, scrubbing my forehead.

"Hello? Dixon?" Mat calls out. "Do I hear growling?"

"I'm contemplating my life choices," I tell my friend.

"Why?" he asks.

"Mat, kitten, my little marshmallow, that is too much information," I say.

He makes a "psh" sound. "This is what friends do, Dixon. They share information. And since I can't see your beautiful face up close anymore, I need the deets over the phone. Which brings me back to my original reason for calling." He pauses to take a breath. "What's the haps with your Greek god?"

"He's not *mine*," I say a little more strongly than intended, not even sure why *that's* the detail I homed in on. "It's fine. We're getting along just fine. Our first scene was *fine*."

"*Oh*."

"Nope," I bark, shaking my head. Even though, as Mat pointed out, he can't see it.

"Yes. Yep. All right, it's happening. Okay, do you want my advice?" he asks.

"What? No! I don't even know what you're talking about."

"Yes, you do. You're developing *feelings*. My advice, Dixon?"

"Jesus," I complain. "It's like no one even hears me anymore."

"Take a chance. Stop choosing *boring*. Try the guy who makes things interesting."

"The one who's going to give me an ulcer?" I ask dubiously, even though, now that I think about it, there have been times when Niko hasn't irritated me. Like when he was talking about his life in the private lounge. And when he was under me.

I clear my throat.

"Yes," Mat says vehemently. "That burning in your gut is butterflies."

"I really don't think that's how that works, Mat."

"Shush," he says, practically cutting me off. "You listen to me. I'm an expert in love now."

"Who said anything about *love*?" I ask in mild mortification.

"You take a chance, Dixon. You hear me? Break the mold!" he says so exuberantly that I can't help but chuckle. Christ, I can always count on Mat to leave me laughing. When he next speaks, his voice is softer, more sincere. "Maybe this guy isn't the one. Maybe you two really aren't a good fit. But Dixon? Maybe this Adonis that you *think* irks you is really just under your skin, and maybe that's not a bad thing. *Maybe* you're fighting it so hard because you're afraid of true intimacy."

"What do you mean?" I find myself asking, even though I'm positive he's full of shit.

"Maybe you chose boring in your past relationships because it was safe, and there was less chance of you falling all in," he says softly. "And maybe you need someone who's going to push, who's going to shake things up so much you don't know which way is up and which way is down. But that's not a bad thing. Because then, when you fall, maybe you won't hit the ground."

"Mat..." I say, a little lost for words.

"And *maybe* I need to eliminate 'maybe' from my vocabulary because I'm positive I just said it a hundred times," Mat says, sensing, I think, that was a little heavy for me. But then he goes and hits me with one more thing. "It's scary giving someone your all. I get it. But, with the right person, what you get back is..." He huffs out a breath. "It's everything."

Christ. I want that, I do. And in some ways, I know Mat is right. Whether it's because of his background as a licensed therapist or because he's just a smartass, I don't know, but I have held back in one way or another with all my past girlfriends. I never felt like I could show my true self because no one seemed to want that person. And not giving my all, not taking that chance, probably had a lot to do with the eventual failing of each and every one of my relationships.

But Niko? Yeah, no. He's not my person.

He's too... Well, okay, maybe not as horrible as I thought. He's confident in himself and his sexuality, which isn't a bad thing, but he's not as pompous as I assumed.

And, now that I think about it, he didn't coast through our scene. He clearly memorized his lines, even though we both went off book a bit, and he did well. *Really* well. He's a much better actor than I gave him credit for. So, maybe he does have what it takes to make it in the industry. I'll give him that.

But even so, he's flashy and makes a point of pushing my buttons. Except most of that snark came about when I was being a dick to him. He's not like that talking to Alex or our other coworkers.

He does smile a lot, though. That's something, isn't it? No one is just that cheerful.

All right, so clearly most of my arguments against the man are thin at best, but there's just *something* about him that rubs me the wrong way. I shouldn't have to defend that. Not everyone clicks. Fireworks shouldn't be because two people ignite like we do. Fireworks should be...I don't know, but I'll know it when I find it.

At the very least, I need to make an effort to temper my mood around the man because I can admit he hasn't done much to deserve my attitude. Besides existing. Which isn't a very good excuse.

I sigh. Even thinking about the peacock of a man is exhausting.

"Thanks, Mat," I finally say. "Even though you don't know what the fuck you're talking about, I appreciate that you care."

Mat huffs a laugh. "Love you, too. Talk soon?"

"Mhm."

When I hang up, I take another look at the script for Monday's scene. Taking a bath with my *boyfriend*. I can do that. Easy.

"This is, by far, the worst thing I've ever done in my life," I complain as Niko lowers his buck-ass naked body in front of me. I try not to let my gaze get lost in his ass cheeks, but it's a hard-fought battle.

He laughs, barely squeezing between my legs in the decently sized soaker tub. "It's not so bad."

I frown. "We're squeezed in here like sardines. Men our size are not meant to share tubs."

He twists his head to grin at me, which *doesn't* make my breath hitch. "You may be right," he says. I go still, and Niko looks at me curiously. "What?"

"You're agreeing with me?" I ask dubiously.

Just earlier, he was being his usual flippant self. Granted, his mere presence entering the break room did send me scowling out of reflex—a fact Alex teased me mercilessly about after Niko left—but that didn't warrant him patting my cheek before he went and saying, "*Whatever did I do to deserve such a handsome boyfriend?*"

It was a miracle I kept my mouth shut.

"Well, when you're right, you're right," Niko replies, facing forward again. I frown at the back of his head. "I can understand the confusion, though. It's probably not a common occurrence for you."

And there it is.

Niko laughs. "I'm *kidding*, my God. I can feel the tension in your body from here."

"I'm *fine*," I say. "Where's Nathaniel, anyway? Can we get this started already?" Before the water turns cold. Shrinkage is real.

"You need to relax," Niko says, spinning to face me. "You're supposed to *like* being naked and wet with me. We're boyfriends, remember?"

"How could I possibly forget?" I answer drolly. Niko grins at me, his thick lashes framing those deep brown eyes looking darker than usual. "Do you wear eye makeup?"

"For the cameras, I do. Does that bother you?" he asks, looking curious.

"No," I answer. It *does* make his eyes pop. My gaze drops to his lips next. Does he wear gloss, too? I'm so focused on his face I don't even notice where his hand is traveling until it lands on my thigh, skating upwards. My breath does hitch this time. "What are you doing?"

His fingertips ghost over my cock, which, like a traitor, perks right up. Niko smiles again. "Relaxing you," he answers. He wraps his hand around my length and pumps me slowly. I can't tear my eyes away from the sight of his fist moving under the water, his bronze flesh contrasting so sharply against my own, darker skin.

I find myself sinking further into the tub. "You're not my fluffer," I point out halfheartedly. We don't even have one employed full-time, although Jerome or Nathaniel bring someone in to ensure arousal if a performer requests it.

Seriously, where *is* Nathaniel? He's supposed to be directing our scene today, but a quick glance around the studio shows he's not yet here. The rest of the crew are waiting in the wings, paying us no mind.

Niko hums in the back of his throat, letting me go, and I miss his touch immediately.

"I didn't say to stop," I grumble, the words popping out before I can filter myself.

Niko's slow smile is blinding, and I internally curse my carelessness. This isn't part of the scene. I shouldn't be wanting this.

Niko scooches closer to me, trailing his hand back up my thigh, but he doesn't make it any further before Nathaniel walks onto set, apologizing and calling the crew into action. Niko makes a sound of disappointment that mirrors my own internal reaction before swinging himself around and settling between my legs once more. Only, this time, my cock is hard and nestled cozily between his ass cheeks.

Christ, maybe I could get on board with baths.

"We ready to go?" Nathaniel asks.

I nod, and Niko answers, "Yep." And, begrudgingly, I note I'm much more relaxed than I was before his wandering hand made an appearance.

Before Nathaniel can cue us in, Niko turns his head once more and whispers, "I'm so glad I can share your worst moment with you."

And even though I can't tell whether or not he's joking, I realize this isn't, by far, the worst moment of my life after all.

Chapter 8
NIKO

My scene with Dixon was a bit of a blur. I'd like to say I was a little more composed than our first time, but that's just not true. Like before, Dixon took me by surprise, and I found myself sinking into the action and forgetting about Nathaniel and Marco and the rest of the crew. Which is, quite honestly, astonishing, considering one of the cameramen was basically up my ass most of the shoot.

Dixon's hands, which I was able to focus on more this time, were softer than I remembered. Softer than I expected them to be. It felt like silk as he dragged them up and down my body, gliding over my chest and abdomen and lower still to wrap around my erection.

And there were his lips, so sweet and tender as they nipped at my neck and shoulder, his breath fanning across my ear as he asked me what I wanted. And then, *God*, those lips wrapping around my cock when I stood up and turned around, bracing myself over Dixon and fucking into his mouth.

I shiver just thinking about it. And after he took me apart and I spent over his chest, I sank down, and Dixon braced his beautiful body far enough up out of the water for me to return the favor, sucking him deep until he shouted and coated my face with his cum.

And the lazy kissing afterward as the water started to cool? Divine. That *was* part of the script, wasn't it?

It's hard to remember now, our scene having happened days ago, even though the memory of Dixon is fresh in my mind. We were supposed to film again yesterday, but the shoot got pushed back because of a couple crew members calling in sick with the flu. Quite unfortunate. For the crew members, that is.

"Are you cold, paidí mou?" '*My child.*'

I look up at my mamá, who's frowning down at me, her brown shawl clutched tightly in front of her.

"Oh, no. I'm fine," I say, chuckling and waving my hand dismissively.

"You were shivering," she says, placing the back of her hand on my forehead to check my temperature.

"I promise I'm fine. I was just thinking about something," I explain rather vaguely, not about to tell my mamá the details of my lust-inducing thoughts.

My younger sister, Elina, snickers from beside me.

"What?" Mamá asks with a frown, her accent heavy, even while speaking English. Although she grew up in Greece and lived most of her life there, Mamá speaks English well because Bampás, our dad, was from America. The two of them met in Greece while he was abroad for his job, and they lived there for many years, until Bampás was offered a better opportunity back in Nevada. We moved when I was about ten. The twins, Ioanna and Sofia, were only one.

I remember a lot about our life back on the shores of that sparkling, blue-green Aegean Sea. That was what I liked best: the water. It was everywhere around our small village, as far as the eye could see. Bampás would take me out swimming in the shallows with a little pail and net, and I'd try to catch fish or dig for treasure. The memories are soaked into my skin and bone, such a part of me I can still hear the waves at times and feel the salt on my skin.

Nevada is, well, a lot different than my home country.

In any case, all of us kids learned both Greek and English growing up.

"It's nothing," I answer my mamá, sloughing off melancholy thoughts of Bampás and Greece and shaking my head at Elina, but she just grins, ignoring my warning.

"What else gives you goosebumps, Mamá?" Elina asks, her tone sweet, at odds with the shit she's stirring up like usual. Elina is twenty and in college. The twins are eighteen now.

"Ah," our mamá says with a knowing smile. "Love."

My eyes flash wide. "There's no *love*. No way," I say, glaring at Elina, even though it's an empty threat. I love my sisters, all of them.

"That's not what I heard," Ioanna says, coming into the kitchen and plopping down at the table where we're gathering pre-meal. The pastítsio—a Greek lasagna dish—is still baking.

"What'd you hear?" Sofia asks, hot on her sister's tail. "How come I didn't hear?"

Ioanna and Sofia are fraternal twins and look no more similar than the rest of my sisters. Cassandra, who's in another room putting Calliope down for a nap, has dark curly hair, like me. Elina's is lighter and significantly straighter, although she shares our brown eyes. Ioanna is the outlier in that regard, her eyes hazel just like our bampás's. And where her and Sofia have the familial dark hair from our mamá's side, Ioanna dyes hers blonde and keeps it straight.

Ioanna addresses her twin. "Cass told me he's been coming home with heart eyes."

"That is patently not true," I say. I do not have *heart eyes* where it concerns Dixon. Sure, I want to win the guy over, and admittedly, I've enjoyed our scenes. But there's a difference between having feelings for someone and appreciating their dick.

"I don't know, brother," Elina says with a sly gleam in her eye. "You were just staring dreamily at the wall for ten minutes."

"He's been doing that at home, too," Cass says, coming into the room and throwing me under the bus.

"Have not!" I defend. I haven't, have I? "Can we talk about someone else's love life? *Not* that I'm confirming I have one," I make sure to add.

"My babies are too young for love," Mamá says, touching each of her youngest three daughters' heads. Then her hand lands on me. "You, on the other hand, I would approve."

Elina snickers again, and I groan.

"Is it someone you work with?" Sofia asks, picking at her painted blue nails.

I'm about to tell her there's no one, no love life to be discussing, but Cass cuts in. "Yes, and apparently, he doesn't like our Niko."

Everyone's heads swing my way. A few *oohs* are thrown.

"That explains it," Elina says with a confident nod.

"Why would anyone dislike Nikolas?" Mamá asks, frowning.

Ioanna swipes an olive from the appetizer tray. "Not everyone has to like everyone, Mamá."

"Besides," Elina goes on. "Niko loves a challenge." That is true. "And he can't *stand* being ignored."

"Hey," I complain.

Sofia nods, looking up at me with a little smirk. Although she's the shyest of the bunch, she's never had a problem needling me, just like the rest of my sisters. "You *do* work in porn. You can't deny you like the attention."

Mamá clutches her shawl tighter around herself, bending down to check inside the oven. "Getting involved with a coworker could be messy, Nikolas."

Elina snickers again, mouthing, "Messy."

I slide my finger across my throat, warning her to shut it. "I'm not getting involved with him. There's nothing going on there. You're all grasping at straws."

Mamá stands up, shutting off the oven and reaching for mitts to grab the hot dish. "You're not getting any younger. It wouldn't be the worst thing."

I throw up my hands. "Which is it, Mamá? I *should* get involved with him or I *shouldn't?*"

Cass presses her lips together, holding in her laughter as our mamá shrugs her small shoulders. "I just want you to be happy, paidí mou. You could use a prince to pamper and adore you."

All of my sisters break into laughter as I drop my head into my hands. No wonder they all think I'm spoiled. Mamá loves us all, but as her only son, she's always treated me a little bit differently. Softer, almost, whereas she's a little more no-nonsense with the girls. I don't understand it, but my sisters love ribbing me for it, saying she treats me like a princess because I am one.

Well, one thing I know for certain is that *Dixon* is not my prince.

Not that I need one.

"Let's drop it," I say, standing up to bring plates over to the table.

"Elina, how's that class on quantum computing going?" Cass asks. I shoot my sister a grateful look as Elina launches into her studies, and she gives me a smile in return.

After our midday Sunday meal is over and I've driven back home with Cass, I retire to my room to check Elite 8's site. My first video with Dixon went up last night—since there's a bit of a delay between shooting and release—and I'm curious about the reception. When I log onto the website, the first thing I see is a still of the two of us with Dixon crowding me against the door, looking at me like I'm a tasty snack. The number of views below the video is huge. It's currently the most popular.

I click the link and watch, a little anxiously, as our scene plays out before me. It's familiar, and yet it's not. Viewing it feels different than living it, but the first thing that strikes me is the way I'm looking at the bigger man there on the screen. It's worlds away from how I looked at the rest of the guys I hooked up with for my videos in the past. I look like I *do* want him to be my boyfriend. Which, yes, was the goal, but I'm not that great of an actor. I have no experience faking it. Sure, I can flirt and turn on a little extra swagger if the situation calls for it. But faking interest like that? That's not something I've ever had to do before.

Which makes me wonder how much of what I'm watching was just for show.

As Dixon tosses me onto the bed, I gulp, seeing that smile of his again. He follows me down onto the mattress, and my heart kicks up. Wow, that's hot. I watch the rest of the video with wide eyes and a major boner, torn between lusty appreciation and a sort of wistful envy for the relationship I'm witnessing on screen, which is ridiculous because it's not even real. And that *is* me on screen. I'm right there.

Besides, I'm not really looking for that in my life right now. I'm fine flying solo. Something about the premise of the video is just throwing me. I feel invested in the story, which is clearly

Jerome's goal with these arcs. I get it because I want to see more, too.

With a heavy sigh and an even heavier cock, I lie back on my bed and rub one out. There's no use thinking about anything else until I take care of the problem in my jeans. It only takes a minute before I'm spilling over my fist, one hand tugging my hair and remembering the way Dixon's hands carded through the strands during our bath scene the other day as he filled my mouth with his cock.

Fuck. I really need to think about someone other than Dixon the next time I jerk off. The man is already occupying too much of my life. He doesn't need to be making appearances in my spank bank, too.

After I wipe myself up, I give Kipp a call, knowing he's been waiting to hear from me.

"*Dude*," he says in lieu of a greeting.

"What?" I ask, reclining back on my bed and using my foot to nudge the drape closed so the low evening sun isn't shining right in my eyes.

"I really want to fuck you right now."

I laugh hard, my stomach hurting with the force of it. "Really? Are you that hard up?" I ask my friend.

"No, not really. But that was *hot*." He emphasizes his point with a low whistle.

"Thanks, Kipp," I say, chuckling.

"I'm not kidding. And that hunk of a man who was pummeling you into the sheets? My God, sign me up. I couldn't decide if I wanted to *be* you or be *in* you."

"Wow, Kipp, thanks. That's some next-level friend shit right there," I reply with an affectionate eye roll.

"I can't believe you get to have sex with guys like Dix," he says, not even bothering to comment about our strange, rather open friendship in which we freely discuss our separate or mutual sex lives. "Please tell me when you're going to fuck Tink. I've gotta see that as soon as it happens."

"I'll keep you in the loop about my business dealings," I tell him.

He snorts. "Was it weird? Being surrounded by guys while you fucked?"

I tilt my head back and forth. "Not really. No different than some of those group parties we went to back in college."

"Ah, yeah, those were some good times," Kipp replies.

"It's a little different having to be aware of my *angles*, though. Knowing where the cameramen are and all that," I explain.

"Hm, I could see how that might take some of the magic out of it."

Kipp's comment makes me think about being interrupted by Jerome during our first scene and how it really did take me out of the moment. But I immediately shut down that line of thought because when it comes down to it, "We're just fucking, Kipp. There's no *magic* happening."

"Well," he says, ever-persistent, "Dix's dick sure looked like magic. Oh, my God..."

"What?" I ask.

"I just got his name. Dix. *Dicks*." Kipp laughs loudly. "That's good."

"As always, your maturity is appreciated."

He scoffs. "Please, neither of us is all that mature for edging toward thirty. You never did say—how'd your second scene with the incomparable Dix go?"

"It was...wet," I decide on.

Kipp groans. "That could mean *so* many things. Seriously, do you wanna fuck? I'm horny as shit now."

I chuckle, and where normally, I'd tell Kipp sure and hop in my car for a quickie at his place, I hesitate. I don't really *want* to fool around with Kipp right now, which is...strange. The only other times that happened was when I was in a relationship. And I'm not in a real relationship. This "fake boyfriends" thing with Dixon definitely doesn't count.

The only explanation I can come up with is that I must be tired and sated after my orgasm minutes ago.

Kipp seems to sense my hesitation. "It's okay if you don't want to."

"Another time? I'm pretty worn out."

"Yeah, that's fine, Nik." He sighs exaggeratedly. "I'll just watch your video again and jerk off."

I chuckle at my horndog friend. "All right. See ya later, Kipp."

"Bye."

When I disconnect the call, I drop my phone next to me and look over at my laptop, which is still open on Elite 8's site and the image of me and Dixon. The video is over, but we're frozen there onscreen, the two of us wrapped around one another, moments after deciding to become exclusive.

With a frown, I remind myself those guys onscreen don't exist. Dixon doesn't even like me.

Yet.

Chapter 9
Dixon

Even though my partner scenes for the next few weeks are blocked off with Niko, I have a solo session Jerome wanted me to film today. We do them occasionally, usually with toys that we receive for promotion, but sometimes with only ourselves. Jerk-off videos never really get old.

My schedule for today just says "Dix Solo," so I'm not sure exactly what's in store, but these solo sessions are always a cinch. No memorizing lines or other performers to worry about.

I'm looking forward to an easy afternoon and then the rest of the day off. But what I don't expect, as I stroll into Elite 8, latte in hand, is to nearly bump into the one man capable of turning my mood on a dime. It's been days since I last saw him, but my reaction is immediate and predictable. I tense up before I can even chide myself for it.

"Sorry," Niko says, holding his hands up and stepping back into the locker room. His hair is wet, hanging in messy waves around his head, and that scent of cloves he seems to carry on his body hits me right in the face. I clench my jaw, doing my best to avoid taking a stronger whiff. Niko plants his hands in his pockets casually. "Didn't see you there, which is pretty funny when you think about it."

I walk through the doorway, intent on ignoring his bait, but those flippant words needle at me until I stop and turn around. "What does that mean?"

Niko smiles widely, rocking on his heels slightly. "'Cause you're basically a wall," he says, waving his hand up and down. I blink a couple times, trying to discern his meaning, certain he's taking a jab at my *icy exterior* or too-tense frame, both of which he's pointed out before. But instead, he takes a couple steps forward and squeezes my arm, his fingers lingering as he says, "You know, like a wall of man and muscle? You're big. That's what I was getting at." His eyebrows raise pointedly before he skirts his hand away from my arm and takes a step back.

I most certainly do *not* miss the contact.

I huff, confused about whether or not that was an actual compliment, and turn to open my locker. When I grab my toiletry bag and spin back around, Niko is still standing there, watching me with an amused expression.

"What?" I grumble.

He shrugs. "Nothing. You do know you're pretty, right, Dixon?"

I narrow my gaze. "What are you playing at?"

Niko laughs lightly, stepping toward me. "I'm being serious. You're very pretty. I'm trying to pay you a compliment. Just accept it."

"I'm not *pretty*," I counter, frowning. If anyone's the pretty type, it's Niko.

Niko tilts his head, shaking it slightly. "You are. Pretty doesn't have to be soft, small, and feminine, you know."

"Why are you being nice to me? What's your motive?" I ask in trepidation.

"I'm always nice," he says, taking another step forward.

"No," I respond. "You're not. You're snarky."

He laughs. "I can't be both?"

"What are you doing here?" I ask, eyes swiping over his wet hair once more. I know he's not partnering with anyone else right now.

"I did a meet-and-greet for the site. You know, 'Hi, I'm Adonis, here's some info about me, and this is my cock.' That sort of thing."

He takes another step toward me. One more step and he'd be up against my body. I resist the urge to back away. I don't want to let him win whatever *this* is.

"Right," I say. "Well, if you'll excuse me, I need to get ready to jerk off."

I'm about to turn around when Niko's palm hits my chest, halting me. He steps in close, bringing that scent of cloves right under my nostrils, looking at me with those big, brown eyes of his.

"Think about me when you come, won't you, griniári mou?" he says, making my breath hitch. He holds my gaze for one second, then two, before patting my chest and walking off, chuckling softly.

I'm left standing there, half-hard and fully confused, as he disappears through the door.

What the fuck was that? Some new way to mess with me?

As I wash the gym off myself, I can't stop thinking about Niko fucking Adamos. The man is like a thorn in my foot, trying, at every turn, to hobble me. It's like he's made it his mission to rile me up. What I don't understand is *why*.

The only exception is during our scenes. Then he's sweet and unguarded and a little needy in a way that goes straight to my dick. And he manages to pull the same sort of thing out of me, transforming me into this different person each time we're together, someone who's not angry and bitter and walking through life with a guard up.

I don't know how he does it, and I don't *like* it.

At least in three weeks' time, I'll be rid of Adonis, the boyfriend, and go back to being just Dix, the guy who fucks for cash and nothing more.

That's easy. That's the job.

The rest of it? Figuring out my life and finding that person who fits with me? Well, that'll come.

When I show up for my solo scene in Studio 3, it's just me, one cameraman named Bill, and a bottle of warming lube.

"Hey, Bill," I greet the man.

"Dix," he says in response, fiddling with the camera stand.

"Just you and me today, huh?"

The man snorts. "Don't let my husband hear you say that. He already thinks I work in a den of lions waiting to pounce."

I chuckle at that. "Jealous type?"

"Like you wouldn't believe," Bill says, rolling the camera into position.

"How does that work?" I ask, curious, as I undress and take a seat on the couch, the bottle of lube next to me. I've experienced my fair share of jealousy, but I never took those relationships to the next level. They wouldn't have survived. Anyone I became exclusive with didn't have a problem with my job.

"With a lot of trust and communication," Bill says.

I hum.

"Ready when you are," he says.

I'm already half-hard from my interaction with Niko in the locker room, so I give myself a couple strokes and then give Bill a thumbs up. I don't have to do much for this video apart from masturbate. Some performers give a spiel about the product or talk to their viewers, but that's never been my style, and people don't seem to expect it from me. The lube will be linked in the video description, and I just do my thing, letting my viewers watch me jerk myself off slowly.

I do make a production of it because that's the whole point. I start slow, humming my approval at the warm glide of my fist over flesh, the properties of the lube making it easy to imagine it's a hot body I'm sinking into instead. And since the last hot body I sank into was Niko's, that's exactly where my mind goes. His bronzed skin, spread out below me. His dark curls, splayed across the white sheets. The way he felt, his body clasped tight around my dick. How well he took me. The way he squirmed for me.

His inky-black lashes, batting when he came. And his broad, smiling lips telling me to "Think about me when you come, won't you?"

Shit.

With a grunt, I unload, aiming so that I come all over my abdomen. The milky white ropes of my release land against my skin, one after another, until I'm drained and slumped against the couch. I wait there until Bill gives me the cue that he's done recording, and then I clean myself up with the tissues waiting off-camera.

I say goodbye to Bill on autopilot, my mind stuck on the image of Niko. And with each step I take back toward the showers, my frustration mounts.

How has this man so firmly lodged his talons in me? He's wreaking havoc, even when he's not around. I need to figure out what it is about Niko Adamos and get him off my back and out of my mind. He doesn't belong there.

"My favorite grumpy bear," Alex says, hanging off my arm.

"Where'd you come from?" I ask, frowning in confusion at the small, bright-eyed man.

Alex pouts, drawing back and looking affronted. "Excuse me, I've been here all morning. Did you not hear me say hello earlier?"

"Uh..." I think back, but no, I can't remember running into him since getting to work about an hour ago. "Sorry?"

"Where's your mind been?" he asks, pulling out a chair and sitting down with a salad in front of him.

Against my will, my gaze travels to Niko, who's lounging on one of the couches in our swanky break room, reading what appears to be a mystery novel.

"Oh, of course," Alex says with a tittering laugh. "Silly me."

"No," I say with a little too much bark.

Alex grins. "You're just precious."

I groan. "Alex, angel, biscuit, the tiniest-ever pain in my ass, I am not *precious*. That is not an adjective anyone has ever used to describe me." I return my focus to my beanless burrito, but when Alex doesn't respond, I look up, surprised to find him watching me with the strangest expression on his face. "What?" I ask, mouth full.

"You *nicknamed* me," he says in near reverence, eyes wide and awestruck. "I've only ever heard you do that with Mateo."

"Ah, shit."

I don't have time to ward Alex off before the five-and-a-half-foot man scrambles onto my lap, wrapping himself around me like a barnacle. He leans close to my ear, his blonde hair tickling the side of my face. "I will treasure our friendship forever," he says softly yet vehemently. "You won't regret this, Grumpy Bear."

"I already regret this," I mutter.

"Shhh," he says, clamping his hand over my mouth and then stroking my head. "No more words. This day has already been perfect."

Alex leans back and looks at me fondly, and despite my best efforts, I can't even manage a scowl. He pats me one more time before climbing off my lap and returning to his side of the table with his sad little salad.

I clear my stupidly tight throat. "That's all you're eating?"

"Shhh," Alex says again. "Don't ruin our moment." I shake my head and dig back into my food, but after a while, Alex breaks. "Fine. If you must know, I'm filming with Trevor today, so I'm eating light."

Trevor, moniker Bruiser, is a beast. Bigger than me even. He's probably six foot four and 275 pounds of muscle. Not to mention he has a massive dick. I honestly don't know how Alex can take it, but take it he does, exuberantly.

"Good luck," I mutter.

"Honey, I don't need luck. Just a whole lotta lube," Alex says with an impish grin before grabbing his empty container and pushing away from the table. "Later, sunshine."

I nod at Alex as he leaves the break room, and then I can't help but glance over to where Niko was lying last time I checked. He's still there, and although he turns his head quickly, I'm almost positive he was looking this way. There's a little smile lingering on his lips, and my gaze gets stuck there before I grunt and return my focus to my food.

The next thing I know, Niko appears like magic, plopping into Alex's vacated seat. "Hey there, *sunshine*."

I sigh, cramming the last bite of my burrito into my mouth to stop myself from responding to his bait, staring at Niko as I do so. What does he look so goddamn pleased about?

"Excited for our scene today?" he asks. When I keep chewing, Niko goes on. "I'm particularly looking forward to having your tongue up my ass."

I cough, choking on my food a little, and Niko grins, his eyes practically sparkling.

"I think that might be my favorite use of your mouth," he says at a near whisper.

"So glad I can be of use to your highness," I grumble. "Anything else you need? Sparkling water? Caviar on blini?"

"Why, Dixon," he says, leaning forward, his shirt dipping to reveal his collarbones. "How very thoughtful of you."

"Right. Guess my 'big head' is good for something," I mutter, still a little salty about Niko's comment on my supposed egotism in Jerome's office.

Niko's gaze drops, though, landing on my lap. He wings up a brow and purses his lips. "That it is."

I clear my throat, busying myself with clearing my trash as I remind my dick that *no*, we do not like this man or his ridiculous comments. "I look forward to seeing you on your back later," I say, standing up.

Niko laughs, the sound light and earthy. "It's a date."

I clench my jaw tight, blocking out the sound of his resounding laughter.

Chapter 10
Niko

"*Fuck, fuck, fuck,*" I chant.

I can practically feel Dixon's smirk against my ass. The man is punishing me. Death by tongue-fucking.

We're spread out on a bed, a different one than before since this is supposed to be Dix's place, not Adonis's. There's a navy duvet that's been thrown to the side, an end table with a lamp, and a picture of a sailboat on the wall.

But none of that holds my attention like the feel of Dixon's thick tongue spreading me open and taking me to the edge, again and again.

I vaguely register Jerome holding up a cue card in the wings, but it doesn't seem important as Dixon slowly and methodically takes me apart. I can barely remember my own name, let alone what we're actually supposed to be doing for this scene.

"All right, move along," Jerome finally calls out when neither of us heeds his direction. "You've been eating him out for fifteen minutes, Dix. Enough."

Dixon grumbles something I can't make out, and then he's working his way up my body. "How do you want it?" he asks as scripted.

I try to remember my own line. "Just like this," I say, pulling up my legs in invitation.

Dixon suits up, covering himself in a condom while I lick my lips and watch. He coats himself in lube and inches forward, eyes intent on me, but then Jerome interrupts once again.

"Cut! Hold on," our boss yells, holding up his hand and looking down at his tablet. He nods a couple times before walking forward. "Yeah, we need to change this part. I forgot you guys did missionary already. Let's switch it up."

Dixon hangs his head, and I swear I can hear him growling. He sits back on his haunches and looks over at Jerome. "What do you suggest?" he asks, voice clipped.

"From behind." Jerome circles his finger in the air before turning to walk off the set. "But same finale! Take it from here and improv."

"I can ask you to flip me," I say quietly to Dixon. "That would probably make more sense than you appearing to change your mind at the last second."

He nods. "Yeah, fine."

"Anytime," Jerome yells.

"*Christ*," Dixon mutters, making my lips twitch into a smile. Somehow, his grumpiness has only become more endearing to me, even though I'd never admit that to the man. He'd probably bite my head off.

Dixon gets back into position where we left off, but this time, I grab his wrist, halting him. "Hold on," I say. "Do me from behind?"

Dixon's mouth curves into this slow, sexy smirk that's like a punch to my gut before he grabs hold of my hips and flips me onto my stomach. I let out a surprised yelp, and Dixon smooths his hands over my backside, his soft palms caressing me before coming to a stop on my ass cheeks. He plumps them, exposing my hole and making me inhale a sharp breath.

"How do you want it, baby?" he asks, the endearment fitting for the scene but causing an inconvenient flutter to pass through my lower belly. "Tender or rough?"

I contemplate my choice for all of two seconds before deciding, "Rough." I don't think I could handle tender Dixon right now. I'm already turned around enough, confused about my feelings toward this man. I need to keep the distinction between Dixon and Dix clear and separate in my head. I need to remember this intimacy is a farce, and that's hard to do when Dixon treats me like precious glass.

My costar hums low in his throat, and then those big hands lift my hips, making me scramble for purchase. I get my knees under me and grip the sheets as Dixon notches himself against my entrance. He enters me slowly, blissfully, the glide easy after he loosened me so thoroughly with his tongue and fingers. I breathe out a sigh of...I don't know, relief? Satisfaction? Mild alarm as my brain goes offline?

I don't have time to dwell on it because as soon as Dixon is fully seated, he leans down and grabs my hands, pressing them into the bed.

And then he lets loose.

And *fuck*, if I thought Dixon face to face was hard enough to handle, having the man bucking into me from behind, his heavy body draped over me like a weighted blanket, is something else entirely. I bury my face in the sheets, knowing I should keep looking to the side for the camera, but I need a moment to close my eyes and *process*. It really shouldn't feel this good.

Dixon's not taking it easy, but he's also not slamming into me as hard as I expected him to. Although the truth is I didn't quite know *what* to expect of rough Dixon, but even though his hips are slapping my ass and his balls are slapping my balls, and even though his pace is punishing, it's like he's pulling his punches just so. And whereas some guys would want him to unleash that last ten percent, I'm not that guy. To me, it's much more intense without the edge of pain, and the fact that, perhaps, Dixon is holding back because I told him I didn't *like* pain is a heady thought.

Or maybe I'm simply reading too much into it, and this is how Dixon fucks all the performers.

I definitely shouldn't assume it means something.

Once I've taken enough solid breaths to feel like I'm on even ground, I turn my head toward the camera and moan. And it's not even fake. The drag of that thick cock inside of me feels fucking amazing. Dixon brushes his lips over the edge of my ear, catching the lobe between his teeth and flicking his tongue against the soft flesh.

"You feel so good," he says against the shell of my ear, his voice soft enough that I wonder if the boom will even pick up the sound.

I nod my head, not even able to articulate words for what I'm feeling.

"I could do this all night," he adds, shifting his weight off my back and kneeling upright, taking hold of my hips and changing the rhythm and angle of his fucking.

I hiss in pleasure. "*God*. You have me. All night," I agree a little mindlessly, the words falling from my lips like breath. I hope they fit the script.

Dixon's hands map the expanse of my back, like he can't help but touch me. One brushes lower, applying pressure over my taint in a way that makes it feel like he's hitting my prostate inside and out. I clench around him tightly as I groan, and

Dixon grunts, giving me a few targeted thrusts that have me seeing stars.

Jesus, it *really* shouldn't feel this good.

"I'm gonna come if you keep doing that," I tell the man.

"Do it," he says, even though he moves his hand away from my taint and up to my chest, heaving me upright in a surprisingly fluid movement. He holds on tight, his other hand enveloping my erection and tugging in quick bursts that match his near-frantic rhythm inside of me.

I grab his arm, hanging on as my body coils tight. My head flops back onto his shoulder, and Dixon's hand moves from my chest to my jaw, turning my face until he can kiss me. It's not the easiest angle, but it does the trick, and Dixon swallows up my moan as I come across the sheets in front of us, my entire body shaking.

He milks me through my release, and then he lets go, pushing me forward on all fours as he pulls out of my body, rips off the condom, and strokes himself furiously. I look back in time to catch Dixon's eye as his body tenses. With a final shout, he shoots over my back and ass, his cum hitting me as hot and heavy as his stare.

I slump when it's over, falling onto the mattress and rolling so that Dixon can join me. There's a sheen of sweat on his forehead from the exertion, and I'm sure I'm not faring much better, but he surprises me by tugging me in close and kissing my forehead. He leaves his nose buried in my hair after that, and I wrap my arm around his waist and snuggle close, shutting my eyes just in time for Jerome's loud "Cut" to pierce the air like a bullhorn.

My body jolts, as does Dixon's. He blinks his brown eyes at me a couple times before rolling away, leaving me feeling cold and a little off-kilter.

"Jesus, you two," Jerome says as one of the crew passes me a robe. "Best pairing yet. You're really selling this love shit. It's perfect."

I hide my cringe, but Jerome doesn't seem to notice. His eyes are on his tablet. I chance a glance at Dixon, but he's turned away from me, tying his own robe closed.

"We're just that good," I say lightly, trying to remind myself what it is I'm doing here. The job. Porn. That's it.

Dixon looks back at me, an inscrutable expression on his face. I tilt my head, waiting for him to say something, but he sets his jaw and turns around, heading out of the studio.

I frown at his retreating form, wondering what he could have possibly been upset with me about this time.

"Nice work, Adonis," Jerome says, having taken to calling me by my stage name, as he does with all of the performers. "I'm glad we have you on board."

"Thanks," I mumble, appreciating the compliment but also feeling a little weird being praised for having sex. I don't know if I'll ever get used to that part.

By the time I catch up to Dixon in the locker room, he's in the shower. I head to my own stall, hanging up my robe and turning on the water.

"Good scene," I tell Dixon as I wash his spunk off my skin.

The man grunts. "You don't have to fill every silence with chitchat."

Right. Back to this.

Dixon shuts his water off, and I rush to finish cleaning myself before he has a chance to get away. I dry succinctly with a towel and then wrap it around my waist. When I open the curtain, he's still at his locker. I breathe a sigh of relief as I walk to my own.

"Do you ever accept compliments?" I ask, dropping my towel and pulling on a pair of clean underwear.

Dixon's gaze strays to me ever so briefly before he tugs on his shirt, cutting off his line of sight in the process. "I was just doing my job."

Ouch.

"You know, I'm not sure I like the new nickname. 'My job' sounds a little impersonal," I tease.

Dixon fixes me with a glare, pulling the laces on his shoes tight like he has a personal vendetta against his feet. "This would be a lot easier if we just focused on our work. We don't need to be friends. In fact, I'm positive we'll never be friends, *Niki*," he throws out, clearly trying to rile me with the new choice of nickname.

I, however, grin, a wash of giddiness rolling through me. I zip up my pants before facing the man, and his eyes narrow as he pops a piece of gum into his mouth, his jaw muscles tight as he chews.

"That's where you're wrong, griniári mou," I say, walking close enough to smell the fresh scent of Dixon's body wash and his minty breath. "One of these days, you *will* admit you like me. And I won't even gloat, I promise."

Dixon grabs his bag from inside his locker before slamming the door shut. "The only way I'll admit to liking you is if I'm trying to shut you up," he says, turning on his heel and making for the exit.

"There are different ways of shutting me up," I call out after him, shaking my head when the door swings shut on his retreating ass.

With a wistful sigh, I shut my locker. I probably shouldn't keep provoking the man, but I can't seem to help it.

I'll admit, when I started this mission to get Dixon to like me, it was a game. I didn't understand why he hated me from the get-go. And I saw no reason why we couldn't be friends, or at least be friendly. But now, it's like this obsession. I *need* him to like me. I crave it.

I shouldn't, but I do.

The thing I don't understand is how Dixon can treat me so differently when we're doing our scenes together. It's like night and day compared to how he is with me otherwise. When we're filming, there's none of that frustration or animosity. He's gentle and intentional, handling me with care. It's sweet. It doesn't feel like he dislikes me or wants me gone. It feels like he's cherishing me, as absolutely cheesy as that sounds.

But then, the minute we leave the set, he goes right back into his *grumpy bear* mode, as Alex called it. He's the guy who can't decide whether he wants to punch me or ignore me altogether. It's confounding.

I know he's not a heartless or cruel guy underneath it all. The way he interacted with Alex just earlier today? It was positively adorable. He played at being surly, sure, but I could tell how much he adores Alex and how much Alex adores him back.

Which makes me wonder—does Dixon truly dislike *me?* Am I pushing too hard to make him like me when that's not a feasible goal? It's entirely possible that the reason he's so amicable during our scenes is because he really is doing "the job." Maybe I should stop trying to push his buttons the rest of the time and just maintain a professional distance with the man.

The only problem with that idea is it doesn't sound appealing at all.

Christ, I don't know what to do about my coworker.

What I do know is that I have groceries to buy, dinner to make, and a niece to babysit so my sister can have a much-deserved video date with her husband.

With that in mind, I finish getting dressed and head toward home, stopping at the grocery store near our house on the way. I make my way up and down the aisles, picking everything out that's on the list my sister and I co-manage via an app that syncs to both of our phones. It's the easiest way we've found to keep things like groceries, chores, and house repairs up to date.

It's near the end of the list, when I'm in the produce section picking out avocados, that I hear, "Oh, shit."

Looking over, I catch sight of a slender guy, younger than me by quite a few years if I had to guess, staring at me with wide eyes behind his square-framed glasses.

"Sorry?" I ask, wondering if he asked me something and I missed it.

The guy gapes at me before looking around and stepping closer. "Are you who I think you are?"

Oh, holy crap. Is this my first fan?

I give the guy a smile. "That depends. Are you trying to serve me papers?"

He laughs nervously, fidgeting with the small basket of groceries in his hands. "You *are* Adonis, right? You have to be."

"Caught me," I admit, winking. I've never had this happen before. It feels strange to be *recognized* by someone who's seen me naked and having sex. Not bad, strange. Just an entirely new experience.

The guy blushes, fiddling with the handle of his basket. "Wow. Okay, well, yeah. I'm a huge fan. Just wanted to tell you that."

"Thanks, I appreciate it."

The guy continues to stare at me, and I wonder—is there an etiquette for this sort of thing? Interacting with fans 101? I make a mental note to ask some of my coworkers what they do in these situations.

Luckily, before I have time to worry over it, the guy stammers a polite goodbye. I wish him a good day, give him another smile, and watch in amusement as he runs into a display case before righting himself and heading toward the registers.

I chuckle to myself. I know my sister, Elina, likes to joke about me being the center of attention, but the truth is that's not something I need. I'm certainly not doing porn for the notoriety. It just seemed like, without any other passion calling my name, it was worth a try. And so far, it's been great.

But I don't need to enter a room and have all eyes on me. That's not something that bothers me if it does happen, but it's not the reason I enjoy being around people, either. I just enjoy people, plain and simple. I like hearing their stories and seeing their eyes light up when they talk about things they appreciate. I like making them feel good because everybody deserves to feel good. And I like the energy I get back when that happens, like karma kickback. Because even after someone leaves with a smile on their face, I can still feel the reverberation of our interaction, like a tangible marker that I was here in this world. That maybe I made a difference, even if it was a small one each day.

That's why I like people. And I think that's why people like me. Because who doesn't want to gravitate towards someone who puts positive energy out into the world?

Dixon, that's who, my brain so helpfully supplies.

And maybe that's why I'm dead-set on turning a new leaf with my soon-to-be-friend. Because I'm determined to spread a little joy to Dixon's life, even if it comes at the cost of driving the man up and over the wall between us.

It certainly has nothing to do with the way he flips my insides like hotcakes.

Chapter 11
DIXON

"Dixon, you sly dog," Marley says, shaking her head as I enter Hyped for my daily caffeine fix.

"What'd I do this time?" I ask, leaning against the counter. For once, the place is nearly empty.

"I had to hear from Jason that you were telling the truth the other day about your 007 life," she says, affecting an accusatory tone.

I laugh. "Hey, it's not my fault you didn't believe me." And that explains the kid's red face. He must've been embarrassed about the topic being brought up if he already recognized me from my videos.

She raises an eyebrow, her barbell glinting under the shop lights. "Of course I thought you were kidding," she defends. "I didn't think my routine-abiding, hazelnut-latte-drinking regular was *actually* a porn star. I thought you were, I don't know, an accountant or something."

I shake my head, trying to hide my smile. "How boring."

"Well," she says, "pretty guys like you *are* usually boring when it comes down to it."

I scowl. "What's with this pretty boy shit? You're the second person to say that to me recently."

Marley scrunches up her face, looking at me curiously. "It's not an insult, Dixon. I just mean you're almost too good for words. It doesn't seem fair that you're also a porn star."

"Careful, Marley, or I'll think you're flirting," I retort.

In all honesty, I'm not really sure how to take her words. Or Niko's, for that matter. I've never considered myself a *pretty* guy.

Marley scoffs, turning the card reader my way. "We both know we're not each other's types."

I raise an eyebrow, but I don't respond. The truth is, generally, no, Marley is not my type. But clearly, I've been picking the wrong types.

At that moment, Jason walks in from the back room, his beanie-covered head lifting. His eyes widen a little when they land on me, and I shoot him a grin. He blushes and looks away.

"You know the drill, Jason. Hazelnut latte for our man of mysteries over here," Marley says.

"Yep," Jason says, getting right to work.

Marley leans in closer to me. "Careful, Dixon," she says quietly. "You'll break his heart if you keep looking at him like that."

I huff a laugh. "Don't worry, Mama Bear. He's not my type, either."

She raises a brow. "Cute isn't your type?"

"Young isn't my type," I amend. "I'm closing in on thirty, doll. I'm looking for something more than cute and fun."

Marley looks gently amused at that. "A romantic porn star, who would have thought."

"Here you go," Jason says, handing me my drink over the counter.

"Thanks, Jason," I tell the kid. He barely makes eye contact before sliding away.

Marley chuckles quietly. "Such a darling, that one."

"I'll see you tomorrow, Marley," I say.

"Same time, same place," she says, giving me a salute.

I wave on my way out. As I'm walking home, I see a notification on my phone from Mat.

Mat: Call me, you dork.

I sigh. I'm guessing he saw the bath video and wants to ridicule me mercilessly. Well, that can wait until later. I pocket my phone and take my time making my way home, walking past the little park a few blocks from my apartment. The weather has gotten cooler now that it's mid-November, and I zip up my sweatshirt to ward off the chill. There are a couple families in the park, kids bundled practically in snow gear, even though it's over fifty degrees.

I watch them for a moment as I pass, wondering, not for the first time, what it would be like to have a family of my own. To pile presents under the tree at Christmas and sit at the kitchen table, eating together nightly, sharing stories and maybe some laughs. To patch up scraped knees and wounded hearts.

It's something I've thought about, on and off, all throughout my twenties. But I don't think kids factor into the future I envision for myself. Maybe part of that has to do with how my own childhood ended, the happier memories fractured now, broken apart just like my relationship with my parents.

But more than that, I'm not sure I'm meant to be a father. I'm not exactly a role model, with my job and the fact that my default mode is being a bit of a grouch. Mat has told me before that it doesn't matter, that I'd never be the kind of person my own dad was, the type of person who'd abandon their child for being different. That my love wouldn't be fragile. But I still can't see it.

When I look to the future, when I think about what I want family to mean, I see a partner. Someone I can share my life with. Someone who accepts me for me.

Some fucking luck I've had finding that. Maybe my dad was right about one thing—maybe fairytale endings aren't real.

A breeze picks up, and I pull my hood tighter, turning toward home and leaving the happy families in the park behind. I take a shower when I get to my apartment and dress casually to head to the studio. I'm not on the schedule today, but I agreed to bring Alex lunch after he frantically texted me about forgetting food, claiming he was ready to wither away because of his back-to-back scenes. The man is ridiculous. He could've just ordered lunch to be delivered, but I think he's taken it on as his personal mission to force his friendship on me ever since Mat left. Which means dragging me out of the house on pointless errands.

The sad part is, besides work, there's not much else I *do* have to do. I should probably develop some sort of hobby outside of working out. Especially because bringing Alex his tiny salad is not a good use of my time. Usually, my spare time would be spent with my girlfriend. But I don't have one of those right now.

When I arrive at Elite 8, the place is bustling with activity like usual. I find Alex in the break room, lying on one of the many deep couches, a sparkling water in his hand. He perks up when I enter the room.

"Grumpy Bear, thank God you're here," he says, springing upright.

I roll my eyes. "So glad I could be your personal errand boy for the day."

Alex grins, snagging the salad, as well as my arm, and bringing us both over to an empty table. I notice Felix in the room, as well, and shoot him a head nod. He smiles in response before sticking his face back into his thick textbook.

"That sounds like the start to a great scene, Dixie." Alex affects a fake, throaty voice. "But sir, I don't have any cash on me. Surely there's something else I can do to pay for this lunch you brought me."

"Christ," I mutter. "Not everything is a porno."

Alex laughs. "Our lives are a porno, Dixon. Embrace it."

"Uh-huh," I mutter, glancing over as the door opens and Malibu walks in. He looks a little harried, his posture slumped.

I squint, watching as he shuffles over to the vending machines. There are two: one for drinks and one for snacks. Both are free for the performers and are kept well stocked. Malibu snags a candy bar from the snack machine and then leaves the room without a word.

"Have you noticed anything different about Malibu?" I ask Alex. I can't recall Malibu ever eating junk food before. In all the years I've known him, he's been incredibly healthy.

Alex chews his bite of food, looking like he's concentrating, and then he shakes his head. "No, I don't think so. Why?"

I shrug, wondering if I'm seeing things that aren't there. "He just seems a little off."

"How so?" Alex asks.

I hum, thinking it through. "During our scene the other day...actually, it was a couple weeks ago now, he was unfocused. And that's not normal for Mal."

"Huh, yeah. That doesn't sound like him," Alex agrees.

"And now he's eating junk food," I say, realizing I sound a little ridiculous because the man can eat whatever he wants.

It's just a candy bar, after all. But something about his behavior is setting off warning bells inside my head.

Alex frowns, looking thoughtful.

"I've noticed it, too," Felix pipes up. Or rather, Emil. Felix is his stage name because the kid looks like a bit of a nerd, in a hot way. "We had a scene together earlier this week, and he seemed really distracted. I wondered if it was just me."

I shake my head. "I don't think so. I think something's going on—I just don't know what."

"We'll keep an eye on him," Alex says, ever the mother hen. "And I'll do some recon later, see if I can get him talking."

"How're you going to do that?" I ask, curious.

Alex grins, looking mischievous. "I have my ways," he says mysteriously. I don't doubt it.

When the door opens again and Niko comes strolling into the room, I do my best to remain unaffected. I really do. But one grin directed my way, and I'm snapping my jaw shut, my body coiling tight despite my best efforts. I return my focus to Alex, whose eyes widen slightly. He gives me a questioning look before turning his head Niko's way, and then his lips spread into a slow smile.

Crap.

"Oh, hey, Adonis," Alex says much too casually. "What are you doing here today? I know it's not a scene with this hunk of a man." He reaches across the table to pat my arm.

Niko grabs a water and shakes his head. "Nope, just a review with Jerome to see how I'm settling in after a couple weeks."

"And how *are* you settling in?" Alex asks cheekily. "Every-one treating you all right?" He adds a pointed glance in my direction.

Niko gives me a once-over, smiling widely. "No complaints thus far. The job has been...satisfactory."

I huff, immediately regretting it when Niko homes in on me. I shouldn't have given him the satisfaction of reacting.

"Something you want to say?" Niko asks, stepping closer. He comes to a stop in front of me, lifting the bottle of water to his lips.

I shrug. "Nah, not a thing, Niki."

He grins at me, unperturbed.

Alex pipes up. "Oh, Dixon, I forgot to mention I met someone who's interested in meeting you."

I look over at him in confusion. "What?"

I finally told Alex last week how Regina and I split. He was asking if we'd want to join him and a few friends out, so I came clean. It wasn't even that I was trying *not* to tell him—I just didn't think about broadcasting it. We broke up. It sucked. That was that.

But after assuring Alex I was okay—I am, really—he asked if that meant I was going to make a move on Niko now that I could. When I practically bit his head off, Alex laughed and said, *"Fine, I'll find you someone else."* I didn't bother correcting him that I'm not ready yet or that it hasn't been long enough because neither of those excuses are true.

"A friend of a friend," Alex answers me. "She's really nice, and I think you two would get along swimmingly. I told her I'd pass along her number, and she's expecting your call." His voice is casual, but I narrow my eyes. He's being fishy.

Niko, I notice, is watching our interaction curiously, a hint of something on his face that I can't quite decipher.

"I don't know, Alex," I tell the man. Do I really want to agree to a blind date?

"Please? You'd be doing me a huge favor," he says, putting his hands together like he's pleading with me.

"Jesus. You're not subtle," I complain. "We both know this has nothing to do with you, and everything to do with meddling in my life."

"Dixon," Alex says with an exaggerated pout. "I'm offended, really. It's not meddling when you care."

I laugh; I can't help it. "Fine," I say, holding out my hand. "Give me the damn number."

Alex looks victorious, opening his contacts and slapping his phone into my palm. I glance up at Niko, who's still standing next to our table, his face pinched. He better not be one of those assholes who judges men for being bi instead of *just committing to men already*. I glare slightly, challenging him to say something, but he doesn't even notice me. His eyes are on my phone.

After a moment, Niko rubs his mouth and takes a step back. "As fascinating as Dixon's dating life is, I have a meeting to get to. See you guys later."

"Bye, Adonis," Alex says melodiously.

As soon as Niko is out the door, I swing my head Alex's way. "What was that about?"

"What?" he asks, shrugging innocently.

"Even I can see it," Emil says, gaze still on his book.

"See what?" I ask.

Emil looks up, and from my peripheral vision, I can see Alex shaking his head.

"The fact that you could use a date to unwind," Alex cuts in. "Call Melissa. I think you'll like her."

Melissa, as it turns out, is all too excited to hear from me. We make plans to meet up right away because Melissa is a nurse and has a rare evening free. I was hoping, by the time I got to our date, I'd be feeling a little more excitement. But the truth is, even sitting across from her now at the tapas bar she picked, the only thing I'm feeling is boredom.

I don't get it. Melissa is very attractive, with a curvy figure, beautiful green eyes, and a nice smile. She's the type of person I'd normally go for. And yet I'm feeling nothing.

"I'm so glad you called," she says, picking a couple items off the charcuterie board between us and placing them on her plate. "I wasn't sure if you would."

"Why's that?" I ask.

She shrugs, wiping her fingers on her napkin and then taking a sip of her drink. "I guess because you look like that"—she waves her hand in my direction—"and work in gay porn." She looks around after she says that and then winces slightly. "Sorry, am I not supposed to bring that up?"

"It's fine. It's my job, and I don't mind talking about it," I tell her, grabbing a little roll of meat and cheese off the board. It's good, despite its minuscule size. The white cheddar is a nice sharp contrast to the cured salami. "And I do date women. I prefer it, actually."

"Why's that?" she asks, sounding more curious than judgmental.

I lean back in my seat and finish chewing, thinking over my answer. "I guess I always assumed I'd end up with a woman as my romantic partner."

She nods, seeming to accept my answer at face value and giving me a smile. I, on the other hand, frown.

I *have* only ever dated women, apart from my one and only boyfriend in high school, which barely counts as a real relationship in my book. Mat used to joke it's because I get enough dick at work, but the truth is a person's parts have never mattered to me. So why has my romantic preference been geared toward women?

I have a sinking feeling, on the heels of my earlier reflections regarding family, that my past has been affecting me more than I realized. My dad was always vocal about what he considered the *right* sort of family to be—husband, wife, good little kids—and that cookie-cutter notion was ingrained in me from an early age.

But those ideals aren't my own, so why the hell have I been clinging to them, even subconsciously? Why have I been choosing the same pattern of women over and over again?

"What do you do for fun?" Melissa asks me, pulling me out of my epiphanic moment.

Ah, Christ. This question. "I go to the gym a lot."

"I can see that," she says with a smile.

"What about you?" I ask, desperate to move the conversation along from myself. "I assume being a nurse is hard. You must do something to unwind."

"I do like to go rock climbing," she says, much to my surprise. "Me and a few coworkers have a group. We meet indoors mostly, but sometimes we go out to Red Rock."

"Sounds intense," I admit.

"It's a lot of fun and safe when you do it correctly. Do you like heights?" she asks.

"Honestly, I don't know. I've never done anything like that." Because, apparently, I *am* boring.

"Ever gone skydiving? Bungee jumping?"

"No way," I say with a little shudder. "There's no chance anyone could convince me to jump out of a perfectly good airplane or off a perfectly good bridge."

"What about a roller coaster, then? Did you ever go to a theme park as a kid?"

"No," I say with a wry laugh. We didn't have enough money to go anywhere. A vacation was spending the night at a friend's house.

"Not a risk taker, huh?" she says, and she doesn't seem put off by it, but her words hit me nonetheless.

"No, I guess not," I say, a slight frown marring my face.

Melissa and I have two drinks together before going our separate ways. She says I'm welcome to call again if I want to, but I think we both know I won't. I can't be the only one who didn't feel even the barest hint of a spark on our date.

By the time I arrive home, it's late, and I start to get ready for bed. As I pass by the living room, I hesitate, seeing my laptop on the coffee table. I decide to check my email, and sure enough, the script for my next boyfriend scene is waiting. I skim it quickly, my blood heating and my cock thickening as I imagine Niko on his knees for me, taking me down his throat, his pretty lips stretched around my cock. I can see it now, how his eyelashes will flutter and his brown eyes will glaze over. How I'll wrap my hand around his neck, feeling myself deep in his throat.

And then, *fuck*, I'm supposed to come on his face before edging him until I'm ready to go again. I slip my hand down my pants, palming myself as I finish reading the script, which ends with me fucking Niko over the back of the couch.

As I bring myself off in real time, I convince myself it's perfectly normal to be so excited about my job. That it has nothing to do with the man I'm working with. And the fact that I couldn't muster an ounce of the same enthusiasm about the prospect of sleeping with Melissa doesn't mean a thing.

Not a goddamn thing.

Chapter 12

Niko

"You're coming to Friendsgiving, right?" Alex asks, popping his head into the locker room.

I just finished showering after my fourth scene with Dixon, in which he gave me a facial and then fucked me into oblivion—something I *refuse* to think about, lest I pop another boner. The man himself is still cleaning off. Another fact I refuse to think about.

I finish tugging on my shirt before answering Alex. "Oh, right. That's tonight?"

"Yes," he says, coming fully into the room and letting the door swing shut in his wake. "And you have to go."

"It's mandatory?"

I remember seeing an email about the cast and crew Thanksgiving celebration here at the studio, but I don't remember reading anything about it being a requirement. Not that I was planning on skipping anyways.

"Well, no," he admits with a pout. "But everyone is going to be there, which means you have to be there, too."

"All right," I say with a laugh, closing my locker. "What time do we show?"

"Seven," Alex replies, running his hand along the lockers and knocking on a couple. He paces a couple steps, lingering, and I cock my head.

"Something wrong?"

"Huh?" he asks, seeming distracted. That is, until Dixon exits his shower stall and Alex perks right up. He claps his hands together, approaching our wary-looking coworker. "Dixon, honeybunch, how was your date last night?"

Dixon's gaze flicks to me before settling back on Alex. He crosses his arms, which makes his glistening muscles pop. "Why are you being such a little shit?" he asks without venom.

"I'm being a *friend*," Alex says, scoffing, kicking at a tile on the floor that's missing a tiny piece of its corner.

"Mhm. A nosy, interfering friend," Dixon replies, opening his locker and grabbing a pair of briefs. He tugs them on under his towel and lets the fabric drop. I take a moment to discreetly ogle his mighty fine glutes.

"A friend who cares, dummy," Alex responds, pushing the man, who doesn't budge. "Emily said Melissa said it was 'fine,' which means it tanked. What happened?"

Dixon sighs, pulling on the rest of his clothes. I make myself busy, retying my boots as I listen. For curiosity's sake, not because I have a vested interest in Dixon's love life or anything.

"There wasn't a spark," he finally says, facing Alex and crossing his arms once more.

"Why not? She's very pretty. Even I could see that."

"She was," he agrees before exhaling heavily. "She was nice. It *was* fine, like she said. There just wasn't anything else to it."

"Huh. Interesting," Alex says, nodding.

"What?" Dixon replies, tone flat, the exasperation practically pouring off him.

Alex shrugs, nonplussed, and purses his lips. "Maybe 'nice' isn't right for you." His eyes flick over to me ever so briefly before he grins at Dixon and plops onto the bench seat beside me, crossing his legs and swinging one.

"Jesus," Dixon groans. "Have you been talking to Mat?"

"Well, sure. We chat."

"Well, stop it," Dixon gripes. "Whatever scheming you're doing, cut it out."

"Fine," Alex says, dropping his leg and standing up.

Dixon looks at him curiously. "Fine? Just like that?"

"Yep," Alex replies, patting Dixon on the chest. "I won't try to set you up with another woman."

"Thanks," Dixon mumbles as Alex walks out of the room. He looks back my way then, seeming to remember my presence.

Honestly, there was no reason for me to stick around, but I couldn't quite resist staying to hear about Dixon's date. It probably shouldn't have made me so ridiculously happy to hear it was a bust, but I'm going to chalk that up to wanting to make sure Dixon stays focused on our boyfriend arc for the remainder of our month together. Sure, that's it.

Dixon turns without a word.

"He's right, you know," I call out before he's out of sight.

He pauses. "About what?"

"You deserve better than nice."

Dixon's brows furrow, and without responding, he exits the locker room. The door closes behind him, and I let out a huff through my nose.

The man may be more prickly and guarded than a porcupine, but I'll win him over yet. In fact, I'll get another chance tonight at Friendsgiving.

Elite 8's Thanksgiving celebration is taking place in Studio 1, just like my first meeting here did. The entire room has been turned into a festive fall-scape, with pumpkins and scented candles and fake leaves strewn about. There's a massive rectangular table center stage, covered in an orange runner, tiny gourds, and more food than I think even our crew could eat.

And, like Alex said, everyone is here: performers, producers, and crew alike.

I set down my offering of baklavá, glad I'd made plenty in preparation for my own family Thanksgiving this weekend, and then I take it all in.

Jerome, in his standard black leather, and Bill, one of the cameramen, are talking animatedly while Bill holds tight to a man at his side, presumably his husband. Alex is hanging off Dixon, who has a little smirk on his face, as Marco, one of the boom operators, regales them with a story that has Alex laughing continuously. Trevor and Emil are standing huddled in another corner, talking quietly and nodding along to something on Trevor's phone. And that's only a few of the individuals spread about. Everyone is mingling, chatting with smiles on their faces or walking around between groups of conversations. Some people have drinks in their hands. Others are glancing longingly at the table of food. Nathaniel snags a roll when no one is looking.

It feels like a family. A slightly odd, incestuous family.

"Hey there, sugar. What's a handsome fella like you doin' all alone?"

I smile at Alex as he hooks our arms together and starts dragging me towards where he was standing moments ago.

"Just enjoying the view," I tell him. "What's with the Georgia peach routine?"

He bats his eyelashes. "Just tryin' it on for size, like my mama's four-inch heels. God," he says, dropping the accent. "No, I can't keep this up. I'll never be a drag queen."

I look at him in amusement. "Is that something you want?"

He waves his free hand. "No, not really. I've just been frequenting this bar near the strip with a friend of mine, and the queens there are life."

"I've never gone to a drag show," I note as Alex and I reach Dixon and Marco.

Alex gasps, looking affronted. "Then you're definitely coming next time."

I chuckle. "Sure."

"Where's my invite?" Dixon asks Alex, brow raised. The man has a seriously impressive ability to raise one eyebrow to scrutinous heights.

"You'll come?" Alex asks excitedly, bouncing once.

"I didn't say that. I just asked where my invite was," Dixon retorts.

Alex pouts. "Sourpuss."

"I did drag once," Marco interjects, surprising us all. "It was uncomfortable."

"Being dressed as a woman?" Alex asks.

"No, the heels," Marco says. "Killed my feet."

Alex grins, and I can only guess where his mouth is about to go—perhaps requesting a personal demonstration—when Jerome calls everyone's attention.

"Hey, assholes. Let's eat."

There are several chuckles as the Elite 8 cast and crew descend on the table. I end up squished between Alex and Dixon, and almost immediately, dishes start flying past. There's so much food, I only take the things that appeal to me most. Dixon's plate, I note, is piled high.

For several minutes, the room is filled with the pleasant hum of chatter and the smells of a Thanksgiving feast: herbs and spices, roast meat, pumpkin and cinnamon. It brings a smile to my face, and when conversation turns to a particularly memorable orgy from earlier this year, I chuckle along with the rest of the table. A couple of the guys are practically in tears as Marco regales us with his tale about nearly dropping the boom on Silver because he was distracted by the man's ability to handle four dicks at once. Before I know it, Alex is putting his phone on speakerphone, and the former performer himself is joining the conversation.

It's heartwarming to see the reception he receives, even miles and miles away. Clearly, he was loved by this little family of sorts, and it makes me glad, once again, that I accepted a job here.

Desserts start making the rounds soon enough, and I notice, with a healthy dose of smugness, that Dixon enjoys *two* pieces of the baklavá I brought.

"Who made the sweet, crispy triangle things?" Dixon asks as he licks the flakes from his fingers.

I turn to him slowly, a wide grin on my face, and he immediately scowls.

"Did you like them?" I ask sweetly, blinking a few times for effect.

"They were fine," he grumbles, looking away and taking a drink of his mulled wine.

"I can make you more anytime you want, griniári mou," I say quietly, brushing my fingers along his arm. "All you have to do is ask."

Dixon's head snaps back around, and he glowers at my hand, but he doesn't remove it.

"Let's do that thing where we go around and say what we're thankful for," someone calls out from the other end of the table.

I sit back in my seat, letting my hand fall away from Dixon's arm, as everyone's attention is drawn to the topic at hand.

Alex claps once. "Yes! It's tradition."

Jerome rolls his eyes, and I imagine Dixon is doing the same, but the boss nods. "Fine, fine. Kick us off, then, Stan."

I listen as person after person lists the things they're thankful for this year. We've never done this in my family, but it's nice to hear. When it gets to Alex, his mischievous grin already has me chuckling under my breath.

"I'm thankful, every day, for this job I love, and to Mateo for being the reason I'm here," Alex says.

"Aww, boo," Mateo's disembodied voice says from the phone beside him.

"And what's more," Alex continues, a sly grin on his face. "I'm thankful for extra-large condoms and the men who wear them."

There's laughter at that, and Alex looks pleased with himself.

When it's my turn, I hum. "Well, I'm thankful for my four amazing, meddlesome sisters. And...for people who accept you for exactly who you are."

I think not only of my family, but of all the people around this table who've made me feel welcome here. There's no judgment or disdain because everyone in this room is in the same boat, working in this industry or loving someone who does.

And, as I glance at Dixon, who's watching me with a cautious expression on his handsome face, I come to a startling realization.

I haven't accepted Dixon for who he's been to *me*. I've been prodding him. Needling. Trying to get a rise out of the man and thaw that chilly exterior. I've been trying anything and everything to bring Dixon around. To make him *like* me.

I thought my behavior was harmless, but now I feel like an ass.

Like Ioanna said, not everyone has to like everyone. Dixon has been professional during our scenes, sure, but he's given me no real impression that he appreciates my attempts at befriending him.

Guilt hits like a brick wall, and I realize I need to make a change. No more pestering, no more poking. I'll be friendly, courteous, and professional right back because Dixon deserves that. And if he wants to be ornery when the cameras aren't rolling, that's fine.

It's not that I wanted him *not* to be a grump. That's who he is. I just wanted him to let me into his inner circle where he's sixty percent, as Alex said, not one hundred.

But that's not fair of me to ask. If Dixon doesn't want to be my friend or...whatever else, that's his choice.

Gut uncomfortably tight, I face my empty plate as Dixon takes his turn, his deep voice rumbling in the space between us.

"I'm thankful for my chosen family," he says, making my chest constrict painfully for reasons I don't want to delve into. "And for you, Mat, even though you deserted."

"Dixon, you big, secretly sweet grizzly, I love you," Mateo says through the phone.

"Yeah, yeah," Dixon grumbles, sounding both fond and crotchety at the same time. "Someone else say some sappy shit now."

The circle of thanks continues until everyone has spoken, and as soon as the meal has been devoured and the table cleared, Alex bounds up with the exuberance of a sugar-high puppy. "I'm ready to dance," he says, bouncing lightly and shimmying his shoulders.

I take in the outfit he wore tonight, the skintight, shiny black pants and sheer white Oxford shirt, and chuckle. The boys will be all over him.

And luckily, since Alex mentioned going to the club after dinner, I dressed up, too, in slim-fitted, rust-colored pants and a deep V-neck t-shirt, topped off with my brown leather jacket. Maybe dancing is just the thing I need to brighten my somber mood and get over a certain coworker of mine.

"I need to sleep off this food," Dixon counters.

"Not allowed," Alex says. "You're coming with the rest of us, or I'll turn you into a pumpkin."

"Yes, fairy godmother," Dixon snarks.

"Now *that* would be a great drag name," Alex notes, ever cheerful as he starts rounding people up to head to the next part of our evening.

Sublime is packed when we arrive, the club already thrumming with a weekend crowd. It's my first time coming here with the crew, but from what I've heard, this is a weekly occurrence. I usually stay home Friday nights, watching Calliope so Cass can have a night off at the end of the week.

The bouncer lets us right through the doors, and as soon as we're inside, the booming bass of the club settles over my skin like a heavy shroud. The whistles and cheers we received outside are nothing compared to the noise and catcalls within. And in the blink of an eye, me and the rest of the gang are surrounded by a throng of horny men.

Holy shit.

Alex keeps his hand in mine as he pulls me along after him, up a roped-off staircase to a VIP balcony above, leaving our fans and their pawing hands behind. "They keep this area saved for us on Fridays," he explains over the cacophony of the club.

I nod, grateful for the temporary reprieve, and within moments, a server appears, wearing nothing but a silver chain around his neck and little red booty shorts that could barely be classified as decent. He takes orders as I look everything over.

The VIP section of Sublime is full of expensive-looking black leather chairs and couches, as well as small tables littering the space. A railing takes up one long wall, which opens onto the dance floor below. The thrum of music is ever-so-slightly muffled up here, but it's still loud enough that I can barely hear myself think. Below, lights flicker over the crowd, creating a dizzying effect as men, and the occasional woman, gyrate against one another.

"This your scene?" Dixon asks, sidling up next to me at the railing.

I glance over at him, trying to hide my surprise that he's choosing to speak to me of his own free will.

I shrug. "I enjoy the club scene on occasion."

He nods once.

"Do you like dancing?" I ask. I wouldn't mind seeing that. Oh, who am I kidding? I'd love to see that.

"Sometimes," he replies, turning around and walking away without another word. He takes a seat next to Alex, who's currently up on his knees, shaking his body to the music. And even though I itch to follow, I let him go, determined to keep up with this new *professional boundaries* plan of mine.

When the server returns with our drinks a moment later, I accept mine and sit near Emil, who I learn is studying psychology. He talks animatedly about it, waving his hands, the excitement evident in his tone. And I share a little about my own life, barely even glancing in Dixon's direction and certainly not thinking about going over there and pestering him.

See? Progress.

I can be *not* pushy. In fact, I'll do my best to ignore Dixon tonight and focus on having fun, instead.

Chapter 13

DIXON

It doesn't take long for most of my coworkers to head downstairs to the dance floor. And even though I join them, I'm not enjoying myself as much as usual. Against my will, my eyes keep finding Niko in the crowd. His hair falls around his face as he smiles and dances, and the lights reflect off the sheen of sweat covering his chest, easily visible because of that ridiculously low-cut shirt of his. It's distracting.

It's also evident, by the swarm of men vying for his attention, that he's the fan favorite tonight. That's not surprising, actually. We draw a huge crowd of Elite 8 viewers here every Friday night, and Niko—or rather, Adonis—is fresh meat. Everyone wants to be the first to sink in their claws.

"Did you say something?" my dance partner practically yells, standing on his tiptoes to reach my ear. His hand is splayed against my chest, and I'm guessing he felt, more than heard, whatever sound I just made as one of Niko's admirers copped a feel. At least Niko shut that crap down, sliding the man's hand away and spinning him into a dance move instead.

I shake my head. "No."

"Do you want to get out of here?" I think he asks.

I give him another quick once-over. I know most people assume, being a porn star, I'm a fan of casual hookups. But the truth is that's not my scene. I much prefer dating. Maybe it *is* because I get regular, meaningless sex on the job. Or maybe I simply want a connection, to find my fabled someone, and I doubt that person will still be playing the field.

"Not tonight," I tell the guy, trying to be as polite as possible.

He pouts but seems to accept my answer, moving on to dance with someone else. I head toward the bar, not because I want a drink, but because I'm really not in the mood to dance tonight.

"Another bourbon?" Remi, one of the bartenders, asks.

I shake my head. "Just a water."

He raises his eyebrows but nods, filling a clear glass with water and sliding it over to me. I thank him and spin around, resting my back against the bar top as I peruse the room. Niko is still dancing with a throng of men, a wide smile on his face like he's having the time of his life. He shed his jacket at some point, and while the leather did, admittedly, look nice on him, the plain tee leaves nothing to the imagination. Every ripple of muscle is visible under the thin cloth as he moves to the beat like liquid sex, the same way he walks and does just about everything else. Like he knows he's hot. Like he's confident in his own skin.

I suppose some people would call that arrogance, and until recently, I was one of them. But I guess now that I've gotten to know him better, I understand Niko a bit more. And that cocky attitude? It's his way of being playful. He's actually quite good-humored most of the time.

It's such a foreign concept to me, and I briefly wonder if that's why I took such an immediate dislike to the man. But then I think about Alex and how he's just as cheerful in his own, different way. I don't know what it is about Niko in particular that's settled under my skin like an itch I can't scratch. At least we get along when we're both naked. Having sex with the man doesn't feel like a battle at all.

And now that I'm thinking about sex, I can't help but wonder if Niko will bring one—or more—of those men he's dancing with home tonight. The idea puts a scowl on my face. If he's going to take advantage of his newfound notoriety, he better be safe.

In fact, I intend to tell him that, to march right over and make sure he knows how these fans can get, but something else grabs my attention before I can make my move. Instead of brown curls, it's blonde ones, spread across the shoulder of a man much larger than their owner.

"What are you doing, Mal?" I mumble, watching as my coworker and friend practically hangs off his dance partner, his body concerningly limp. The bigger guy seems to be holding Malibu up, and after a moment, he starts to lead them off the dance floor. I follow before I can second-guess my judgment. The situation seems sketchy as fuck.

Malibu and the man head toward the back hall. I lose sight of them when they turn the corner, but I push my way quickly through the crowd of people, ignoring the occasional person calling my name.

When I turn down the hallway, I don't see either of them, and my stomach sinks. Quickly, I debate my options. It doesn't look like the back exit has been opened. I wasn't too far behind the duo, and if they went out that way, I'd expect the door would still be closing, as it's on slowing hydraulics. Instinct tells me the man was trying to go somewhere private, so I don't think they went upstairs. And I don't see them among the men hanging out in the hallway, kissing or doing other things in the dim lighting.

I head for the bathroom. It's full when I push inside, several men hooking up, a few actually using the urinals. There are three stall doors, and I look underneath for Malibu's bright green Converse. I've never been more glad for his ridiculous choice in shoe wear because I spot him right away.

I storm up to the stall door and bang on it. "Malibu?"

"Go away," Mystery Guy says gruffly.

"Open the goddamn door," I growl. A few people in the room stop to watch, curious about the spectacle I'm creating.

"'S'fine," Malibu slurs, his voice much too gone for my liking.

"It's not fine," I practically yell. "Open the goddamn door before I rip it off its hinges."

"Oh, I'd like to see that," someone comments from behind me.

I bang a few more times.

"Leave us alone," the guy says. "Your friend wants to be here."

"I'm not taking your word for it, mate," I growl, getting a lot frustrated at this point, my worry for Malibu only increasing. "Open the fucking door, or I'm getting the club owner, and you'll be banned for life. *After* I kick your ass."

That threat seems to do the trick, as a second later, the door swings open an inch. I push it wider, my heart kicking up when I find Malibu slumped against the wall, his head back, eyes barely open, blinking slowly at me.

"Mal, you okay?" I ask, shoving past the man who's attempting to block my entrance into the stall. There's barely enough room for the three of us, but I don't give a shit.

I grab Malibu's face, tilting it toward me. His eyes are glassy and unfocused, but after a moment, he smiles loopily. "Hey."

"See?" the guy says. "He's fine."

"He's not *fine*. He's either way too drunk for whatever activities you had in mind, or he's drugged." Adrenaline-high, I whip around, pressing the guy against the opposite side of the stall. "Did you slip him something?" I grit out, watching as his eyes shoot wide.

He holds up his hands in surrender. "No way, man! It's not like that. We were just dancing. Your friend is the one who suggested coming in here."

"If you gave him something, I swear to God—"

"I didn't! Fuck," the guy stammers, looking relieved when I drop my hold on him.

"Come on," I tell Malibu, turning around and hooking my arm around his shoulders. He leans heavily on me. "We're getting out of here."

I walk Malibu past the gawkers, leaving stall-guy behind. It feels like I'm holding most of Malibu's weight myself, his head lolling against my shoulder with each step.

"Jesus, Mal," I say quietly. "What did you get yourself into?"

"What's going on?" a voice asks as we're passing by the stairway.

I look over, finding Niko watching us with curiosity and some alarm.

"I don't know," I tell him, continuing to walk Malibu out toward the front of the club. "I think he's wasted."

"I'll grab some water," Niko says, peeling off toward the bar.

I wait near the door while Niko grabs a bottled water, and a minute later, the three of us break out into the cool night air. I shuffle Malibu a few dozen feet down the sidewalk, where the sound is more dimmed, and lean him against the wall. He slumps down to his butt, and the neon lights of the club sign play off his skin, casting him in a reddish glow.

"Malibu," I say, crouching down and holding his chin.

He blinks several times like he can't focus, but then he smiles. "Hey."

"Did you take something?" I ask.

"Huh?"

"Drugs. Did you take drugs? Or do you think someone might have slipped you some?" I ask, watching as Malibu's lids lower like he's about to fall asleep. "Shit," I mutter, slapping his face lightly.

Malibu perks back up, and I uncap the water, holding it against his lips.

"Come on, drink," I tell him.

He manages a few swallows before leaning his head back against the exterior of the club, the lights above making him look flushed. "No drugs," he says quietly. "Just alcohol."

I blow out a breath of relief, but it's short-lived. Malibu is definitely not okay.

"We should get him home before he's sick," Niko says.

I nod, not even arguing the *we* as I pull out my phone to order a rideshare. It's only three minutes out. I encourage Malibu to hydrate as we wait, and when the car pulls up, I tug him upright. He follows without question. Niko does, too. Before maneuvering Malibu into the car, I grab his wallet to give the driver his address. By the time Malibu is tucked into his seat and I'm buckled in next to him, Niko is already strapped in up front. I don't even complain.

It doesn't take long to arrive at Malibu's. He lives in an apartment opposite a small park that reminds me a little of my own place, at least from the outside. Niko helps me get Malibu upstairs, and I grab his keys from his pocket to let us in.

As I flick on the light, I note that the place is nice. Or, rather, it *would* look nice if it weren't almost entirely empty.

There's a small couch, a single lamp, and dozens of nails in the wall without a single picture hung upon them. I could imagine this space being filled with vibrant art or personal photos, but at the moment, it looks devoid of life. Even the kitchen is sparsely outfitted, without any visible pots or pans to cook with. I have a feeling if I were to open the fridge, I wouldn't find much inside.

I've never been to Malibu's apartment before, but I can't imagine that this is how he normally lives. It doesn't fit the guy I know who's colorful and happy and full of life and love. It doesn't mesh with the guy who's put together, eats healthily, and talks about yoga like it's a spiritual experience. There's nothing chakra-cleansing about this place. It's a depressing void.

As soon as we get Malibu settled on the couch, I push the water into Niko's hand. "See if you can get him to drink more. I'm going to look for something for his impending headache."

Niko nods as I walk off. I check the bathroom first, but there are no meds in the cabinet behind the mirror. I look through all of his drawers, as well, but they're nearly empty. The only items I find are toothpaste, a toothbrush, and a couple towels.

I check the kitchen next, but it's more of the same. I don't even see Band-Aids or a first aid kit anywhere. And, as expected, the contents of the fridge are depressing.

Reluctantly, I head into Malibu's room and look through his drawers, doing my best to avoid displacing his stuff. However, he doesn't have much stuff to displace. His clothes and small collection of brightly colored shoes make up the entirety of his possessions. There are sheets and a comforter on the bed, but they're thrown in disarray, and the end table is empty. There's nothing on the walls, no trinkets or jewelry on the dresser.

I rub my head as I walk back into the living room, a pit lodged deep in my stomach. Something is off about this whole situation. Unless Malibu is getting ready to move, it makes no sense for his apartment to be this barren.

What's more, I've *never* known Malibu to get drunk. Never. Not once. Not even close. He's always been careful about his intake, only accepting a single drink whenever we're out. It's a habit I've noticed time and time again. So for Malibu to get wasted enough that he could barely stand and to follow—or lead—a guy into the bathroom for who knows what? That's not Mal. He could've easily been taken advantage of, and he wouldn't have had the wherewithal to fight it off.

I don't have the slightest clue what's going on with my friend, but it makes me uneasy.

Niko looks up as I walk into the living room. Malibu is slumped on his side, groaning lightly, probably starting to feel the unfortunate side effects of alcohol.

"Anything?" Niko asks.

I shake my head.

"I can run out," he says, hopping up.

I blink a couple times. "What are you doing here?"

The question comes out ruder than I intended, but Niko simply cocks his head. "I just want to help."

I open my mouth to tell him there's no reason for him to help. That I have it under control. But the truth is I'm worried. My mind is running wild with scenarios that could explain Malibu's recent behavior and whatever is going on here in his apartment, and not one of them makes me feel an iota of comfort. My friend may be spiraling or in trouble or who knows what. I have no idea.

Should I have pushed more? Tried harder to get Malibu to open up about what's wrong?

I don't know. But I do know there's no way I'm leaving Malibu's side tonight. And the thought of not being alone in this, of having someone else here, is a relief, even if that solace comes in the form of the last man I would've expected.

I blow out a breath. "You sure?"

"Yeah, of course," Niko says sincerely. "I saw a convenience store a couple blocks down. How about I grab some Gatorade, meds...and maybe a little food for later?"

I nod. "Not a bad idea. Thanks, Niki."

He looks as surprised by the nickname use, void of any snark, as I feel at having said it. But he nods and heads off without another word.

I sit next to Malibu, who's half-dozing on the couch. Brushing some of his hair back from his face, I wonder aloud, "What are you getting yourself into?"

Chapter 14

NIKO

No one could ever again convince me that Dixon is an unfeeling, cantankerous ass. Not that I thought that anyways. I could always tell his grumpy bear routine was a bit of a façade.

But seeing Dixon worry over and tend to Malibu all night and on into the morning was like being given a brief, precious glimpse into who the man is at his core. He relentlessly persuaded Malibu to drink the Gatorade I bought. He held his hair back when Malibu eventually emptied the contents of his stomach into the toilet. He had him drink another Gatorade once he'd settled. He tucked him into bed when it was clear Malibu was too exhausted to keep his eyes open any longer. And he stayed next to him all night, periodically checking to make sure Malibu was comfortable and well.

Honestly, it was endearing as all get out. I remember when I first met the man, I accused him of having his exes wait on him hand and foot. Granted, he *did* make some snarky-ass comment about me doing just that as his fake boyfriend. But clearly, that's not the type of person Dixon is, and if anything, I bet it's the opposite. I bet he likes taking care of people, maybe even pampering them a little.

I shouldn't like that notion as much as I do.

I left in the early morning before Malibu had woken up—because I'd promised Cass I'd be home to babysit so she could meet a friend for kid-free brunch—and when I texted Dixon to check in later that afternoon, he replied simply that Malibu seemed okay but didn't want to talk about it. I don't know the guy well, but if Dixon says this isn't normal behavior for Malibu, I believe him.

And I'm glad he has Dixon, among others, in his corner, whether or not he wants them there.

"You look miles away, paidí mou," my mamá says, calling me "my child" like she always does.

"Guess I am," I admit, refocusing on the bechamel sauce I'm making for the papoutsákia, a stuffed eggplant dish.

We're preparing a big feast for Thanksgiving like we do every year. Greeks don't celebrate the holiday, but we always have because of our bampás being American. We don't do a turkey, though. Instead, we put together a traditional Greek spread. The exception is pumpkin pie because who doesn't love pumpkin pie?

It's still early, midmorning, but everyone is gathered at our mamá's to help prepare the food because that's another one of our traditions for the holiday. As well as the fact that we now have it on a Sunday because it's easier for all of us to get together that way.

"Where's your head?" Mamá asks while cutting up vegeta-bles for a salad.

"I bet I know," Elina, Miss Middle Child, chirps. She's sitting at the table, Calliope in her lap while Cassandra helps Sofia with her laptop. Cass has always been good with technology.

"Hush," I say, even though I know the troublemaker won't heed my warning.

"Do tell," Ioanna says, loving gossip, as always. The snarky twin is standing at the other end of the L-shaped, terracotta-colored counter, preparing the pie, her blonde-dyed hair up in a bun atop her head.

Our mamá's kitchen is large, which affords us plenty of space to cook big meals like this. Counters run along two walls, and a massive, oval table takes up space near the third. The last wall is comprised of a large archway that opens into the hall and then the living room. There are dried herbs, peppers, and other things hanging in the kitchen, and they create a beautiful array of greens and browns and reds that dangle in front of the cream-colored walls. It's all very warm and inviting, fitting for the Nevada desert, apart from the blue, Greek-inspired tiles acting as a backsplash over the countertops and running along the archways between rooms. The whole house is like that: a mix of desert colors and nods to our Greek heritage.

"There's nothing to tell," I cut in, wondering how Elina even *has* the gossip. Must be from Cass. Or...

"You should see this guy," Kipp says, flouncing into the kitchen. "No wonder Niko's head is in the clouds. He's built like a god."

"Kipp," I moan.

"No, really. Look." He holds his phone out towards Elina. Her eyes widen.

"Please tell me you're not showing her a picture of..." I don't even want to finish my sentence.

Kipp smirks. "Don't worry. It's his profile picture, and he's *clothed*."

"I wanna see," Sofia says, Cass at her heels. Before I can stop it, everyone, including our mamá, is peering at Kipp's phone. I hang my head, resigning myself to the inevitable.

"Oh, wow," Ioanna says.

"Very handsome," Mamá adds with a nod.

Cass gives me a little smile, shaking her head as she takes Calli back into her arms.

"Nice catch, bro," Elina says, smirking up at me. Her and Kipp have that smirking thing in common.

"He's not *my catch*," I clarify. "He's just my coworker. There's nothing going on between us."

"So you claim," Kipp says, tucking his phone back into his pocket. "But the videos say otherwise."

"Nope, keep that out of this house. My family doesn't need to hear those details," I tell Kipp, leveling him with a glare.

Ioanna wrinkles her nose. "Yeah, seriously. I try not to think about it as is."

"Fine," Kipp says, holding his hands up in surrender, even though I know he'd never actually share details about my work in front of my family. He simply likes to give me crap.

And I love him for it. Kipp is like a brother to me, evidenced by the fact that he's here today. Ever since college, he's tagged along for the holidays. His own family moved back to the Midwest, and even though Kipp has traveled there on occasion, he and the rest of his family aren't on good terms, so visiting isn't high on his list of wants. My family, however, has always accepted him with open arms, folding him into our holiday dinners like he belongs.

Exactly like a brother. Except, when I think about it, maybe that's not the best term for what Kipp is to me, considering we do fuck on occasion.

"Speaking of gods, though," Kipp says, drawing my attention back to him and the sly gleam in his eye.

"Kipp," I warn halfheartedly.

He grins. "Did you ladies hear what Niko's new porn name is?"

"Is that like a pen name for porn stars?" Sofia asks.

"Surely not," Elina says, swiping her finger into the pumpkin pie mix and stealing a lick.

Ioanna whips her with a towel. "I don't think you can retain your anonymity when people can literally see who you are."

"It's like an alias," Cass says, bouncing Calli on her hip. "Or a stage name, like Cher. What's yours?" she asks me.

All of my sisters look my way, but I glare at Kipp, who is enjoying this far too much, a large grin on his face.

With a heavy sigh, I face the firing squad. "Adonis."

There's a beat of silence, and then the kitchen erupts into laughter.

"See what you've done?" I complain to Kipp through the hoots and comments about my "pretty face" and Elina opening her phone because she just *has* to "text every single one of our cousins." Kipp comes over and slaps me on the back, unperturbed by the chaos he's bestowed upon me.

"Very fitting," Mamá says, squeezing my shoulder after Kipp has retreated to sneak some cheese from the appetizer board on the table.

I shake my head, chuckling under my breath. At least my family is supportive.

By the time dinner is ready, I've listened to countless friend-ly jabs about my job. But as we all sit down around the food-laden table, the teasing stops, and my family and I enjoy a meal together. We talk about what's going on in our lives, about Bampás and Greece and the family we miss, and it's nice. Even Kipp shares some memories from years ago, about other times we've gathered like this, all of us together. I can tell it means a lot to him, having this surrogate family, and I give him a smile which he readily returns before stuffing his face with the baklavá I brought.

Of course, that makes me think about Dixon stuffing his face with my baklavá, too. I wonder what he's doing today. I wonder if he has family he spends Thanksgiving with every year. I wonder the same about Malibu, who's still on my mind.

Once it's late and everything has been cleaned up and the remaining food portioned into containers for all of us to take as leftovers, Kipp, Cass, and I head home. We'd carpooled together since it was easier than driving the hour to Mamá's separately. On the way home, Cass and Kipp talk a bit about some sort of coding system that makes no sense to me, but seeing as they both work in software development, they have a lot of joint knowledge to share.

When I pull up to the house Cass and I share, my sister extracts her daughter carefully from her car seat and carries her inside to put to bed.

"Want to come in?" I ask Kipp.

"Yeah, sure," he replies, sticking his hands in his pockets and following me to the door.

I pass through the kitchen on my way in and grab a bottle of tsípouro, two glasses included. Kipp is already sitting in the living room when I get there, so I join him on the couch, pouring some of the anise-flavored drink into each glass and sliding one his way across the coffee table.

"Yamas," I say, holding up my glass. *'Cheers.'*

Kipp repeats the Greek toast and we clink our glasses together. As we sip our tsípouro, Kipp looks my way.

"Thanks for letting me join you today," he says.

My brows draw together. "Of course, Kipp. You know you're always welcome." He shrugs, but I can tell something is on his mind. "What's up?"

"Don't you think...once you find someone, that will change?" he asks.

"What do you mean?" I turn more fully toward my friend. He looks a little forlorn.

"When you start dating or get married. It'd be kind of weird for your former fuck buddy to show up at family gatherings." He frowns slightly, taking another sip of his drink.

Oh.

"Kipp," I say, inching closer and putting my hand on his thigh, squeezing lightly. "You *are* family. You're always welcome, and anyone I end up with won't have a problem with that. Because if they do, I won't end up with them, all right?"

"How can you say that?" he asks, leaning back against the cushions and tilting his head my way. His short, dark hair is styled up away from his face today, and his blue eyes look sharp in the dim lighting. "You can't help who you fall for. It might be someone who's jealous."

"Well, they'll have nothing to be jealous of," I say. Kipp winces, and I immediately backtrack. "You know what I mean, Kipp. If I'm with someone, I won't be sleeping around. The past will be in the past."

"Yeah," he says simply, looking away, and I don't know what exactly has my friend so bothered, but I don't like it.

"Hey," I say, tapping his chin until he looks my way. I open my mouth, but I don't get a chance to say another word because Kipp swings his leg over my lap and presses his lips to mine. I "oomph" against his mouth, instinctively grabbing Kipp's waist with my free hand, holding my drink out of the way with the other.

He kisses me almost frantically, and the familiar feel of him, the familiar taste, has me drifting into that zone we've been in countless times before. Where we get off, using each other's bodies to fulfill our sexual needs.

Except something feels off this time, and the minute I tense against Kipp's lips, he stills and pulls back. He's still settled over my lap, half hard, just like me. But he must sense something in my expression because he shifts away and reclaims his seat on the couch, picking up his drink and downing the remainder.

"You really like him, huh?" he says, reclining back against the cushions and adjusting himself.

"I..."

"Sorry," Kipp adds, voice low.

"What for?" I ask, setting down my own unfinished drink. "I should be the one apologizing."

"No," he says with a wry chuckle. "I should've asked before I attacked you. I had a hunch you really did like this Dixon, but I guess I was feeling a little lonely tonight, and it overrode my common sense."

It's on the tip of my tongue to tell him I *don't* like Dixon, that it's not like that, but I hold back. A more concerning thought enters my head.

"Kipp, do you have feelings for me?" I ask.

We've always been very open with one another, but that's one question I've never asked because I thought I knew the answer. Maybe I just didn't want to know.

Kipp looks over at me again, his head rolling on the couch cushion, a sad sort of smile on his face. "No, Nik, I don't love you. Not like that." Relief floods my body. I don't want to lose Kipp as a friend. "I'm just in a weird place right now. Everyone is settling down, you know? And even though I don't think I want that, I feel like I don't really know what I'm doing with my life. I'm not *unhappy*. I just wonder if something is missing."

"You don't have to want what everyone else does, Kipp. It's okay if you don't want a romantic relationship," I say.

"Yeah," he says softly. "Maybe. I should get going." He sits upright.

"If you're sure," I say, feeling a little off-kilter.

"Yeah. Just tell me one thing. *Do* you like him?"

I look over at my friend, his blue eyes holding my gaze. I think about Dixon, about his warm, chocolate irises and how his eyes crease at the corners when he's irritated, which is often. I think about the way he smiles, every once in a while, and how it's almost like he's fighting it. Like he doesn't want to admit when he's happy. I think about the way he cares about his friends and how he's always watching, paying attention even when no one realizes it. And how he tries to hide how much he feels, as if he's purposefully putting himself on the other side of a glass wall, thinking it'll protect him. I think about his amazing body and the fact that even though he *knows* he looks good, he's never once acted like it matters. In fact, even though he always dresses nicely, often in those button-downs that do delicious things to highlight his chest and arms, he doesn't try to flaunt it.

I open my mouth to tell my friend that I can't like him because Dixon has made it clear he doesn't like *me*, so there's no future there. No reason to hope.

But I realize I can't deny it.

Kipp nods, like he understands what I'm not saying. "Keep me in the loop, yeah?"

"Yeah," I say a little numbly.

"I'm happy for you, Nik. If it works out for you, I'd be happy."

"Thanks, Kipp," I say around a tight throat.

He nods before slipping on his shoes and exiting out the front door. A moment later, his car pulls away, and then there's silence.

I wasn't supposed to like Dixon as more than a friend and coworker. I really wasn't. But now that I might, I'm not sure what to do about it. The man can barely tolerate me. Asking for more, well, I wouldn't stand a chance.

Doesn't stop me from pulling out my phone and looking at his latest text, though. Fingers flying like they have a mind of their own, I send him a new message.

Me: I hope you caught up on your beauty sleep today. You looked pretty tired last time I saw you.

After he stayed up all night tending to Malibu, being a wonderful friend and human being. I smile fondly.

Dixon's response comes through quickly, my phone pinging as I'm brushing my teeth.

Grump: Is that your way of telling me I looked like shit?

I snicker, both at Dixon's name in my phone and at his words. After putting away my toothbrush, I turn off the bathroom light and head across the hall to my room. I plop into bed before typing back.

Me: You never look like shit.

Grump: You're up to something.

I bark a laugh.

Me: Swear I'm not. Night, boyfriend!

Shit, I'm supposed to be playing nice, not needling.

Groaning, I let my phone fall onto the bed next to me. I might not be on Dixon's short-list for boyfriend—or even friend—and I *might* have feelings Dixon himself will never reciprocate, but that doesn't mean I can't be perfectly amicable and *subdued* toward the man.

With a sigh, I resign myself to doing better tomorrow.

As for Dixon, I'm not surprised he doesn't respond before I fall into sleep.

Chapter 15
DIXON

"I don't know what to make of it, Mat, but I'm worried."

"Yeah," my friend says, sighing into the phone. "It doesn't sound good. What did he say?"

"Nothing," I reply with a huff of frustration. "He refused to talk about it in the morning."

I couldn't get anything out of Malibu at work yesterday, either. I didn't need to go in, but I did because I wanted to check on him. But Malibu spent the entire afternoon evading me.

"The best you can do right now is make sure he knows you're there if he needs someone. His behavior does sound unusual," Mat says.

"This isn't him."

"Just be a friend, Dixon. That's the best you can do."

"Yeah, you're probably right," I concede.

There's a pause and then, gleefully, Mat says, "I'm sorry, could you repeat that one more time? Bad connection on my end."

"Fuck off."

"There we go. That sounds *so* much more like the Dixon I know. I don't think I've ever heard the words 'you're right' come out of your mouth before," he says, and I'd smack his face if he weren't a thousand miles away.

"I said 'you're *probably* right,'" I clarify.

"Oh, of course," Mat says around a huff of laughter. "My apologies. So... How're things going with Adonis?"

I sigh. "Can you stop calling him that?"

"Fine. How're things going with *Nikolas?*" he asks, saying the man's name all breathily.

"You are the worst. And I mean that, Mat. I don't even know why we're friends," I tell him, stopping outside Hyped while I finish my call. It's a cool day, and I have my post-workout sweatshirt on to ward off the chill.

Mat laughs loudly. "You tell me that about ten times a year."

"Because I mean it."

"I bring joy and fun into your life, and you know it," he says. "I'm like a goddamn candy cane."

"That's...a strange analogy."

"Because I'm motherfucking cheerful. You can't help but smile when you see me, like I'm all the best and most comforting memories you've ever had, rolled into one. I'm the epitome of sweetness and mirth," he says, and I have to bite my tongue to keep from laughing. I refuse to give him the satisfaction. "And I'm good to lick."

"Aaand you ruined it," I grumble, shaking my head.

His laughter rings in my ear. And even though I know Mat was just joking around, something about his words, about him being fun, pokes at my brain, making me remember something else he said to me recently.

"Why did you have to tell me I'm boring? I was perfectly fine not knowing that," I say, my tone a little sourer than intended.

"What?" he asks, sounding genuinely confused.

"You told me I was *boring*, and now I can't get it out of my head," I repeat, thinking back to my conversation with Melissa when it hit home that I don't *do* anything fun. That my life is full of routine and not much else.

"Dixon, love, I didn't say *you're* boring. I said your relationships are. Or were."

"Well, you might've well said as much. 'Cause I am. Why did you never tell me how boring I am?" I grumble.

"Wait," Mat says. "First you're mad I called you boring, and now you're mad I didn't? I'm confused."

"I just... Christ, Mat. What do I have going on in my life other than work? Nothing."

"Dixon, I don't think that's true. You have friendships, and you do things every day that you enjoy. Like, I know for a fact you just finished working out, and now you're probably waiting to get off the phone with me so you can go get your coffee," he says, nailing it.

"Right, the same things I do every day," I point out.

"Well, so? If you enjoy those things, who cares? Every day, Hawthorne wakes up, collects eggs from the chickens, milks the goats, and then goes to work at the ranch. He comes home, takes a shower, there's definitely some sex in there at some point, we have dinner together, and then he starts it again the next day. He's very much a man of habit, but he's happy. Are you happy?" my friend asks.

I pause, admitting quietly, "I'd be happier with my own Hawthorne."

"You can come visit Texas again and pick one up yourself," he says, making me laugh.

"I get what you're saying," I tell him. "I think I'm happy, most of the time. But I'm missing something."

"I understand," Mat says. "Just keep yourself open, you know? Don't try to shove something into that space if it doesn't fit."

"Yeah, I hear ya."

"All right, say you love me so I can hang up and you can get your caffeine. I can tell you're getting cranky," he teases.

"Yeah, yeah. Say hi to your man for me."

"By-eee. Love you."

When I pocket my phone and push into Hyped, I'm greeted by the warm smells of coffee and peppermint. There are a few people in line, and I take my place in back, looking over the specials board. There's a spiced holiday latte on there that makes me think of Niko and his smell of cloves.

"Dixon," Marley greets me when I reach the counter. She's looking down, not making eye contact.

I narrow my gaze. "Marley. How're you today?"

"Just fine," she says, tapping away at the monitor in front of her. "Your usual, I presume?"

"Mhm. Is there a reason you're avoiding eye contact?" I ask.

Marley's eyes ping to me before she winces and looks away, seeming guilty.

I sigh. "You watched my videos."

"I'm sorry!" she says, covering her face. "I'm never going to be able to look you in the eye again."

"I know the feeling," Jason says as he walks by, delivering a drink to another customer.

"What's the big deal?" I ask. At least now I have confirmation for why Jason's always been a little sheepish around me. "I'm sure you've seen naked men before."

The customer next to me looks over in surprise before averting their gaze.

Marley lowers her voice. "Sure. But Dixon, you know I don't mean this in a flirtatious way, but you are *fine*. And now that I've seen the goods, I'm not sure I can ever imagine you as a mere mortal."

She swings the reader my way, and I pay for my drink, adding a hefty tip.

"I'm just a guy," I say, shaking my head. I'm not unused to the attention, to being recognized as a porn star, but usually, it's not by people I know beforehand.

Marley meets my gaze head-on, raising a brow. I notice she has a ring through her nostril today instead of the stud that's normally there. "Yes. Just a guy. Who's been gifted with a huge"—she cuts herself off when another customer looks over curiously—"talent."

"Please never say that again," I groan.

Marley laughs. "We'll never speak of this. I'll bleach my brain."

"Much appreciated," I grumble before stepping to the side.

Jason hands me my drink, attempting a paltry smile.

"Don't strain yourself," I tell him, amused when he laughs, a real smile making a brief appearance on his face. He shakes his head before disappearing.

I wave at Marley as I leave the coffee shop, the smell of holiday spices staying behind as the late November air greets me. Just a couple more days before December hits. Just two more weeks until I'll be done with this boyfriend arc crap.

The thought isn't as welcoming as I'd imagined it'd be. The holidays must be dampening my mood more than usual this year. That's probably what happens when your girlfriend dumps you at the beginning of November, right before the three most nostalgic days of the year: Thanksgiving, Christmas, and New Year's. The lonely single's sadness trifecta. One down, two to go.

I sigh, internally chastising myself for putting the blame on Regina, when I know it's not really her fault.

When I get to work, I swing into the locker room to shower off my workout and then head to the break room, where Teddy and Marco are sitting at a table, discussing some new movie release I'm unfamiliar with. I settle into one of the deep, comfy chairs and browse the news on my phone while I finish my morning caffeination.

When the door opens, I glance up in time to catch Niko strolling in. He heads to the vending machine, picks out a green tea, and uncaps it. Just as he's turning around, bottle at his lips, we lock eyes. Niko swallows and nods his head. "Morning," he says casually before heading back out of the room.

I narrow my gaze after him, wondering what the catch is. He never misses an opportunity to pester me. In fact, sometimes I swear he goes out of his way to do just that. He's never given me a simple greeting and then *left*, without so much as a parting shot. I'm suspicious, but Alex comes into the room next, derailing my thoughts.

"Any luck?" I ask as he walks up. He sits on the armrest of my chair, forcing me to move my hand out of the way lest it end up under his ass. "Excuse you."

Alex ignores my complaint. "No luck," he responds, fiddling with the hem of his sleeve. "He laughed it off, like everyone is simply overreacting to him getting drunk at a club."

That makes me growl. "We're not overreacting."

Alex gives me a look. "Put away your claws, Grumpy Bear. *I* know, but Malibu either doesn't see the problem or he's refusing to acknowledge it."

I shake my head. "He was so out of it, Alex. If you could've seen him in that bathroom...the way he was barely responsive? That guy could've done anything to him."

Alex frowns, his worry mirroring my own. "Let's do the drag show this weekend and invite Malibu. That way, we can keep an eye on him while we're out."

"You think he'll agree to go?" I ask.

Alex shrugs. "I don't see why not. He always joins in when there's something going on."

"Okay," I say, nodding. "Let's give that a shot."

Alex grins.

"What?" I ask.

"That was so easy, getting you to accept the invitation," he says.

I roll my eyes. "It's not like I'm going to leave you to watch him alone. Besides, it won't be my first drag."

"That's right," he says. "I forgot you and Mat used to go on occasion. Well, it'll be a blast." He claps his hands together. "I'm going to see if I can catch Malibu on my way out. Have a good scene today with your naughty little elf."

I hang my head back and groan. "Get out of here."

Alex laughs as he skips out of the room, and when I check the time, I realize I need to get a move on. Studio 2 is lit up like Christmas at Macy's when I arrive. There are lights *everywhere*. On the walls, hanging from the ceiling, and piled meticulously on the floor, ready for my scene with Niko.

We're decorating. For fake Christmas. As boyfriends.

If I weren't worried about the legal—and fine, moral—ramifications, I might've been inclined to make sure Jerome couldn't write another scene for me ever again. First the bathtub. Now this.

But alas, Jerome is also here, unharmed, looking over today's scene on his tablet. I bypass the man and head toward the living room set, where a Christmas tree is already up and decorated. The overhead lighting is set low so that the string lights create a nice, soft glow, and Niko himself is sitting in front of the tree, his face lit by the twinkling strands.

He's wearing a soft red sweater, and his hair is tied back in a bun. There's a smile on his face, aimed at something one of the cameramen is saying as the two of them untangle the last of the lights, and my breath hitches. Seeing him there on the floor in front of the pine tree, fake presents, and imitation snow, with the smell of cinnamon filling the room from the candles burning for added ambiance, reminds me, once again, that I don't have anyone this year. No one to sit in front of a tree with. No one to call my own.

I'll be alone for the holidays.

Mat, of course, invited me to stay with him, but I declined. I know he loves me, and he didn't invite me out of pity, but I don't fit in there with his boyfriend and their huge, Texan family. I'd rather spend the day alone than in a place where I'd feel like an interloper.

I'll probably just order in, watch movies, and pretend the day isn't anything special.

Pretend I don't wish I had someone in a comfy, warm sweater to huddle with as the night falls dark.

"Hey, Dixon," Niko says, drawing my focus, even though I was already staring right at the man.

I grunt my hello.

Niko pushes off the ground, dusting some glitter off his hands, before he walks over. "Ready for this one?"

I look Niko's face over, confused for a moment because something seems different. And I realize it's because he's just *gazing* at me. He's not grinning or batting his eyelashes or doing any number of other ridiculous things I've come to expect from the man over the past few weeks.

He's simply...neutral.

I don't like it.

I don't trust it.

"Sure, I'm ready," I say, narrowing my eyes slightly.

Niko gives me a pleasant smile. "Cool."

He walks back into the living room set, and I follow, perplexed.

"All right," Jerome calls out. "We're going to spend several minutes with the two of you hanging lights. Do cutesy things, kiss, all that crap. We'll edit it for the best parts."

"All that crap," I mutter. Sounds about right.

Niko chuckles, drawing my attention to the soft slope of his lips.

"Anytime!" Jerome yells.

I roll my eyes and hop to, grabbing a strand of lights. Niko and I work together to hang them around the room, Niko handing me little removable hooks while I stand on a low stepstool and attach them, and the lights, to the wall. Every once in a while, he swoops in to give me a kiss or playfully withholds the hook until I come after him. Before I even realize it, I'm laughing, playing along, shaking a glitter-covered ornament over Niko's head in retaliation. He doesn't seem to care; he just shuts his eyes and tilts his head up, letting the glitter fall on his face as his hands hold my shirt, bunching it in his grasp like he doesn't want to be anywhere else but here with me.

When he lowers his face, it sparkles under the Christmas lights, the flakes of glitter catching and reflecting the light like little disco balls. It looks ridiculous, and yet...

I kiss him, cupping his face and tugging us together until there's not an inch of space between us. Niko's hands, still clenched in my shirt, smooth around to my back, his fingers digging into my skin and pulling me closer. He smells like spices, like the holidays. And something else, maybe honey. His lips are soft and sweet and so very welcoming, and he hums against my mouth, broadcasting his pleasure.

My hands start shaking against his cheeks, and I drop them quickly, grabbing Niko's hips instead. This kiss feels too...*real*.

It has to be the setting. The fact that we're hanging lights and standing near a tree and pretending that we're boyfriends. It's messing with me. It's making me want things I can't have. It's making me wish this were real, that this is how my holidays could be.

It doesn't have anything to do with Niko. It's just the circumstances.

Except, as he gently pulls back, looking into my eyes with a softness that feels painfully genuine, I realize I don't believe myself. These scenes we've been playing, this boyfriend act, it doesn't feel like an act at all.

In these moments, under these cameras, it feels real. It feels like Niko is mine, and he wants me to be his, too.

Our kisses, his touch, that look in his eyes—I don't want it to end. But it will. We're halfway done with our arc together, and after that final camera stops rolling in a week and a half, I'll have to face the fact that Niko fucking Adamos isn't mine to keep.

Because this man, this Adonis, isn't even real.

Chapter 16
Niko

Something is going on with Dixon. He's covering it well enough, but I can tell. Ever since that deep kiss, he's been intense. He's still playing the scene, but he's a little more quiet, and he keeps staring at me like he's doing quantum mathematics in his head.

When Jerome gives the cue to move on from our cutesy light-hanging stuff, Dixon descends without hesitation. I had just spritzed him with a holiday-scented air freshener when he swoops towards me, lifting me in his arms with ease as I squawk in surprise. He deposits me on the couch and tosses the air freshener aside.

"Joke's on you because now you're about to smell like a peppermint pattie, too," he says, rubbing his face all over my neck.

I laugh, the sensation of his mouth, nose, and stubble tickling me. "Nooo," I mumble halfheartedly. "The horror."

Dixon grins against my skin, tugging my sweater lower to nip at my collarbone before he sucks a bruising kiss against the tender flesh of my neck. I gasp, not having expected that in the least, and Dixon raises his mouth, capturing my lips once more.

I wrap my arms and legs around his bigger body as he kisses me, pressing me into the couch cushions. He *does* smell like peppermint, but underneath it is still Dixon, manly with a subtle kick of his fresh soap that's scented like clean laundry. He kisses me for what feels like an eternity, grinding against my erection, his heavy body comforting over top of mine as I run my hands over whatever skin I can find beneath his shirt.

Before long, we lose the clothes, taking turns tearing them off one another piece by piece. Dixon's boxers have little reindeer on them, and I laugh loudly before flinging them away to land on the prickly branches of the Christmas tree next to us.

When Dixon sits back on the couch, I settle over him. The crew is still around us. One cameraman at the entrance to the room, capturing a wide angle. The other a foot behind me, likely zoomed in on my ass in Dixon's lap. Marco is standing just off-screen, holding the large boom over us to catch each pant and moan and whispered word. And Jerome is nearby, monitoring it all.

They're all here, but I only see Dixon.

He's directly in front of me. Under me. Holding me in his arms as we writhe together on the couch. He's the only one who deserves my focus.

Dixon takes us in his big hand, squeezing our dicks together as I buck against him. I could happily come just like this, but our scene calls for me riding him instead. Which, honestly, doesn't sound like a hardship at all.

Dixon grabs the lube, snaking his hand around my body to prep me. I lift enough so that he has easy access, and the instant he touches my hole, I relax, knowing Dixon will take his time, making sure every step of the process feels euphoric. We talk as Dixon preps me because Jerome wanted more dialogue in this scene.

It's simple stuff like "Yeah, right there" or "That feels good—you always make me feel so good," but it's also the truth, which makes it easy to say.

When Dixon rolls on the condom, he pauses, taking my face in his hands. He tugs me forward for a featherlight kiss, and then he helps position himself at my entrance, holding my gaze as I sink slowly down onto his thick, hard-as-granite cock.

I rock slowly, a moan pulling from my lips at how *deep* he is. Dixon watches me with parted lips, and I realize some of that glitter he shook onto me transferred to his own face. It makes me smile, seeing it there. Not only because Dixon and glitter seem like a rather unlikely duo, but because *I* put it there, like a mark, however temporary.

"What're you smiling at?" he asks, rubbing his thumb over my cheek and lower lip, a little smile gracing his own face that makes my breath rattle a little shakily from my lungs.

"You look festive," I say, swiping at some of the glitter, although it doesn't budge. "It looks good on you."

"Yeah?" He hitches his hips up as I start riding him a little faster. "*This* is a good look on you."

"Being naked?"

I run my hands over Dixon's impressive pecs and abdominal muscles, and my dick bobs as I fuck myself down on the man. I ignore it for now.

"Mmm," he hums. "On my dick. Like you're mine."

My tempo falters.

"I am," I finally say.

"Good," he grumbles from low in his chest, spearing his hands into my hair and unsettling my bun. "Only mine."

Fuck.

I nod mutely, letting Dixon pull me in for another long, lasting kiss. He's meeting me thrust for thrust now, and our bodies slap together, the sound mixing with our labored breaths. When I lean back for better leverage, Dixon reaches between us, rolling my balls in his hand and watching my every move. I slow down, moaning as he plays with my sac, broadcasting my approval even louder as he rubs along my taint.

When he starts palming my cock, I speed up again, knowing the end is near. Sweat is beading on my brow, and my legs start to shake with the continued exertion of this position, but even though we're supposed to finish our scene just like this with me riding Dixon, it's like he can tell it's wearing on me. Or maybe he simply wants to take control. Whatever the reason, he grabs my hips, stilling my movements. Then he braces his feet down on the ground and takes over, slamming up into me.

"*Fuck*," I call out, dropping my head back and hanging on for dear life as Dixon rails into me from below.

"Stroke yourself," he grits out, watching me intently.

I reach down immediately, dragging my hand over my cock as lightning shoots down my spine. "Close," I breathe out, listening to the sounds Dixon is making—the grunts and groans—as we race to the finish.

"Do it," he says. "I wanna taste you."

"Oh, God."

With a final thrust and twist of my hand, I'm painting Dixon's chest. He doesn't hesitate before dragging a finger through my release and sucking it into his mouth. The image alone has my cock throbbing, another dribble of cum leaking from the tip.

Dixon lifts me in his arms then, and, carefully, he lowers me onto the floor in front of the Christmas tree. His cock stays nestled inside me until I'm settled on the ground. Then he pulls out, rips off the condom, and braces himself over my body, jerking himself closer to orgasm. One of his hands is linked with mine, pressing it to the floor, and his eyes are locked on my face, seeing God only knows what in my expression.

He opens his mouth like he wants to say something, and then he's coming, his face awash with blissful agony.

I squeeze his hand as he finishes, and he squeezes back.

"You...are the best present," he says softly, voice hoarse. With an exhale, he leans his forehead against my chest, and I blink up at the twinkling lights overhead, my thoughts running wild, my heart even wilder.

All I know is, if I ignore the confused emotions swirling around inside my head, this moment feels like tranquility. My hand in Dixon's, his breath fanning across my skin, our legs tangled together as the soft sound of Christmas music filters through the room. It feels a lot like something I didn't know I was ready for. Something significant.

A moment of connection. Of peace, like the lulling of wind and waves.

It feels like home.

That is, until Jerome calls, "Cut," and the reality of the situation comes crashing back in.

"I think that turned out well," I say conversationally, scrubbing myself down and taking extra care to wash the glitter off my face and out of my hair.

Dixon hums.

"I liked that thing you did when you took over," I add, wincing slightly, wondering if it's weird to comment on someone's work-related fucking abilities. Without being able to see Dixon's reaction from the shower stall next to mine, I add, "Saved my ass. I was getting tired."

There's a beat of silence, and then Dixon hums again.

His water shuts off, and I finish cleaning myself before drying my body quickly and squeezing the excess water from my hair.

"You're good at hanging lights," I say as I come out of the shower stall. Dixon is half-dressed in front of his locker. Once I get to mine, I drop my towel and pull on underwear. "Have lots of practice?"

He looks over at me with an incredulous expression on his face. "It's not that hard," he says gruffly, pulling his shirt on and adding, in a lower voice, "but no, not much experience."

"No?" I ask. "You don't hang decorations for the holidays?"

Dixon makes a sort of scoffing sound, and honestly, I'm surprised when he continues answering my questions. "No. No reason to decorate when it's just me."

I purse my lips, drying my hair some more as I watch Dixon gathering his robe and towel to toss into the laundry bag. He's not meeting my eyes, and I don't know if that means he doesn't want to talk about it or he's just not *used* to talking about it.

But he's not running away like he usually does after our scenes. In fact, it feels like he's lingering. Making an effort to be cordial.

"What about when you lived with your friend?" I ask. "Mateo?"

He shrugs. "He'd put up lights. I didn't help."

Huh, okay.

"I like decorating with lights," I say, nodding to Teddy as the man walks by. "My mamá always uses colored lights, like the multicolored strands?" Dixon nods like he knows what I'm talking about. "I like the soft white ones, though. And real trees. Don't even get me started on the fake kind." I chuckle, shaking my head. "But I like to layer those small strands, like the ones we used today, with big bulbs. It makes it look really special, like there are pops of brightness amidst all those twinkling lights. It reminds me of the stars," I say fondly.

Dixon watches me for a moment. "You like the holidays, huh?"

"I do," I respond with a nod. "You don't?"

"I used to," he says.

What changed?

"I'm lucky. I know that," I say softly, plopping down on the bench seat in front of my locker, straddling it as I face Dixon. "I have a whole bunch of people to spend the holidays with, and my family is really great. My mamá, my sisters, even Kipp."

"Kipp?" Dixon asks, interrupting me.

"My closest friend," I answer. "He and his family don't get along anymore, so we've basically adopted him."

Dixon grunts.

"Are you close with your family?" I ask, chancing it since Dixon seems to be in a conversational mood. For a beat, I don't think he's going to answer the question.

But then he faces me, his sharp brown eyes shuttering a bit. "No."

"Can I ask why?"

Dixon's brows furrow, but he answers me again. "You can."

A slow smile overtakes my face. "Was that a joke?"

He scoffs, but I can see a smile tipping his lips ever so slightly.

"Why?" I ask, getting back to the topic at hand.

Dixon's little smile slips away, and he exhales. "My parents disowned me when they found out I was bisexual. I was nearly eighteen, so practically an adult in the eyes of the law, but we didn't have an amicable split." His voice is devoid of any emotion, but I can only imagine how difficult that must have been for him and probably still is.

"I'm sorry, Dixon," I say sincerely.

He watches me, arms crossed in front of himself, waiting like he expects a punchline. But I would never joke about something I know is a sore spot for the man. No one should be judged for their sexuality, and hearing that's what happened to Dixon—that he doesn't have family to spend the holidays with anymore—makes my chest physically ache. I can understand now why he's not that thrilled about the festivities. Add onto that the fact that his friend is gone this year, and it must be even harder. I want to invite him to come to Moapa Valley with me for Christmas, but I know he'd decline.

This may be the closest I've gotten to breaking through Dixon's walls, but it'll take more than one real conversation to develop trust. Maybe, with a little time, I could get him to say yes.

I stand up, closing my locker.

"Well, I, for one, am hoping Santa visits this year. I've been a very good boy," I say lightly.

Dixon raises a brow. "Somehow, I doubt that."

I chuckle as I head toward the door. With my fingers clasped around the handle, Dixon's voice halts me.

"Niki."

"Yeah?" I say, turning around and doing my best not to beam at that nickname I've come to love.

"Alex is spearheading a trip to a drag show this weekend. You should come."

Alex already invited me before my scene today, but the fact that Dixon is making a point to invite me himself? Yeah, that just about makes me happier than a clam.

"Yeah," I say with a nod. "I'll be there."

Dixon nods, and I exit the room, feeling all sorts of warm and cozy after my winter wonderland scene with a certain reluctant charmer, our subsequent conversation, and my hope that Dixon and I are on our way to some sort of understanding.

Maybe we could be friends after all.

Chapter 17
Dixon

I don't know what sort of switch flipped between Niko and I, but we seem to have come to a truce. Niko doesn't take shots at me like he's on a mission to see me crack, and I don't growl every time he enters a room.

We're practically best buds.

Except for the fact that *something* about the man is still embedded under my skin. I find myself watching those deep, brown eyes of his as he smiles at our coworkers. Or the light dusting of stubble around his broad lips, and the way his cheeks dip in when he's laughing.

It's like I'm waiting for...something. I don't even know what. A catch? The other shoe to drop? For things to go back to the way they were when every move the man made had me wanting to throttle him?

What's even worse is that I kind of, just a *little* bit, miss those snarky remarks of his. It makes no goddamn sense. But it's like he's dimmed his light a little around me, and now I feel guilty that, perhaps, I'm at fault. Like my surly attitude was so off-putting, he decided he'd rather not even deal with it. Which was what I wanted, wasn't it? For him to stay away?

Except he's not avoiding me. We may not *actually* be best buds, but there is a friendliness there, or at the very least a neutrality, that didn't exist in the first few weeks of working together.

I should be happy. This is a good thing. This is exactly how I wanted my interactions with my coworker to be. Professional. Companionable.

Boring.

That fucking word again.

Admittedly, though, I don't find Niko boring, even when he is being this weird, passive pseudo-Niko. It's infuriating that even now, I can't seem to ignore the man.

"I'm going to grab a snack from the break room," Niko says, tugging on his clothes.

We just finished another scene together. One in which Niko swallowed my dick for nearly twenty minutes, until his jaw was sore, and then I ate his ass until he was a shaking, mumbling mess. Definitely not boring, either.

"Want to join me?" he asks after I've failed to respond due to my wandering thoughts.

"Uh, yeah. Sure."

Niko looks a little surprised by my answer, but he doesn't even take a jab about us becoming besties or anything. He simply motions for me to follow as he heads out of the locker room, dropping his used laundry on the way.

"I love the free snacks here," he says on the short walk. "It's a nice perk."

"Yeah, much better than the complimentary spa treatments," I mutter.

He looks back at me, confused. "Spa treatments?"

"From the lovely Raylin."

Niko laughs loudly. "Ah, you mean the mandatory torture sessions. Gotcha."

I snort a laugh from my nose as we make our way into the break room. It's nearly empty, apart from Josh, one of the performers who has a limited schedule and is only here a couple times a month.

"At least neither of us gets a full hair removal. I heard horror stories from Mat," I say, watching as Niko chooses a bag of chips and a tea from the vending machines.

Niko shudders. "No kidding. I think you'd have to have a pain kink to enjoy that."

I follow Niko over to a table, a granola bar in hand. "Right. And that's not your thing," I note.

"Definitely not," he agrees.

He opens his chips, crunching for a minute before my curiosity gets the better of me, and I ask, "Why are you doing this?"

Niko stills, a chip hovering in front of his mouth. "Eating?"

"No," I say with an eye roll, even though I can't blame him. My question wasn't specific at all. "Porn. Why are you doing porn?"

"Oh," he says, chomping down on his chip and settling back into his seat. "Why not? I didn't have anything else going on that I was all that invested in, so when my friend put the idea in my head, I decided to give it a shot."

"What were you doing before?" I ask, biting off half of my granola bar in one go. Niko looks at me in amusement. "What? I have a big mouth."

I fully expect him to make a joke—I mean, come on, I left myself wide open—but he doesn't take the bait. He only shakes his head and answers, "I was a management consultant."

"The fuck is that?" I ask, not at all filled with smug satisfaction when Niko barks a laugh.

"Basically, I looked for ways for companies to cut costs and boost revenue."

I crinkle my nose. "That sounds..."

"You can say boring." He laughs. "I didn't hate it. It was like a puzzle. But I also didn't love it."

"And you love this?" I ask, finishing off my snack.

He shrugs. "It's interesting, to say the least. I don't know if I'll do this until my balls are sagging down to my knees, but for now, it feels like the right thing."

I contemplate his words and the easy attitude with which he delivered them. "It doesn't bother you, not knowing what's next?"

Niko looks at me curiously, his gaze sharp, even though his smile is soft. "No, that doesn't bother me. Like I said, I like puzzles. And half the fun is in the process. I'm okay not knowing what's at the end."

"Huh," I grunt.

"You don't like that," he says plainly, like he's learned how to decipher my various sounds.

"No, not really," I admit. "I want my happy ending."

The truth leaves my mouth without conscious thought, and Niko looks at me in surprise before dropping his eyes to the table and smiling. "That's sweet."

I scowl, immediately regretting my words and how vulnerable they make me feel. "I'm not sweet."

"Okay," he replies, again not pushing it.

"Take it back," I press.

"You're not sweet," he says dutifully.

I narrow my gaze, not trusting this amicable yes-man routine. "And you?"

"What about me?" Niko asks.

"Are you sweet or salty?" I ask, figuring that *has* to earn me some snark.

Niko bites his lips like he's actively holding back before he clears his throat and says, "Probably somewhere in the middle. No one's one hundred percent good."

I wait a beat. "That's it?" I ask in frustration.

Niko looks up at me. "Huh?"

"What is going on with you? No 'Why, Dixon, surely you know whether or not I'm salty' or 'Put me on your tongue and find out?'"

"What?" Niko asks in amusement, eyes wide and glittering.

"You're being all...amicable or some shit. Are you trying to butter me up for something?" I glare when Niko starts laughing harder.

"You *want* me to be argumentative?"

"I just don't want you to..." I wave my hand around, searching for words. "Fade away," I settle on.

Niko braces his elbows on the table, leaning toward me and shaking his head slightly. "You are the most confounding human I've ever met." I can feel my face pulling into a frown, but Niko reaches forward, grabbing my wrist lightly and squeezing. "That's a compliment," he says before letting go and sitting back in his seat.

"If you say so," I mutter.

"Ask me again," Niko says.

"Ask you again?"

"If I'm sweet or salty."

I roll my eyes. "All right. Are you sweet or salty?"

Niko's face stretches into a slow, sly grin. "I'm everyone's flavor, baby. Maybe you should try me sometime."

I shake my head. "*Christ.* That is just the worst thing I've ever heard. And I mean that."

Niko doesn't respond, and when I look up, he has the strangest expression on his face.

"What?" I ask.

He leans forward, dragging his finger along the corner of my mouth, making me conscious of the smile resting there. Immediately, it slips away.

I try to control my breathing as Niko removes his hand, my skin tingling slightly in the wake of his fingers. His lips are pressed together, tipped up, and he looks pleased. Smug, even, like something as simple as making me smile left him personally satisfied.

"Nothing," he says at last, shaking his head slightly. "I was just thinking that mouth would look good wrapped around me."

"Oh, fuck off," I grumble, shoving his shoulder. Niko laughs, looking at me as if I just confessed my undying love. "Jesus Christ, I'm out of here." I stand up and push my chair in, my hands strangely clammy. "See you tonight?"

Niko nods. "Wouldn't miss it."

I thought Niko being his normal self would put us back on even ground. But for some reason, I feel just as unbalanced as ever.

When my Uber driver drops me at Django's With A Big Fat D—referred to as just Django's by most everyone who knows it—I nearly bump into a familiar blonde who's stepping out of the club.

"You're here!" Alex exclaims happily, squeezing my arms. He's wearing a brightly colored jumpsuit I couldn't pull off in a million years.

"The party can start now," I joke. "Is Malibu inside?"

Alex nods. "Just arrived a bit ago. Head on in. I'm just waiting to make sure Teddy finds his way."

"Want me to wait with you?"

"Nah." Alex gives me a nudge toward the door. "Our group is near the stage. Just wait until you see what your Adonis is wearing," he says, waggling his eyebrows.

"He's not *my* Adonis," I grumble.

Alex's tinkling laughter follows me through the door.

Inside the drag bar, round tables are staggered all the way from the center stage to the back wall. The stage itself is grandiose, a massive wooden semicircle that's lined with small lights that gradually change colors, rotating through every hue of the rainbow. A short staircase leads down onto the floor, and maroon, velvet curtains hang along the walls. The seats are nearly filled, since showtime is approaching, and I can see our rowdy bunch taking up two tables right near the front, where Alex said they'd be. I make my way there, bypassing the bar.

Even though there's a good dozen of our crew here tonight instead of at our usual haunt, Sublime, my eyes lock right onto the one person who seems to have the singular ability of making my blood heat, for better or worse, with barely a glance. And I have to admit that Alex was right. The man looks fine.

He's in all white tonight, his pants matching the long-sleeved top that's undone nearly to his navel. The shirt gapes open as he sits with one arm over the back of his chair, exposing the sleek muscles of his torso. His hair is down, falling in thick, wavy curls to his shirt collar, and it appears to be styled some, product holding it back from his face. Even from a dozen feet away, it looks as if he's wearing eyeliner, his thick lashes framing those cunning brown eyes of his. His stubble is shaved close to the skin, and as he turns his head and catches my gaze, he smirks like he *knows* he looks good. Like he knows I think so, too.

I clench my jaw tight, just barely managing not to scowl at the man as an automatic response.

"Dixon!" Marco calls out, pulling me in once I reach the tables.

"Hey, man," I reply, accepting the seat next to Marco and, coincidentally, Niko.

"I'm so excited for this," he says. "I heard Fanny May is making an appearance tonight."

"Oh yeah?" I answer, even though I have no clue who that is.

"She likes to pull people in from the audience," he says. I nod, but the rest of his words barely register because at that same moment, Niko shifts, causing his spicy scent to smack me in the face. I glance his way, and my eyes immediately drop to his exposed chest and the light dusting of hair there. And when he crosses one leg over the other, hanging his ankle at his knee, his pants pull tight enough at the crotch for me to make out the bulge there. Niko clears his throat pointedly, and I avert my gaze, ignoring his soft chuckle.

A server shows up to take my drink order, thankfully disrupting the moment, and me and several others order a round. The reprieve is short-lived.

"You look nice tonight, griniári mou," Niko says quietly from my right.

I glance his way, noting how his eyes are drifting lazily down my body. I'm not wearing anything fancy, just a sleek, charcoal-colored button-down paired with black slacks, but I know they fit me well.

Not for the first time, I wonder what it is he's calling me. My guess is something less than flattering, but I haven't been able to bring myself to ask.

I grunt my acceptance, and Niko's eyebrows raise.

"Wow, look at that," he says. "You're learning how to take a compliment."

Instead of responding, I point to where his shirt is laying open against his tanned skin. "You missed a couple dozen buttons."

Niko laughs, smoothing his fingers down one side of the open placket. "Nah, I think this is good."

"Hmm," I say, neither agreeing nor disagreeing with his claim.

Our drinks arrive, and I take a moment to discreetly check on Malibu. The man is sitting at the other table with a smile on his face, looking relaxed. I breathe a quiet sigh of relief to see him appearing like his normal self.

Alex and Teddy show up a minute later as the house lights flicker to gather everyone's attention. There are a few stragglers in the room, but they quickly make their way to their seats before the overheads dim. When a spotlight hits the stage and a bedazzled queen struts out from behind the curtain, the audience goes wild. She eats up the attention, fanning her face and her fake cleavage and then waving off the applause.

"Thank you, thank you," she says into the mic, clutching her chest. "Y'all know how to welcome a lady." When the clapping dims, she adds, "Well now, I didn't say to stop."

There's a round of laughter and some more cheering, but it's Niko's chuckle that draws my attention the most, the sound seeming to cut above the rest of the din. He shoots me a little wink when he catches me staring at his mouth.

The show starts with Miss Penelope Beauregard regaling the crowd with a short comedy routine and her rendition of "It's Raining Men." When the next performer takes the stage, after a round of boisterous applause for Miss Penelope, Marco slaps my shoulder.

"That's Fanny May," he says excitedly.

I don't recognize the drag queen, but by the deafening roar of the crowd, I'd say she's a fan favorite. Her midnight-blue ball gown swishes around her feet as she approaches the front of the stage, mic in hand like a warrior going out to battle.

"Now, now," she says, waving her hand in a downward motion and shushing the crowd. "I know you're all excited by my magnificent presence, and I don't blame you one bit. But you're going to have to wait a while longer for my performance. I'm here on a little errand."

There's some cheering at that as Fanny May puts a hand over her eyes and scans the crowd. I'm not sure what's going on, but I see several people waving their hands in the air. She steps slowly down the stairs, coming to a stop at the bottom, right next to Malibu's seat.

"My, oh my," she says, turning her attention to our two tables. Most of the crowd is comprised of women, including three separate bachelorette parties, so we stand out, our group of all men, most of us gay porn stars. Fanny May fans her face. "Sweet Daddy Efron, what do we have here? It's a buffet."

There's laughter as she pretends to faint. When she runs her hand along the back of Malibu's chair, he stiffens.

"Hello, darling," she purrs, singling him out.

"Uh, hi," Malibu stammers into the microphone Fanny May shoves in front of his face.

"A man of few words, I can appreciate that." She holds her hand over her mouth and whispers into the mic, her words loud and clear, "Who needs conversation when they look this pretty. Am I right, ladies?"

The crowd cheers, but Malibu slinks a little lower in his seat, face paling. Instantly, my hackles go up.

Look, for as carefree as Malibu comes across most of the time, and for as comfortable as he is in his skin doing the type of work we do, I know for a fact he gets stage fright. One time, a couple years ago, he had to go up in front of a crowd at an industry convention to accept an award. The man barely got out a word of thanks before he rushed off stage, having a panic attack that lasted a good ten minutes.

Filming in front of a small group of trusted coworkers is not the same thing as being put on the spot in front of a crowd. And seeing Malibu's face leech color like a berry-stained rag being washed and wrung dry has me reacting without thought.

"What do you say, handsome?" Fanny May asks a pinched Malibu. "Will you be my volunteer prey tonight?"

"I'll do it," I call out, already out of my seat.

Fanny May's head swings my way, her eyes widening. Malibu forgotten, she strides up to me, taking a handful of my arm and squeezing. "Oh, *honey*. Yes, you'll do. You'll do just fine."

Ah, shit.

What have I gotten myself into?

Chapter 18

Niko

To say I was shocked at Dixon volunteering to go up on stage would be an understatement. The man disappeared twenty minutes ago and has yet to make a reappearance with Fanny May. I've tried to enjoy the show in the meantime, but I'm undeniably curious about what's going on behind the scenes right now.

"I hope he wears heels," Marco says during intermission as I'm nursing my rum and coke. The room is bright and the stage empty.

"Didn't you say that was the worst part?" I ask, remembering Marco's brief conversation about doing drag in the past.

"Yeah, but c'mon. Dixon in heels? I would pay to see that." He grins, and yeah, he's got a point.

I finish off my drink, the dregs tasting mostly like melted ice, as the lights flicker overhead, drawing a hush from the crowd. A spotlight hits the stage once more, and Fanny May struts out from behind the velvet curtains, now wearing a sparkling baby blue gown with a slit up to her hip. Her three-inch heels tap on the floor as she strides to center stage.

When the hollering has quieted, she brings the mic to her mouth with a flourish. "Ladies and hopefully-not-so-gen-tle-men, have I got a treat for you. Please join me in wel-coming"—she pauses for dramatic effect—"Miss Dixie to the stage!"

Fanny May spreads her arm backwards, and Dixon emerges from behind the curtain, stepping onto stage with his massive form clad in the slinkiest red dress I've ever seen. The fabric is positively glued to Dixon's broad chest. And his stomach. And around his thick thighs, where the hem stretches worrisomely. Dixon's long, hairy legs are on display, and even though he's not in heels, he does have pointed red flats on his feet. There's a scowl on his made-up face and a bright white wig that's cut in the shape of a bob.

I gape, unable to form a single word, sound, or comprehen-sible thought as I take in the manliest drag queen I've ever had the pleasure of witnessing. Marco, from beside me, is laughing so hard he's wheezing.

Catcalls and whistles pierce the air, and Alex stands up on his chair, clapping as Dixon reluctantly walks forward, his muscles flexing under the tight, shimmering red fabric.

Fanny May waves to him like he's a game show prize. "Isn't she just precious?" There's renewed cheering. "Now sweet, dear Miss Dixie has agreed to join me for a song. What do you say to that?" She cups her ear, and once satisfied by the volume of the crowd, she nods, passing her mic to someone offstage. She holds out her hand to Dixon, and he steps forward, look-ing like he'd rather be anywhere else than at the other end of the drag queen's manicured clutches.

When the opening chords to "Baby It's Cold Outside" start and Dixon begins mouthing the counterpoint to Fanny May's lip-syncing, I just about lose my tongue. Dixon's unenthused attitude seems to thrill the audience to no end, and he's cheered on, the crowd going wild and laughing every time Fanny May dances around him or strokes his stiff arm. Dixon, for his part, stands stock still as he plays along, sulkily mouthing each and every word.

And me? Well, I think I lose a little piece of my heart.

It was obvious to me why Dixon offered himself up as bait, even though he wouldn't have, in a million years, chosen to do so otherwise. It was for Malibu. To take the heat off him because Malibu was clearly uncomfortable with the attention. I think there may be a story there that I'm unaware of, but the fact that Dixon so quickly and easily stepped in to take the bullet tells me loads about the man I'm coming to know more about each day.

This *like* I'm harboring—the one I wanted to deny to Kipp, my family, and even myself—is treading quickly onto dangerous ground.

When the song comes to an end, Fanny May grabs Dixon's hand and the pair of them bow. The drag queen says something to Dixon, and then he turns around to walk offstage. My eyes drop straight to his ass.

"My God," I mumble, watching his taut globes make their way behind the curtain.

Alex slides into Dixon's seat next to me, his eyes wide and excited. "That was the best thing I've ever seen in my entire life," he whisper-shouts, clutching my arm.

"It was something, that's for sure," I agree.

Alex grins at me as Fanny May finishes her routine and leaves the stage. There are a few more performances after that, which I'm barely able to pay attention to, and then the show comes to a close. The room is bright by the time Dixon reappears, his dress, wig, and makeup gone.

Alex jumps up and runs right to him. "Dixie!" he shouts.

Dixon hangs his head as our whole crew parrots Alex's shout, a chorus of "Dixie" echoing in the air. And even though Dixon scowls, there's a hint of a smile at the corner of his plush lips.

"You guys can't use this against me," he grumbles, coming back to our table and downing the remainder of his forgotten drink.

"Yeah, sorry, but I can't make that promise," Alex replies, to which Dixon groans in frustration.

"All right. I need another drink," Dixon says.

Malibu slides up next to the man. "On me," he says, giving Dixon a pointed, appreciative stare.

Dixon nods. "Deal."

With nearly everyone from our group on board, we head down the neon-lit street to another bar, our night far from over.

"Shh," Alex says, nearly tumbling into me as we walk down the hallway to Dixon's apartment. I steady him.

"Why are we whispering?" I ask, looking around.

"So we don't get caught."

Dixon looks back at us, eyes narrowing at Alex. "I know you're there, baby boy."

"Oh," Alex replies, standing more upright. "I thought we were being sneaky."

Dixon shakes his head. "You've been following us since we left the bar, and you're about the least subtle person I know."

Alex shrugs, not looking perturbed by that bit of information. The motion seems to make him wobble, however, and he grabs my arm for support. "I'm kinda tipsy," he whispers again.

"You don't say," I reply with a laugh.

Dixon glances back, rolling his eyes before he sticks his key into his door and lets us inside, Malibu included. Dixon's apartment was closest, and, at the time, it made sense to share his ride instead of going our separate ways. Drunk logic may be slightly flawed, but I'm glad to have a place to crash for the night. I'm far too buzzed to drive back home.

"We should get some food," Malibu says before face-planting onto Dixon's couch. Malibu, I noted with relief, didn't drink at the bar.

Alex swats his leg until Malibu makes some room. "Agreed. Dixie, make us some dinner."

"It's nearly four in the morning," Dixon grumbles, rolling up his sleeves and putting his nicely toned arms on display. "We're long past dinner."

"Brunch?" Alex asks hopefully.

"How about we order some food?" I suggest, sliding onto one of the vacant chairs in the living room.

My eyes feel heavy, but I take a moment to look around. Dixon's place looks like him, in a way. The minimalist colors and cool affect. It's calming, serene in the way a moonlit sea is at night, crisp and gentle and never-ending. It reminds me of Greece.

"Pizza?" Dixon asks.

There's a murmuring of agreement. Malibu slips off the couch and walks down the hall, presumably to the bathroom, and Dixon sits in his vacated spot, pulling out his phone to order food. Alex scoots over, laying his head on Dixon's lap. I try not to be jealous about that—realistically, I know there's nothing to be jealous about—but I can't help but wish I was in Alex's place.

"He seemed okay tonight," Alex notes quietly, his eyes slipping shut even though he's clearly awake.

"Yeah, he did. I'm still worried, though," Dixon says while tapping away.

"You're a good man, Grumpy Bear," Alex responds.

I agree, but Dixon simply grunts.

Malibu reappears and slides onto the couch next to Alex, smooshing him into the couch back and putting his feet on Dixon's lap.

Alex grumbles, lifting his head out of the way. "*Hey.*"

"Oh, didn't see you there, small fry," Malibu says, laughing when Alex pinches his leg.

"Children," Dixon chides, making me snort.

God, he really is pretty sweet under that gruff exterior.

Dixon's eyes lift to mine, and he glares slightly, as if challenging my inner thoughts. "Pizza will be here in twenty," he says, laying his head back against the couch.

"All right," Alex says, climbing over Malibu and sitting down onto the floor. "That gives us plenty of time."

"For what?" Dixon asks with some trepidation.

"Truth or dare."

The rest of us groan.

"What are we, sixteen?" Dixon grumbles.

"Come on!" Alex persists, tugging Malibu until the other man joins him on the floor, sitting cross-legged.

Malibu brushes back his hair. "Only if you go first."

"Fine," Alex says. "Dare."

Malibu thinks for a moment before saying, "I dare you to run buck naked up and down the hall."

"Agreed," Alex says immediately, standing up and proceeding to strip off his clothes. "But you can't cheat and try to wake up the neighbors or anything."

"Deal," Malibu says, laughing when Alex drops his jock-strap on top of his head.

Dixon rubs his hands over his face as Alex opens the front door, Malibu right behind him. "I'm gonna get kicked out," he says flatly.

I snicker, watching the open doorway as Malibu laughs and Alex streaks by at a fast clip.

"Those darn hooligans," I tease.

Dixon shakes his head, his lip twitching up at the corner. He watches me for a moment before clearing his throat and looking away. Half a minute later, Alex runs back in, hands shielding himself before he slips his clothes back on.

"Have you no shame?" Dixon asks.

"None whatsoever," Alex answers, looking proud of the fact. "All right, your turn, Niko."

"Why me?" I ask.

"Because I'm running this game, and I said so," Alex responds before skipping off to the kitchen. He returns with waters, passing them out.

"If I must," I sigh, even though I honestly don't mind. "Truth." I take a few long sips of my water as Alex taps his chin, doing his best to look evil.

"What's the kinkiest thing you've ever done?" he finally asks.

"Does my job count?" I ask.

Alex laughs. "No."

"Okay, hmm." I lean back, doing a quick mental rundown of my sexual encounters. Dixon, I notice, is watching me intently. Malibu, on the other hand, looks half-asleep, curled up on the couch with his head on the armrest. "When I was in college, my friend Kipp and I went to this sex party. They had this darkroom where the purpose was anonymity. One of the hosts blindfolded me before I went in, so I couldn't see anything when the door opened, and the agreement was to do the same on the way out. To this day, I have no clue who I had sex with," I admit.

Dixon makes a noise deep in his chest that almost sounds like a growl. "I hope you used protection."

"Yes, Daddy," I say with an eye roll, chuckling when Dixon's glower intensifies. "I've always been safe. I was on PrEP even before I started at the studio. Used condoms for blowjobs, too, if I didn't know the person. Happy?"

Dixon looks away, but I swear there's relief in his eyes. Or maybe a tiny, hopeful part of me is simply projecting the fact that I want him to care.

"Your turn, then," I tell the man. "Truth or dare?"

Dixon lets out a long sigh before saying, "Truth."

I grin. There are so many things I could ask him, but I decide to go easy. "Did you have that song memorized already, or did you have to learn it before going on stage?"

Alex grins, watching Dixon with rapt attention.

Dixon, on the other hand, looks like my question offended him on multiple levels. "I already knew it."

Alex titters, leaning over to swat Dixon's leg. "Secret softy, told you." Dixon doesn't reply, just rolls his eyes, and Alex gives Malibu a swat. "Mal, wake up."

"'M'awake," he says.

"Truth or dare?" Alex prompts.

"Truth."

Alex puts his hand back on Malibu's leg, holding it there and squeezing as he asks, "Are you okay, boo?"

Malibu opens his eyes, blinking down at Alex, a small frown on his face. To everyone's surprise, he says, "I don't know."

"Do you want to talk about it?" Alex asks, scooting closer and rubbing Malibu in a comforting way.

For a moment, Malibu looks like he might. But then the buzzer sounds, and he closes his eyes. "No. I'll be fine." Alex looks like he wants to press the topic, but Malibu swings his legs off the couch and heads toward the door. "I'll get the pizza."

Dixon and Alex exchange a glance, both of them frowning, and after a moment of contemplation, I hop up, catching up with Malibu as he walks into the kitchen. He starts grabbing plates, attempting to balance them on top of the pizza boxes in his hand.

"Here, I got it," I say, saving Dixon's dishes.

Malibu mumbles a thank you.

I run my finger along the edge of a plate as I quickly debate what I want to say. I don't know how much my words will mean to Malibu, considering out of all of us, he's known me for the least amount of time. But that defeated look he had on his face a moment ago was all too familiar to me, and I get the sense Malibu feels alone, when I know that's not the case.

Maybe it won't help, but I have to *try*.

"So, my sister Cass, she's married," I say.

Malibu frowns briefly, looking confused by the non sequitur. "Oh?"

"Yeah." I nod, grabbing some napkins and adding them atop the pile of plates in my hand. "Her husband, Carlos, is deployed in the Armed Forces."

Malibu leans against the counter, listening. "That must be tough."

"It is," I agree, nodding. "Cass is tough, though, too. She puts on a brave face and gets shit done because what's the alternative?"

Malibu doesn't respond.

"Sometimes I hear her crying," I say softly. Malibu swallows roughly at that, looking down. "So I hug her and remind her that she doesn't have to be brave all the time. That it's okay to accept help. That she's not alone."

Malibu nods once, looking at the floor.

"You're not alone, either, Mal."

He blinks several times, and I want to prove it to him. I want to point out Dixon and Alex in the other room, who have his back, even if he doesn't know it. I want to tell him that even though we just met, I have his back, too. I want him to truly understand he has people in his corner, even if he can't see it for himself.

But Malibu clears his throat, says, "Yeah," and slips out of the room before I have a chance.

With a sigh, I follow him out of the kitchen. Malibu is wearing a forced smile when I step into the living room. But he encourages everyone to dig in, and even though Alex and Dixon shoot him occasional concerned glances as we eat, no one pushes the topic of his personal life again. Discussion turns to happier subjects, and by the time the pizza boxes are empty and our chatting has dried up, it's early morning, nearly time for the sun to rise.

Dixon is the first to stand, scrubbing at his face sleepily. "There's a guest room and a couch. Do what you will with that," he says before disappearing down the hall.

Alex grabs Malibu's arm and drags him into the guest room without a word, and I take a quick glance at the couch before following the hallway to Dixon's open door. The man is already lying in bed in his boxers, one arm thrown over his eyes. I knock gently before entering.

"Are you really going to make me sleep on the couch?" I ask.

"It's comfortable," he replies, not answering the question.

I'd like to say it's the lingering effects of the alcohol emboldening me as I take a step inside his room, but that's not the truth. The alcohol has been out of my system for hours.

The truth involves feelings I'd rather not name. And the fact that Dixon told me he doesn't want me to *fade away*, which was the sweetest, and most shocking, way he could have possibly told me to be myself.

Well, what my self wants most right now is to slip into bed with Dixon. Thinking about Malibu and my sister and Carlos, I don't want to be alone tonight. I want to be with this man who, somehow, makes me feel safe.

Realistically, I know there's a good chance Dixon doesn't and won't like me the way I seem to like him. But *sometimes*, I swear I see a fire in his eyes that has me wondering. It's entirely possible he's simply trying to burn me alive with the heat of his gaze, but lately, I've felt a shift in our dynamic that has me thinking otherwise.

The smart thing would probably be to sleep on the couch. To maintain a professional distance and let those pesky feelings I've been harboring fall by the wayside.

But since meeting this big, lovable grump, I haven't been known to do the *smart* thing. He makes me a little reckless.

Case in point, I take a step closer. "The bed looks more comfortable."

Dixon frowns, but I can sense the moment I've won. "Do you snore?"

"Not that I'm aware of," I say, hiding my relieved smile as I shuck off my pants and lay them over a dresser drawer that's half open.

As I'm unbuttoning my shirt, Dixon asks, "Kick in your sleep?"

I huff a laugh. "I don't think so." I hang my shirt over my pants and then slide under the sheet in Dixon's bed, subtly inhaling the scent that's reminiscent of the man himself, like fresh laundry and mint. I sigh happily.

"If you get handsy, I'm kicking you out." He pulls the sheet over his lower half.

"I promise not to maul you in your sleep," I say. *Hopefully*.

Dixon blinks at me a couple times before huffing, "Fine."

With a victorious smile, I slide my hands under the pillow and close my eyes before Dixon can get annoyed with my face and give me the boot.

I hear him huff once, but then he's quiet. I don't know if he's watching me or if his eyes are closed, too, but I don't dare check. I let the soft sounds of his breathing lull me to sleep, and when I wake up cold sometime later, I settle myself against Dixon's broad, warm chest, and his arms wrap around me like a vise.

Chapter 19

DIXON

When I blink my eyes open, it takes me a second to reconcile what I'm seeing and feeling with reality because it resonates like a dream. My first fleeting thought is that Regina is in my arms, but the person I'm wrapped around is much too large, and Regina and I aren't together anymore. I know this.

No, the person in my arms is definitely a man. I inhale sharply, his spicy scent tickling my nostrils.

Niko fucking Adamos.

I'd like to say I jump away immediately, not tighten my arms around the man while my brain supplies the unhelpful thought that he feels good tucked against my body. I'd like to, but I can't, which pisses me off.

Niko is lying on his side, turned into me, one of his arms over my stomach and his knee dangerously close to my morning stiffy. And I can't even place all of the blame on him in this scenario. Because even though I'm on my back, my arm is curled possessively around the guy, and my other hand is holding tight to the forearm across my belly. I don't know who started it, but clearly, I'm just as guilty of perpetuating this sleep-snuggle situation.

I turn my head as slowly as possible, so as not to wake the man, and eye the gentle curve of Niko's back and the way his ass pops underneath his tight, white briefs.

Goddamn it.

When my eyes travel back up to Niko's face, I'm surprised to find him awake and grinning softly. "Well, this is cozy."

I push him off of me, retracting my arm and grumbling something about him attacking me in the night.

Niko laughs. "We've been in much more intimate positions than this, Dixon. A little cuddling is nothing to worry about."

What he's saying is true, in a way. We have been much closer before—I've been inside him, for Christ's sake—but more intimate? I'm not sure about that. I've always thought there's something incredibly intimate about sharing a bed, so I'm not sure why I allowed Niko to climb into mine last night.

"What time is it?" I ask instead, grabbing my phone off the nightstand. "Jesus. Eleven."

Niko hums, swinging his legs over the edge of the bed and stretching his back in a way I find distracting. "That means we only got, like, six hours of sleep."

"I missed my workout," I say idly, watching Niko's muscles flex.

He looks back at me, and I avert my eyes. "How often do you work out?"

"Every morning," I answer him, checking my messages and finding one from Mat demanding details about Miss Dixie. *Christ.*

"Every *day*?" Niko asks. "Geez. I only do twice, maybe three times a week. I guess that explains all that," he says, swiping his hand up and down my body.

I try not to preen under the praise. "Yeah, well, not today, clearly. I need my coffee." I rub my eyes.

Niko gets off the bed and walks to the dresser. He tugs his clothes from last night back on, the white ensemble looking ridiculously over-the-top for a morning commute. "I need the bathroom," he says before disappearing out the door.

After shooting a quick text to Mat to stall for time, I head down the hall myself. At the bathroom door, I come up short.

"What are you *doing*?"

Niko spits into the basin, catching my gaze in the mirror. "Brushing my teeth."

"With my toothbrush?" I ask incredulously. I mean, *really*?

Niko grins lopsidedly at me. "We've shared plenty of bodily fluids before," he comments before going back to his task.

"But that's my toothbrush," I defend. "That'd be like me using your..." I flounder for an appropriate comparison, "underwear."

Niko's head turns slowly, a wicked smile curling his lips. "And how would you use my underwear?"

I huff. "You are the most ridiculous person I've ever met."

Niko rinses his mouth and my toothbrush before setting it back in the stand. He shakes his head a little, shooting me a surprisingly apologetic look. "Sorry, I'll stop."

I spin on my heel, heading back down the hall to get dressed, and in confusion, I realize I don't want him to.

"The fuck is wrong with me," I mutter to myself.

After kicking everyone out of my place yesterday morning—the lot of them moving like comatose sloths—my day was already shot. I didn't get my latte until the *afternoon*, at which point I was irritated past the point of no return, and the remaining hours of daylight were spent in much the same frame of mind.

It didn't help that my thoughts kept wandering back to Niko and wondering *why*, of all things, I liked waking up next to him.

Mat would have a field day, but I'm not ready to tell him. I did, however, have to begrudgingly regale him with my tale as a one-time drag performer. He could barely stop laughing long enough to get a word in, and he took immense joy in hearing my reaction when he forwarded along a couple pictures Marco took of me.

Red and skimpy is not my thing.

I also couldn't stop worrying about Malibu. His tone of voice and that forlorn look in his eyes when he told us he wasn't sure he was okay concerns me. But I don't know how hard to push. I want Malibu to know we're here for him. I don't want to alienate him away from coming to me or one of the other guys if and when he needs help.

Niko and Malibu; they're both problems I don't know how to solve. But one thing I can accomplish this Sunday morning is getting my coffee fix *on time*.

There are different baristas that work the weekends at Hyped, and they're no Marley and Jason. The guy manning the register gives me a polite nod as I walk to the counter, entering my order only after I tell it to him. Marley never has to ask. And even though it's good, it just doesn't quite taste the same as my weekday lattes do. I'll have to ask Jason his secret.

I take the long way home, a light jacket keeping me warm now that we're into December and it's dipping towards the forties. I'm passing the park near my apartment when I catch sight of something that makes me stop and stare.

Can't I catch a break?

At first, I think Niko is here alone, which doesn't make any sense. Why would he be at the park near my apartment when he lives outside the city? Then I see a baby in his arms, bundled in a warm coat, and I'm even more confused. The child looks young...maybe three months old? And there are dark curls, just like Niko's, sticking out from underneath the hood of his or her coat. Niko has a firm hold around the baby's waist as he guides them down the slide slowly, and with a gut-wrenching jolt, I question—could that be Niko's child?

I have no idea. Because I've never asked if Niko has children. And when a dark-haired woman approaches Niko and he smiles up at her, I'm hit with the truth that there are a lot of things I don't know. Niko could be married, or, at the very least, in a relationship. It seems likely, watching the scene play out before me, that this *is* his family. His wife, maybe, and his child.

What I don't understand is why that thought hurts as much as it does. Why I feel duped, when I have no right to feel that way. Why I have this ache in my sternum, wishing I could go back and unsee this. Wishing it weren't true.

There's so much I have yet to learn about my new costar, and until now, I didn't realize how much I wanted that information. But that's my fault, for being such a prickly, self-absorbed ass that I never asked Niko the basics of his life.

Except I do know some things. He talked about his sisters and mom. Surely he would've mentioned a wife? And Niko said he's gay. Unless that was a lie? And what about the other night, when he cuddled me in his sleep? I suppose I can't fault the guy for that. It could've been accidental, and cuddling doesn't necessarily mean anything. But I would hope, if he *is* married, he wouldn't go around sleeping in other people's beds.

God, it's all a jumbled mess of thoughts in my head. I don't know which way is up, and I intend to get away before any of them can see me, but I don't make it in time. Niko turns in my direction, and with a double-take, recognition hits, and he smiles.

I take a few deep breaths as Niko jogs over lightly, the little baby in his arms, their hands covered in tiny pink mittens. A girl, possibly.

"Dixon?" he asks, tilting his head at me. "I didn't expect to run into you."

"Right," I say, clearing my throat. "Well, you know I live nearby. I was walking home." I hold up my Hyped cup as an explanation.

"Ah. We're heading to the aquarium," he says, and I nod because I know the one he's referring to that's a few blocks away. "We stopped here to sit and have a quick bite to eat beforehand."

I look over at the bench the woman is now sitting on and notice the paper lunch bags next to her. She's watching us curiously, but so far, she hasn't made a move to come over.

"Family trip," I say, more of a statement than a question. My throat is tight, and I feel like a fool. I have no reason to be this upset.

"Yeah," he says, looking down at the baby fondly. "This is Calliope." He makes her tiny hand wave, but the little girl doesn't pay any attention to me. She makes a smacking noise before punching her fist into the air. Niko snorts.

"Looks like you," I say, hoping it comes across casually.

"I guess so. Familial resemblance and all," he replies. "And that's my sister, Cassandra." The words hit like a blast of cool, refreshing air as Niko calls out, "Cass, come say hi."

The woman gets up and walks over, stuffing her hands in her pockets as she approaches. I find myself breathing a little easier now that I know who she is. Ridiculous. Why am I so relieved?

"Cass, this is Dixon, my coworker," Niko says, introducing us. "Dixon, this is my eldest sister, Cassandra."

"Hi," I say with a nod, reaching forward on autopilot. Cassandra shakes my hand in a soft grip.

"Hi, Dixon. Nice to finally meet you," she says, a welcoming smile on her face. "I've heard a lot from our Niko."

"Cass," Niko groans, eyeing his sister.

Cassandra laughs, sounding much like her brother, although her expression is a lot less mischievous than Niko's tends to be. "What? The porn isn't a secret," she says to me.

"La, la, la," Niko says, holding his hand over Calliope's ear.

Cassandra snorts a laugh. "Please, she's too young to understand anything."

"Then for my sake, *please*," Niko says.

Cassandra rolls her eyes and stage-whispers to me, "Quite a prude for someone who has sex for a living, no?"

Niko hangs his head back and sighs, and I can't help but chuckle.

"I don't know about that," I hedge. "I don't think prudish is a word I've ever associated with Niko."

Cassandra grins as Niko pins me with a playful glare.

"Anyways," he says loudly, cutting us off. "We should probably get going, Cass. Our ticket time is coming up."

She nods, holding out her arms. "Give me my daughter, then, so you can have a proper goodbye with your agápi."

"Cass," Niko warns, but he hands off the child nonetheless.

"Nice to meet you, Dixon," Cass says, ignoring her brother. "I hope I'll see you again soon."

"Nice to meet you, too," I respond.

Niko watches her walk away before turning back to me, rocking on his heels a bit.

"What did she call me?" I ask, too curious not to.

"Agápi?" When I nod, Niko sighs. "Love. Like a term of endearment because of the whole fake boyfriends thing at work."

"Ah," I say, wondering why I kind of like that. "So Calliope is your niece."

He mentioned a niece before, didn't he? I should've realized.

"Yeah," Niko says, nodding before his eyes go wide and he huffs a laugh. "Did you think she was my daughter?"

I shrug. "Honestly, I wasn't sure what to think." I try not to make my tone accusatory. "I realized you could have a whole family I know nothing about."

"I do," he says simply. "Have family, I mean. I told you about my sisters. My mamá. Kipp. But no children of my own. And I'm not in a relationship."

I shouldn't feel such a strong sense of comfort at hearing those words spoken so clearly and reassuringly, but I do. "I'm sorry for not asking," I say, not sure what else *to* say.

Niko looks at me curiously. "I told you, I'm an open book."

I nod, knowing I can't say the same. And that's my problem, isn't it? It's part of why my own relationships never seem to work out.

"Well, I'll let you get to it."

I start to spin around, but Niko's words halt me. "Dixon. You *can* ask. If there's ever anything you want to know."

I nod, unsure what to do with that piece of information. Niko's lips twitch into a small smile, and then he's gone, turning away and walking toward his family.

I turn, too, wondering what questions I'd already have answered if I weren't too stubborn to ask.

Chapter 20

Niko

This past week has gone by too quickly for my liking. And I'd say I don't know why that is, but I'd be lying.

I'm not ready to say goodbye to my fake relationship with Dixon.

On Tuesday, we filmed a shower scene together, the two of us practically battling it out—wet hands flying over equally wet skin until we were boneless and sated—since the producers wanted something a little less tender. We're down to one more scene together, and unless Jerome decides to keep our arc going, this is the end.

It doesn't help that the scene on today's agenda reminds me of the position I woke up in almost a week ago, amidst soft, cozy sheets with Dixon's even cozier arms around me. I'm lying on my side again now, Dixon close behind me, as we get ready for "spontaneous" morning sex. It's almost as if we're getting a do-over. A *what if* chance to find out what that morning could have been if Dixon and I were an actual couple.

We're not. I'm not that delusional. But it feels nice. And as Dixon nuzzles against the back of my neck, I realize I want this to be real. I really do.

I want Dixon. Simple as that.

I *care* for him, a lot more than I expected to.

And I don't even want to deny it anymore. I want to tell him, but I think I have to move with caution. Dixon's not like me. He likes order and calm control, and my life is chaotic. I have no real plans for my future, other than working in porn until something else comes about. I live with my sister and her baby, but even that isn't permanent, seeing as I'll likely move out once Carlos comes home. My family is loud and in your face and meddlesome, and I know it can be a lot, even though I love them with all of my being.

And, the truth is, I'm not sure Dixon trusts me yet. If I come right out and tell him I want to take him on a date, I'll likely either scare him off or get punched. I need to be patient and show him what we could be. I need to show him that I care before I tell him.

It's almost funny when I think about it. Here I assumed, all those weeks ago, that I'd win Dixon over by force. That I'd chip away at the man until I made him like me. I was convinced that was all there was to it, and it was a game, a challenge I wanted to win. A puzzle I wanted to solve. But now I wonder if I was lying to myself all along. If, maybe, these feelings were there from the get-go. If that crush was a little more powerful than I'd realized.

If, instead of chipping away at Dixon until he cracked, I was only revealing more and more of the man to myself, until *I* was the one feeling smacked upside the head, not knowing what hit him.

I guess that's karma.

I don't know if Dixon could feel the same. I'd like to think so. I'd like to believe some of these moments we've shared have meant more to him, too. That I haven't imagined that look in his eye. But I won't know until I ask.

And I can't ask while we're about to fuck in front of a crew of men.

"This feels nice," I say quietly as Dixon's arms wrap around me.

Much to my relief, he doesn't tense, but he does scoff. "You don't have to sweet-talk me. We're already in bed together."

"My *God*," I complain, momentarily forgetting my plan to continue winning Dixon over with kindness instead of attitude. "It's like you're incapable of believing a word I say. You assume I'm trying to fuck with you."

"Maybe because you usually are," he counters. Which, fair. But that was past Niko.

"It's the truth," I say, wiggling back against the hard planes of his body. "This does feel nice. I like having all that muscle against me."

Dixon grunts, but I can feel the unmistakable hardness of *another* part of his body, and I smile to myself.

"All right, we're going to get started," Nathaniel says, moving back behind the cameras. I lay my head down and close my eyes, and from the stillness of Dixon's body, I'm guessing he's done the same. "Action."

Dixon stirs against me, making an adorably sleepy sound before rumbling deep in his chest, his hand sliding down my abdomen and under the sheet covering our waists. I almost jolt when he wraps his fingers around my erection, stroking slowly before he nuzzles my ear.

"Wake up," he says softly.

I blink open my eyes, smiling and stretching out my limbs. The move upsets the sheets, revealing what Dixon's hand is doing to my dick. How it's gliding slowly, almost teasingly along my length.

"Morning," I mumble, turning my head enough to seek him out. He reads my intent and leans forward, and I nip at his lips, reaching my arm back to hold him in place.

"We need to get ready for brunch with your parents," he says, sliding his mouth along my jaw and lower still to my neck. He sucks a small kiss there, and I gasp.

"How much time do we have?" I ask, pumping my hips into Dixon's fist.

"Enough," he answers, brushing my hair out of the way to lay a gentle kiss on my temple. My heart skips a beat at the tender display, but I try to remind the organ that this is work, even if it doesn't feel like it.

Dixon lets go of my erection and reaches for the lube. Once he's slicked up his fingers, he guides my leg forward at an angle, giving him room to stretch me open. I lean further forward, settling into the sleepy, hazy feeling of the scene, letting myself melt into the bed as Dixon rubs the lube over my hole. I hum pleasantly, the sound turning into a moan as Dixon inches a finger inside.

He takes his time, stretching me slowly, one digit and then two. His lips leave a trail over the skin of my back and shoulders. A little press of his mouth here, a flick of a tongue there. By the time he pushes a third finger in, I'm trembling.

"'S'really good," I mumble, face pressed half into the pillow.

Dixon adds a fourth finger, his thick digits spreading me wide, getting me ready for his even thicker cock. It really does feel good, the way Dixon preps me. How he always takes his time, how he crooks his fingers *just so* to drive me wild and drive away the edge of pain. The hurt never quite surfaces with Dixon. He soothes it away with his careful, clever fingers.

"Ready?" he asks.

I can only nod. Dixon removes his fingers slowly, and then I hear the crinkle of the condom wrapper. Not a moment later, Dixon drapes himself against my side, his leg thrown over mine, as he guides his cock to my entrance. It's a smooth, slow glide as he presses in, and I exhale deeply, enjoying every inch as he brushes against my inner walls. Dixon's arm comes around my chest, clutching tightly when he bottoms out.

And then he fucks me. Slowly. Sweetly. Never moving from our spooned position. He talks to me all the while, telling me how good I feel, how he'll never get sick of this. And I wonder if this is what it's like to feel truly loved, for sex to be something more than bodies joining together to get off.

I've had relationships before, but nothing has felt like this. No one has compared to Dixon.

I return his sentiments, telling him I feel the same, telling him how cherished he makes me feel. And not a word of it is a lie.

The cameramen disappear. Nathaniel and the rest of the crew might as well not be here. I don't even notice them. All I know is Dixon and the way his hand caresses over my chest, his thumb rubbing firm circles against my nipple. The way his hips are flexing against me, pressing me into the mattress each time he hits home. The way his warmth is blanketing me, from my neck downward.

I only hear *him*. I only feel *him*.

And it terrifies me, that singular focus. The way I feel when Dixon and I are connected like this. Because what if it truly is one-sided? What if, to Dixon, this doesn't mean a thing? I think it might crush me.

But as Dixon's hand travels lower to clasp my dick, he tucks his face into my neck and whispers, "Niki," and I know—I *know*—Dixon is here with me.

"*Fuck*," I gasp out, my gut tightening at that one little, massive word. I tip over the crest of that slow-climb hill, wave after wave of honeyed bliss rolling through me as I orgasm onto the sheets below.

Dixon groans as my body tightens around him, and after a few more shallow thrusts, he tenses, unloading into the condom. I reach back and grab whatever part of him I can—his leg—and hold on, tying him to me. He seems to get the hint and doesn't pull out, not yet. He simply lets his weight blanket me more fully.

I could lie here forever. In this warm, dreamlike suspension, with Dixon's body against mine. With him holding me like I mean something. With his dick buried inside of me, a steady reminder that he's here. That he wants me, too.

But, of course, it's wishful thinking. Because Nathaniel calls, "Cut," the lights come up, and with a sudden, sickening loss of heat, Dixon rolls away from me. My body breaks into goosebumps at once, and I accept the robe one of the assistants hands me.

When I stand up, slipping it on, I glance over my shoulder. Dixon hasn't run away yet, which is a surprise. He's standing there, too, almost like he doesn't want to go. Our eyes connect for the briefest of moments, but then Dixon nods and turns away, and the bond is broken.

With a sigh and shake of my limbs, I follow him toward the locker room.

We're quiet as we shower—separately, of course—and we're quiet as we get dressed. I know why I'm feeling somber, but I'm less sure about Dixon. Regardless, I force myself to speak up while he's tying his shoes, before he has a chance to leave. I don't want this to be the end.

"So, are you ready to be rid of me?" I tease lightly, desperate to know the answer yet afraid of it all the same.

Dixon looks up, one brow arched. "Is it that easy, being rid of you?"

I huff a laugh. "Hey, I can't force you to be my boyfriend anymore. All you have to do is say the word, and I'll be out of your hair." I really hope he doesn't say the word.

He shakes his head. "Like I believe that. You're too persistent."

I smile to myself, relieved he's not actually telling me to get lost. "Aw, thanks. What a nice thing to say."

As I close my locker and plunk onto the bench, Dixon watches me. His shoes are tied, but he hasn't made a move to stand.

"Can you twist anything into a compliment?" he asks lightly.

"Why, sure."

"All right," Dixon says, clearly calculating. "You're a peacock."

"Colorful and majestic, thank you."

He crosses his arms, but there's an amused uptick in the corner of his mouth. "You have no shame."

"Confidence," I say with a shrug.

He looks me up and down. "You're too...proportional."

"I'm sorry, what?" I laugh.

"And your eyes," he continues, his tone gruff and yet almost tender. "They're too pretty."

My heart kicks an extra beat inside my chest, and I bite my lip, trying not to grin too widely. "These don't even sound like insults anymore," I say, leaning forward onto my knees. "Admit it."

Dixon huffs. "Admit what? That you're ridiculous?"

"That you don't hate me," I say slowly, my pulse beating heavily, steady and strong like a battle cry.

Dixon rolls his eyes. "Just because you're like a barnacle that's latched on and refuses to sink into the sea, that doesn't mean I enjoy your company."

I hum. I swear Dixon enjoys the banter. "Let me prove you wrong."

"Huh?"

"We both have the day off tomorrow. Let's hang out. And I'll prove you can enjoy my company."

Dixon looks suspicious. "Why?"

"Because, like you said, I'm persistent," I tell him. "Unless you're afraid you'll lose and fall madly in love with me. I *am* very lovable, you know."

Dixon snorts, but there's a hint of a smile in the corner of his lips that sets my heart racing again. "Ridiculous," he grumbles.

"You have nothing to fear then," I say, clapping my hands together. "I'll pick you up at noon. Don't eat lunch."

Dixon looks at me dubiously, but he doesn't say a word, which I take as enthusiastic assent.

I'm already running through options of how I can show Dixon I like him, that I *really* like him, when the door opens and Malibu comes breezing into the room.

"Hey, Malibu," I call out cheerfully.

He looks over, a smile on his face as his hand rises to greet me, but that smile is wiped clean when Dixon jumps off the bench, taking two swift steps towards the man.

"What the fuck?" Dixon growls. Malibu's eyes go wide when Dixon reaches forward, only to stop shy of touching skin. "What is that?"

Now that I'm looking, I see exactly what Dixon is so concerned about. There's a ring of bruising along the base of Malibu's neck, like a macabre necklace. My gut sinks.

"Nothing," Malibu says, his face shuttering as he steps around Dixon.

"That's not *nothing*, Mal. That looks like someone was choking you," Dixon says, his voice low but laced with a tinge of fear. He follows after Malibu.

"It's not like that, Dixon. Let it go." Malibu opens his locker and swiftly starts to strip.

"I'm not going to *let it go*," Dixon growls. "Tell me what happened. *Please*."

Malibu shakes his head, not answering.

"Malibu, you can talk to us," I urge gently, but he doesn't respond to me either.

Dixon spares me a wide-eyed, worried glance before stepping closer to our coworker. "Mal," he says softly, "you're scaring me."

Malibu seems to deflate at that. He finishes pulling on his ridiculously short jean cut-offs for his scene, and then he glances over at Dixon and me. "I agreed to it," he says, voice low. "Don't worry about me, okay? I'll swing by Raylin's before my shoot so she can cover it up."

"That's not what I'm worried about," Dixon says as Malibu shuts his locker.

"I'm fine," Malibu insists, smiling, even though it looks brittle. Before either of us can formulate a response, Malibu breezes out the door.

Dixon slumps, rubbing his forehead before he shouts, "*Fuck*." He storms out of the locker room, and I can't help but agree that Dixon's concern over his friend seems entirely appropriate. Something is definitely going on.

But if Malibu doesn't want our help, I'm not sure what any of us can do about it.

Chapter 21

Dixon

"Fuck, I'm losing my mind," I say into the phone, pacing my living room.

"Dixon, calm down," Mat says gently.

"No, something is seriously wrong. That's not Malibu. The guy is goddamn rainbows and sunshine and coconut suntan lotion. He's not into getting dangerously drunk or BDSM."

"You're right. It doesn't sound like him," Mat says. "But he *could* be into BDSM. Not everyone appears kinky on the outside."

I growl out my frustration. "I just...I *know* him, Mat. And something is wrong."

"I believe you," he says, placating me slightly. "But you also can't force him to admit it. It doesn't work like that."

"He had fucking bruises around his neck," I nearly shout, fully aware my voice is cracking but not giving a damn.

"I know," Mat says gently. "You told me."

"What do I do?" I ask, needing an answer. Needing a way I can help.

"Be his friend," Mat says, not for the first time.

"I feel like I'm failing at it," I admit.

"You're doing your best."

My buzzer goes off, and I curse. I didn't realize how late it was.

"Food delivery?" Mat asks as I'm walking toward the door.

"No, much worse," I respond, hitting the button to let my most exasperating coworker into the building. "It's Niko."

Mat laughs. "Oh, it's *Niko*," he says, voice all breathy again.

"Cut that shit out."

Mat laughs harder. "Do you guys have a date?"

"Mat, peaches, baby doll, little light of mine, you *know* I hate the guy. Why would this possibly be a date?" I grumble, propping the door open and walking back to the living room.

"You don't hate him, Dixon. Otherwise you'd never be doing whatever-the-fuck it is you're doing with him," he points out. "Which is what, exactly?"

"I don't know," I admit between clenched teeth. "I didn't get the details. I was too distracted by Malibu."

Mat hums just as Niko walks through the door, wind-swept and looking like he walked off a magazine cover, with his brown suede bomber jacket on over a cream-colored Henley, jeans cuffed at those fancy-ass boots of his, and an olive-green scarf wrapped around his neck. He notices I'm on the phone and gives me a nod, heading into my kitchen as if he's right at home.

"Dixon?"

"Huh?" I ask.

Mat laughs. "Right. Well, I'll talk to you later. Have a good date."

"It's not a date," I whisper harshly, but Mat is already gone.

When I tuck my phone into the pocket of my jeans and make my way around the corner, Niko is in front of the fridge, drinking a bottle of water.

"Help yourself," I mutter.

He ticks his head up in acknowledgement. "Ready to go?" he asks once he's done.

"No," I lie, heading to the closet to grab a jacket. It's cool today, so I pick my double-breasted wool one, pulling it on over my dark purple sweater.

Niko follows me. "That's nice."

"What is?" I ask, swiping my keys.

"That jacket. It looks nice on you," he says, waiting by the door.

I eye him suspiciously, but he seems sincere. "Let's do this."

"I love the enthusiasm," Niko says cheekily, following me into the hall.

"I don't even know what we're doing," I point out as I lock up.

"That's half the fun," Niko responds.

"I sincerely doubt that."

Niko laughs. "We're getting a bite to eat first. And then a surprise."

I sigh, even though I find myself curious what Niko could possibly have in store for us and wondering why he's even going through the effort. Surely, it can't be because of my chipper company.

Niko leads us to his car and drives about ten minutes away, to this little place I'd never have noticed myself.

"Tacos?" I ask, looking up at the little neon taco-shaped sign where the restaurant name should be.

"The *best* tacos," Niko says, opening the door and gesturing me inside.

There's a counter up ahead and large, school-style tables spread throughout the space. Even though there are empty seats, there are no completely empty tables, and I get the impression it's kind of a free-for-all seating situation. When I glance over my shoulder at Niko with a questioning lift of my eyebrows, he gives me a grin.

"Come on," he says, grabbing my arm gently and pulling me forward. "You order at the counter, and they bring it out once it's ready."

I let Niko go first as I skim the options from the menu board. Admittedly, it does look good. There are interesting choices like beef barbacoa, cilantro lime shrimp, and chorizo with poblano corn relish. Niko orders four tacos, and I do the same. Then we get a little folded number to bring to our seats. Niko doesn't even hesitate. He walks right over to a half-occupied table and plops down. I have no choice but to follow.

"So, this is nice," Niko says once I've taken a seat across from him.

I raise an eyebrow. "I feel like I'm at school again," I mutter, unsure how to react with people I don't know right next to me.

Niko chuckles. "You know, considering what you do," he says with a bounce of his eyebrows, like he doesn't want to use the word *porn* in polite company, "you're surprisingly reserved around people."

I think about Marley and Jason and the men and women at the gym who I have no problem chatting with, but I don't bother to correct Niko. He's not exactly wrong that I don't like forced proximity in situations that are out of my routine and comfort zone.

"This is a surprise to you?" I ask.

He huffs a laugh. "I guess not, Grumpy Bear."

"You, on the other hand, have no problem being around people," I note, ignoring the nickname he stole from Alex.

He shrugs. "Not really, no."

Our food shows up, much more quickly than I was expecting, and Niko thanks the server before picking one of the small plates off the tray and sliding his tacos onto it.

"Can I ask you a question?" he asks before biting into his food and moaning a little.

I avert my gaze, gathering up my own lunch from the tray between us. "Sure."

"How do you deal with fans?" he asks.

"Hm. I guess I engage in polite conversation until they move on their way," I answer, trying a bite of my beef barbacoa taco with fresh pico on top. I barely hold back a moan of my own, surprised by how much flavor is packed into one tiny bite. The meat is rich, tender, and salty, but the acidic notes from the salsa add a fresh touch.

"So you don't offer to sign their cleavage or anything?" Niko asks.

The woman next to him widens her eyes slightly, but she doesn't look over. I chuckle.

"Those aren't generally the type of fans I get," I point out.

"You know what I mean," he says around a laugh.

"You don't owe them anything," I say, wiping my mouth with a napkin. "Some of them are a little over the top, I'm not gonna lie. Some get kind of clingy. But you have to remember that they think you're Adonis." I speak quietly, keeping our conversation as private as possible. "You're an image to them and they just want to, you know—" I poke my finger through my open fist, and Niko snorts. "They don't know the real you, and I guarantee you, they don't want to."

Niko hums. "I hadn't thought of it like that."

I shrug. "So, yeah, I keep it short and impersonal but cordial. I don't talk about myself, ever. I try not to let the interaction linger, and if they get all clingy or inappropriate, I politely wrap things up and go on my way. But you do you," I add. "If you want to sign some ass cleavage or whatever, that's your choice."

Niko snickers, and I try not to notice the way it makes my chest hum in satisfaction.

"Do you ever... Never mind, that's personal."

My curiosity is piqued. "What?"

He finishes his mouthful of food before asking, "Do you ever sleep with your fans?"

"No," I say, shaking my head.

He huffs a laugh. "That was a fast answer."

I shrug. "Well, it's the truth."

"Surely you've hooked up with *someone* who knew who you were beforehand," he presses.

"I doubt it. I haven't hooked up in years, and I only dated women," I say, immediately regretting it when Niko's mouth drops open.

"You haven't hooked up in *years*?" he asks incredulously. "When was your last relationship?"

I swallow my bite of food, giving myself a moment before I answer *that* question. It's not even that I'm all that upset over losing Regina anymore—which, incidentally, makes me feel a little better about the split, since clearly I didn't feel as strongly about her as I thought—but I am a little bitter over the fact that none of my relationships have stuck. I know I'm not the *easiest* guy to be around, but I did care for each of the women I've dated. I did my best to show them that. I guess that wasn't good enough.

"My last girlfriend and I broke up a little over a month ago. The weekend before you started working at Elite 8 Studios," I answer.

Niko grimaces, and I'm not sure why until he hangs his head, looks up at me sheepishly, and says, "I was a dick."

I bust out laughing. I can't even help it. My abdominals get a field day, and try as I might, it takes me a minute to pull myself together. Niko watches me with amusement all the while.

All this time, it's like I've been waiting for him to admit it. It's what I thought at first, too. I hated the guy, and I wanted him to own up to being a douche. But now that he has, my first instinct is to assure him he's *not* a dick because I know him better now, and it's not the truth.

Still, I find myself grinning and saying, "A little bit."

Niko doesn't even seem to mind. He grins back at me, but then his face softens. "I *am* sorry for what I said. Something about your exes."

"I believe," I say, wiping my mouth with my napkin, "you were going to ask them for recommendations on what oil I preferred having rubbed over my big head."

"That was it," he responds in amusement, his smile returning now that he can see I'm not upset about it. Not anymore. I can't blame Niko for reacting to my bad attitude.

I shake my head, amazed to realize I'm thinking of that moment almost fondly now.

"Can I ask you another question?" he asks.

"You just did."

"God, you're insufferable," he teases, his eyes lighting with that mischievousness I kind of don't hate. "Why have you only dated women?"

"You know," I say slowly, wiping my hands clean now that my tacos are gone, "I've been thinking a lot about that lately."

"And what have you come up with?" Niko asks, crossing his arms on the table and watching me like he has all the time in the world. The small group beside us gets up, taking their trash with them, and it leaves just Niko and me, in our own little bubble.

"I think...I was holding onto the one thing that might make my parents proud of me," I admit quietly.

"What do you mean?" Niko asks.

Looking up into his face, I see only curiosity there and kindness. It makes it easier to talk about.

"I didn't have the *best* childhood," I say. "But I thought, at the very least, my parents loved me. We never had much money, so we didn't go on vacations or go out to eat or do the things some of the other kids did. But my dad, even though he was a hardass, would play football with me in the street when it wasn't busy, and my mom would let me sit on the counter and watch her make dinner. And the holidays..." I smile a little sadly. "Christmas was my favorite time of year, with the lights and the roast and that magical feeling in the air." I pause, blowing out gently, as if I could somehow expel the stained memories with my breath. "It wasn't much, just the three of us in a small, drafty house, but it was okay because it was family, you know?"

Niko nods, and I go on.

"I knew my dad wouldn't like me being bisexual—he believed in much more traditional values—so I hid it. But then he saw me kissing this boy my senior year of high school. We'd been dating in secret for months at that point. And when my dad found out, he just started screaming at us. He practically dragged me home, and then, once I was inside the house, he started throwing punches. I was so *shocked*," I admit, shaking my head, "so completely blindsided, that I didn't even react at first. I couldn't believe my dad was this guy willing to beat up his own son. I knew he'd be disappointed, but I thought I'd get a lecture or be grounded or, I don't know. I never thought..." I clear my throat, letting the images in my head wash away. "He got a couple hits in before I stopped him. I was bigger than him even then. He kicked me out after that."

"Dixon," Niko says softly. "I'm sorry."

I can't bring myself to acknowledge his words. "I stayed at a friend's house those last few months until I graduated. Before I left town, I stopped at my parents'. My mom answered the door, and she told me to go. And that was that. I never saw them again."

It happened so long ago, but I can still picture it. My dad's anger. My mom's cold dismissal. It used to hit sharply, like a poignant ache. Now, it's just a bruise, only sore when I press it. Mostly, I barely feel it anymore.

"But you still wanted to make them proud," he says.

"Yeah," I breathe out, nodding. "It's ridiculous. I see that now. I knew we were never going to have a relationship again, but I think I was afraid of closing that door on my end, you know? If I dated a guy, that was it. I was never going to have that *normal* life where I...I don't know, visited my parents with my partner during the holidays," I say quietly.

"I get it," he says, watching me much too intently. "That longing for approval."

I blink in surprise. "Yeah?"

He nods. "My bampás was always happy, always making people smile. And I looked up to him a lot. I wanted to be like him. Wanted to make him proud. I still do, even though he's long gone."

"Sorry, Niki," I say gently.

He shakes his head. "I know our situations are different—vastly different—but I understand what it's like to hang onto those feelings from childhood. They don't just go away with time. Sometimes, even still, I wonder what my dad would think of me. If he'd be proud."

I clear my throat, lips twitching into a smile. "I bet he would. It sounds like you got your charisma from him."

Niko barks a laugh. "Is that what we're calling it now?"

I shrug, Niko's sparkling eyes making me feel too warm. Too *seen*. "Anyways, I think I'm ready to leave the past behind now. Mat would be so proud."

Niko smiles softly. "I think I'd like this Mateo I've heard so much about."

I groan. "You two can never meet. It would be a catastrophe."

"Why? Because we'd gang up on you?"

I neither confirm nor deny it, and Niko laughs.

"Thank you for telling me all that, Dixon. Truly. Now come on," he says, standing up, not giving me any time to feel uncomfortable about everything I shared. "On to part two."

"Oh Lord. What's part two?" I grumble, although my question comes out sounding eager instead of apathetic.

"Let's just say this," Niko says, grinning at me. "Where we're going, you can punch me or pin me. Whichever your heart desires." With that, he winks and walks away, leaving me floundering in his wake.

"What?" I call out, my heart beating fast, my mind stuck on an image of Niko pinned under me. My dick takes interest, and I force my mind blank as I toss my trash and follow Niko out the door, wondering what the hell this troublemaker has in store for me today.

Chapter 22

NIKO

"So, gentlemen, any questions about the rules?"

"Nope," I say, punching my giant blue mitts together in front of me. "We've got this."

Dixon stands across from me, hands loose at his sides and pushed out a couple feet from his body by his suit, his face set in what can only be described as the worst scowl he's ever attempted. His lips keep twitching like he's trying to hold in his laughter, even though he's doing his best to appear stoic and bored.

"All right, have at it then!" our inflatable sumo wrestling guide says before stepping out of the ring.

"This is, by far, the worst thing I have ever done," Dixon grumbles, making me laugh.

"I've heard that claim before," I point out, immensely glad I found this pay-by-the-half-hour sumo gym. Dixon's face when we walked up was priceless.

"Yes, well, do you sense the theme? Both times have involved you." He quirks a brow.

"And I'm *honored*. Now come on, put your hands up," I taunt, holding my gloves in front of me in as close to a fighting pose as I can manage with my huge, blown-up sumo suit around me.

Dixon raises his red mitts in front of him, grumbling all the while. "This is ridiculous."

"You're ridiculous. Now hit me!"

I wobble toward Dixon, punching him right in his big, puffed-up belly. He doesn't even move an inch. I give him a shove, and he finally responds, mumbling something like, "My God, I can't believe I'm doing this," before planting his feet and shoving me back.

I dance back a couple steps before powering forward again. This time, he's ready, and Dixon swipes my arm away when I try to punch him. Pretty soon, he's fully invested, and we're swinging at each other wildly, our gloves doing zero damage to our heavily padded bodies. When Dixon manages to push me hard enough that I tip over like a Weeble, he erupts into tear-filled laughter.

I smile widely, the sight of him so damn happy doing funny things to my insides.

"Think we should convince Jerome to get a couple of these for the studio?" I joke.

Dixon scoffs. "No way. I'm sweating my balls off. And no one could pull off sexy in these things. Here," he says, holding out his hand. I grab on, and Dixon helps me up, although I keep my thoughts on how Dixon looks sexy doing just about anything to myself.

We play together for another twenty minutes, both managing to successfully take the other down a couple times. It's the most fun I've had in a while, but I find myself wishing all this padding wasn't between us. I'd much rather have Dixon's hard body sending me to the floor.

"Got you again," Dixon says from on top of me, his suit squeaking against my own. "You know, for all that game you were spouting, I thought you'd be better at this."

I grin up at him. "Who says I didn't want to be caught?"

Surprise flashes across Dixon's face, and I use it to my advantage, rolling to the side and sending him to the floor. I spend a minute rocking myself onto my feet while Dixon does the same, and by the time we're both standing again, I'm out of breath from laughing so hard.

Dixon's eyes travel over my face for a long moment as I catch my breath, but before I have a chance to question what he's looking for, our guide reappears, letting us know our time is up.

"So?" I ask as Dixon and I are stripping off our gear.

His lips twitch. "It did feel pretty good punching you."

"Brutal, but honest. I can dig it."

Dixon tugs his jacket back into place as we head outside, and I wrap my scarf around my neck. The sun is shining, but it's still chilly. For Las Vegas.

"Any other surprises I should be worried about?" Dixon asks on the way back to my car.

"Nope, I'm done torturing you. Unless you *want* more surprises, in which case I can definitely oblige."

Dixon shakes his head, but he doesn't immediately answer with a *no*, so I take that as a win. To be honest, I feel like today has been full of them. Dixon sharing more about his past with me at lunch. The carefree way in which he let loose at the inflatable sumo place. The fact that I've seen him smile and laugh more today than during the entire time I've known him.

Maybe he already fell over that wall from hate into...well, *like*, at the very least.

I'm not going to press my luck and ask him, though.

Dixon looks surprised when I walk with him up to his apartment door, grumbling something about "chivalry, my ass." But I don't mind. I've come to learn that grumpy-fond harassment is Dixon's love language. Or like language, whatever. I'm glad to be part of the inner circle now.

"Thanks for humoring me today," I tell him outside his door.

He pauses there, turning to me after it's unlocked. "It was all right."

"Like a poet," I say affectionately.

Dixon just rolls his eyes. "Did you want to come in?" he asks hesitantly, probably out of politeness more than anything else.

"Nah, that's okay." I'm not going to push it. Not yet. "I'll see you at work."

"Yeah, okay," he responds.

Before he can turn away, I lean in, brushing my lips against his cheek. He freezes, and when I pull back, he looks a little stunned.

I walk away with a smile on my face.

When I get to work, the weekend behind me, I'm hit with the fact that this is my first day filming with someone other than Dixon. It feels real now, not like some distant possibility. And I have no clue what to expect. I have first-day jitters all over again.

But before my scene, I'm scheduled to meet with Jerome to discuss the conclusion of my boyfriend arc with Dixon. And on my way to his office, right in front of the giant neon Elite

8 Studios sign, I bump into Alex, who's coming out of Raylin's station.

"Hey," he says cheerily, taking a step back before we actually collide.

"Hey, Alex," I reply, just as warmly.

"You have a scene with Emil today, right?"

I nod. "Yep, Adonis and Felix. First time topping here."

"Fun, fun," Alex says, waggling his eyebrows.

I laugh lightly. "Is that what you prefer? Topping?"

"Oh, Heavens no," Alex says with a little shudder. "Bossy bottom all the way, thank you very much." I chuckle, and he leans towards me conspiratorially. "Are you glad to be done with our grumpy bear?"

I snort a laugh. "He's not so bad."

Alex's eyes light up just like those Christmas decorations Dixon and I strung up a couple weeks back. "Honey, do tell."

"What makes you think there's anything to tell?" I ask, grinning as Alex rolls his eyes dramatically.

"Come on. I'm a bloodhound for this shit. You might as well spit it out." He curls his hand in a *gimme* gesture.

I wait until one of the crewmen passes, a giant box of industrial-sized lube in his arms, before speaking. I figure there's no harm in telling Alex. I get the distinct impression he's been pushing Dixon towards me for a while now, so if anyone will be both happy about this news and keep it quiet, it'll be the blonde ball of energy.

"So, I maybe, *possibly*," I add for dramatics, "like Dixon."

Alex squeals incredibly quietly. "I knew it. Give me more," he says, bouncing on his toes.

I chuckle. "There's not much else to tell. I'm working on it, okay? We went wrestling a couple days ago."

Alex looks confused. "And you survived?"

"Inflatable sumo wrestling," I clarify.

Alex's face freezes for a moment before he starts cackling. "Oh, *please* tell me you took pictures."

"Nope," I say, laughing, too. "It was adorable, though."

"Oh, God," Alex says, clutching his chest. "You think Grumpy Bear is adorable. This is too perfect for words."

At that moment, Dixon turns the corner, his pace faltering as he sees us standing near one another.

"Hi Dixie-poo," Alex greets him.

Dixon mutters a hi as he approaches, his eyes sweeping between the two of us. "What's going on here?"

"Oh, just gossiping," Alex says.

"Uh-huh," Dixon says, looking rightfully suspicious. He faces me. "Well, come on. Jerome wants to see us."

Alex sighs, shaking his head as he walks off down the hall. "It's just like day one again."

Dixon rolls his eyes, but I reply, "He's not wrong, you know."

With a huff, Dixon grabs my hand and shakes it forcefully, just like how Alex did when we first met. "Hi, Niko. Good day. How're you doing? Great, let's go see Jerome." He lifts an eyebrow. "Better?"

I grin. "Much better."

He drops my hand and shakes his head, fighting a smile the entire way down the hall to Jerome's office.

Dixon and I take seats beside one another in the large, burgundy armchairs, much like the first day we were in here. Jerome is sitting behind his desk, and Nathaniel is in a chair kitty-corner, watching us all with his trusty tablet in hand, one leg hooked over his khakied knee.

"Let's get started," Jerome says as soon as my ass hits the chair. "We haven't finished putting out the last of your videos, but the response has been really good. Great numbers, lots of hits, lots of requests for more."

"What does that mean?" I ask, my heart galloping away. Will we get to continue our scenes?

"It means we're going to consider revisiting it in a couple months." My heart sinks. "You're new here, Adonis, and we want to show the viewers more of you. More versatility. So you and Dix will do separate scenes for a few months, and then we'll consider another handful of videos to continue your boyfriend arc. Like a second season."

"Okay," Dixon says slowly. "Why, specifically, would none of our scenes be together in the meantime?"

"Because you, as a couple, garnered so much attention that we don't want people to see you both together *outside* of that role if we intend to put you back into it. It'll break up the believability of you as a lovey-dovey duo," he explains. "Fans want to believe."

"And if you decide not to continue the boyfriend arc?" I ask.

Jerome shrugs. "Then we'd pair you together on occasion."

I nod.

"Questions?" Jerome asks.

Dixon and I both shake our heads, eyeing each other briefly. I can't help but wonder if Dixon is as bummed as me knowing we won't be sleeping together for another couple months. Well, unless my plan to woo the man goes off without a hitch. One can hope.

"You guys did good," our boss adds, leaning back in his chair, his leather jacket hanging behind him. "You work well together, which, I'll admit, was a shock. Now get out of here and keep doing good work."

I salute the man and head out of the office alongside Dixon.

When he shuts the door behind us, I pause. "Well."

"Yeah, well," Dixon says.

We stand there awkwardly for a moment before I shake my head and take a step back. "See ya, boyfriend."

Dixon doesn't bother correcting me as I turn and walk away.

I have my scene with Emil, alias Felix, and it goes off without a hitch. We jibe well enough, there's minimal fumbling or weirdness, and Nathaniel only has to interrupt once to do some repositioning. It's fine, but it's perfunctory at best. Definitely not the same as my scenes with Dixon. And it convinces me, even more, that what I'm feeling for him is real. That it's been there all along. I just have to figure out how to make Dixon see it, too.

When I get out of the showers and exchange a polite good-bye with Emil, I stop by the break room for a quick snack. Fucking always takes it out of me. I'm surprised to see Dixon there, sitting in a chair and swiping through his phone. His eyes lift when I come through the door, and there's a flicker of something there—trepidation?—when he sees me.

"Hey, I didn't think you'd still be here," I tell him, knowing he's not on the schedule to film today. Sue me; I checked.

He just grunts, setting down his phone. "Good scene?"

I take a closer look at the man, noticing the tension in his frame. The way his eyes are slightly pinched and how his fingers are digging into the armrest beside him. Is he...*jealous?*

I hide my blossoming smile as I grab a cinnamon roll from the vending machine, schooling my features before I turn around.

"Yeah," I say, walking over and sitting across from Dixon on the arm of another chair. "It was fine."

Dixon nods, lips pursed tightly together.

"Different," I add, pretending to be absorbed in my cinnamon roll.

I pick at it as Dixon asks, "Different how?"

I shrug. "Not the same as you." I glance up in time to catch Dixon's expression of surprise and, if I'm not mistaken, relief. Then a smug little smile pulls at his lips, and I can't help but laugh. "Go ahead, gloat."

"I wasn't going to," he says, brushing imaginary lint off his shoulder.

"God, you're such a dick." I shake my head fondly before standing up and tossing my wrapper in the trash. I stop at the door and make sure Dixon is looking at me before I add, "But that's okay. I happen to like it."

Then I walk out, grinning the whole drive home.

Chapter 23

Dixon

Everything is back to normal. Or, should I say, BN. Before Niko.

I've had a couple scenes with other performers—nothing lovey-dovey—and my job is just how it used to be. The sex is a little rigid. A little detached. It's fine. It's simple.

But what's not simple are my feelings for Niko.

The man has made a point of continuing to be friendly, of joking around and pushing my buttons in a way that feels decidedly less antagonistic than it used to, and I swear he's even been flirting. I don't know what to make of it or the fact that I can't stop staring at his mouth. I miss *kissing* the guy, which is just so ridiculous it makes me want to punch something.

I should be glad things at work have settled back into a routine I'm used to, where I can simply go through the motions, but I'm not. I find myself wishing for more scenes with Niko. For that spark of whatever it was that made things different with him. I find myself looking for him in the halls and the break room. Imagining him next to me in the showers, or *with* me in the shower.

He's invaded my brain, and when he invited himself over to "hang out" today, I didn't even object. Which is how I find myself, Saturday afternoon, tidying up a little before he arrives.

What am I even doing? What is *this* we're doing?

I don't have time to dwell on it before I'm buzzing Niko in and cracking the door, my heart thumping in some sort of nervous excitement.

"Honey bear, I'm home," he calls out, nudging the door wide as he comes through, a large box in his hands.

"What the fuck is that?" I ask, not even bothering to call him out on his idiotic greeting.

"A clay molding kit," he says, a wide grin overtaking his face when he peers around the box.

"I'm sorry," I say, shutting the door behind him. "I thought you just said 'clay molding kit.'"

"Then your hearing is superb," he retorts, nudging the box against me until I grab a hold of it. Niko takes off his shoes, setting them neatly to the side, right next to mine, before standing upright. "You're not talking. Did I break you?"

"This is—"

"By far the worst thing you've ever done?" he finishes for me, grinning when I scowl.

"What's even in here?" I ask, begrudgingly bringing the box into the living room.

Niko follows me, flopping onto my couch like he lives here. I don't hate it. "There's clay, of course, and a spinning table thing."

"A spinning table thing," I repeat.

Niko motions his hand in a circle. "Yeah, like a wheel that spins. You know, goes around in a circle?"

"I know what spinning means," I huff out, pushing his legs out of the way so I can sit down.

Niko swings his feet to the floor; then he leans forward and opens the box, proceeding to pull the contents out and make a mess of my coffee table. I watch him for a minute before I can't stand it anymore.

"Niki, why the hell are we spinning clay? Is there something about me...something about my person...that screams *pottery lover* to you? Because if so, please tell me so I can remove it."

Niko laughs, his eyes twinkling as he opens a small instructional booklet and begins setting up the spinning table thing. "I thought we could have a *Ghost* moment."

"Isn't that, like, a romantic thing?" I ask with a frown.

He winks. "Broaden your horizons, Dixie. You never knew you'd love drag until you tried it."

"I didn't love drag," I point out. "I tolerated it. Barely."

"*Loved* it," Niko claims. "Looked hot, too," he adds in an almost offhand way.

"I..." I falter. "Did you really think so?"

He stops fiddling with the clay molding kit and turns toward me. "I mean, I can't say the dress and wig were what did it for me, but the fact that I could make out every single one of your muscles, glutes included?" He purses his lips and makes the hand gesture for *okay* before returning to his task. "Plus, your singing voice was divine."

I laugh at that, considering we both know it wasn't me singing, and Niko looks victorious, his eyes sweeping over me lightly.

"So," he says, holding up the clay, "we're going to make a bowl."

"Sounds ambitious," I mutter, still stuck on the fact that Niko finds me attractive.

"It's not, and that's why we're making it," he says matter-of-factly. "We'll need some water."

I stand up and grab a bowl from the kitchen, filling it with water and wondering why I'm even going along with this. Making pottery. Ridiculous. I grab two beers while I'm at it, figuring I'll need it.

"Drink?" I ask when I come back. I set the bowl of water down on the coffee table and hold out one of the bottles.

"Sure," Niko says, accepting it. "Would you have drank both if I refused?"

"Oh, definitely." I pop the top on mine. "I need to get through this somehow."

Niko laughs, shaking his head and making his hair fall all around his face. My fingers twitch with the urge to brush it back—I still can't believe Niko doesn't like his hair—but I catch myself and keep my hands to myself.

"Okay, so, looks like we get the clay wet and just…spin the thing," Niko says, frowning down at the instructions.

"Have at it, Michelangelo."

"You are so damn sassy under that grumpy exterior of yours," he says, shaking his head with a little smirk, like he likes that fact.

"You're one to talk," I point out.

"I'm not grumpy at all," Niko counters.

"That's not what I meant and you know it."

Niko laughs. "Even now, you're growling while you're sassing me. It's cute."

"Cute?" I ask incredulously.

Niko's eyebrows pop up. "Can't I call you cute?"

"Not if you're sassing me back," I say, trying to get my bearings. Sometimes it feels like Niko is running me around in verbal circles. It's hard to keep up.

"Well then," he says, "I'll repeat myself. It's cute."

Niko takes a long drag of his beer, and I freeze, really damn confused about whether or not he's being serious or just taking the piss.

"Here we go," he says, getting down to business. "Let's make some magic."

Niko grabs a large blob of clay and wets it down with his hands until it's more malleable.

"Can you tug up my sleeves?" he asks.

I do as he asks, trying not to let my fingers linger on his warm, bronzed skin. Niko thanks me and presses the soon-to-be-bowl over the middle of the spinning wheel where it protrudes upwards.

"This feels weird," he says as he starts spinning the contraption, the gray clay oozing out between his fingers a bit.

"Looks great," I mutter. "Very bowl-like."

Niko huffs a laugh. "Help me out."

"Help you how?" I ask.

"Put your hands over mine," he says completely seriously.

I look at him, waiting for the punchline, but he's looking down at the clay, focusing on shaping it into a bowl. "I think you've probably got it."

"Come on, Dixon," he says, just shy of a whine. "We're supposed to be doing this together."

With a sigh, I lean forward but pause. "How am I even supposed to fit?"

Niko scooches forward to the end of the cushion, and without overthinking it, I climb into the empty space behind him and mold my body to his back, bracketing him between both my legs and my arms as I reach for the clay. I do my best not to inhale his intoxicating scent, but it's impossible to avoid, and as I lean my chin atop his shoulder, the aroma of cloves settles around me like a warm winter snack.

Niko doesn't even flinch as I curve myself around him, much like his hands are doing to the clay. And placing my palms against the backs of his hands feels a lot less weird than I thought it would. He's warm in my grip and against my body, and even the texture of the gooey clay against my fingers isn't enough to erase how *good* this feels.

"Are you loving it?" Niko asks, kind of ruining the moment, but kind of not.

"No, this is horrible," I say softly.

Niko hums. "I'm loving it."

"Are you always so honest?" I ask.

"Yeah, I guess so."

"Doesn't that, I don't know, scare you?"

Niko turns his head slightly, his lips ghosting over my cheek. I don't turn, but it's a near thing. It'd be so easy to slot our mouths together, to get that taste of him I've been missing. My heart pounds rapidly, and I'm grateful for the clay hiding the moisture forming on my palms.

"No," he finally says before facing forward again.

I think about how Niko told me he'd always tell me the truth. All I have to do is ask. And even though it terrifies me somewhat, I do it.

"What is this? Right here. Right now. Why are you here?"

Niko turns his head again, his breath fanning across my cheek lightly. He stops the wheel, and our hands rest idly on the soft clay. "I'm wooing you, Dixon," he says with all the casual confidence of a man who knows exactly what he wants and goes after it, unaware of the chain reaction his words are setting off in my body and my mind.

I've never had anyone woo me. I've never had anyone *try*. I'm shocked and excited and terrified to realize how much I want that. I'm almost dizzy with it.

But on the cusp of that revelation is the terrible foreboding that I'm going to mess it all up. The worry that he'll see what's underneath the surface and realize it's not so great after all.

It's what's happened before. Time and time again.

No one stays.

I don't want to go down the same road with Niko. If I allow this man in only to lose him, I have a feeling it would leave the deepest wound yet.

"Why?" I ask quietly. "Why me?"

"Oh, griniári mou," he says softly. Those words again, whatever they mean. "Don't you see? I *like* you."

Three simple words. Three simple, profound words.

"But I was such an asshole to you," I say, having a hard time believing this is real. That it's not just another one of our scenes.

But Niko chuckles, leaving a soft kiss on my cheek, his stubble crisping against my skin amidst the velvet-soft press of his lips. "I was one, too," he says softly. "Would you kiss me?"

My pulse kicks up like a drum, and I turn my head slowly, finding Niko impossibly close, regarding me with a soft, hopeful, and somewhat heated expression. I lean forward, and the moment our lips touch, he inhales, and then he shifts his body and kisses me back.

It's so familiar, the feel of his mouth on mine, and yet this is the first time we've done this just for *us*, which makes it completely new. The earthy scent of damp clay hangs in the air, but more than that is Niko himself. How he smells, spicy and warm. How he tastes, a little minty underneath the edge of hops, like he took the time to brush his teeth before he came here. How he sighs gently against my lips in a way that feels like home.

Niko shifts again, standing up only long enough to turn around and climb onto my lap. He holds his hands out carefully, draping his arms over my shoulders as our mouths meet again. I want so badly to tug him to me, to grip him and *feel*, but my hands are covered in clay, too, and honestly, I have no clue how hard this stuff is to wash off. So I keep my hands to the sides, carefully like Niko is doing, and I try to convey the urgency I'm feeling with my mouth alone.

It seems to be enough. Our tongues tangle, teeth come out to nip, we battle and clash until breath is a necessity. Even then, we don't part. Our mouths slow, our tongues tease, until, finally...finally, we pull back.

"Fuck," Niko says, leaning his forehead against mine, his hair tickling my face. I ache to wrap my fingers into it. "I want to date you."

I squeeze my eyes shut, inhaling sharply as his words coast over me like an electric jolt to the heart.

"We're gonna get so much shit," I reply, which is maybe not the best response when someone tells you they want a relationship, but it's the first thing that popped into my mind.

Luckily, Niko laughs, accepting my strange acquiescence for what it is, his eyes crinkled at the corners as he pulls back and levers himself off of me. I miss the contact immediately.

"Yes, we are. Now come on." He pries the blob of bowl-ish-shaped clay loose. "We need to put this in the oven."

I wash my hands, wondering how it was so easy to go from *then* to *now* with just a few simple words, as if, when it mattered, Niko and I synced up and all that combativeness, teasing or otherwise, simply fell away. It's still on my mind when I set the oven to bake and Niko situates the bowl inside, declaring it perfect. Looks pretty janky to me, but I'm not going to say so. Niko washes his hands when he's done, and then, together, we clean up the clay molding supplies.

"We're both in porn," I muse aloud, trying to work through some of the thoughts that have been running rampant inside my mind ever since Niko's gentle declaration. *I want to date you.*

Niko looks up at me. "Yes."

"Is that going to be weird?"

"Do you think you'll get jealous?" he asks, sliding close and hooking his arms around my waist. I definitely don't dislike that.

"I don't think so. I'd have no right to be," I say, realizing it would be such a double standard if it did bother me.

"Were you jealous when we talked about my scene with Emil?" he asks, a cheeky little smile twitching his cheek up. "You seemed a little growly."

I turn my head and exhale, but Niko pulls me right back around to him, stealing a kiss from my lips.

"You have nothing to be jealous of," he says, which does help to soothe some of my ragged nerves.

"I think I was mostly nervous," I admit.

Niko tilts his head. "How so?"

"I didn't want to admit that I didn't hate you. And I was worried to find out that, maybe, what I'd been feeling wasn't reciprocated."

Niko smiles, running his hands up my back and clasping my shoulders. "You like me," he says softly, not even a hint of gloating in his tone.

Doesn't stop me from glowering, though. "Clearly," I mutter.

He grins, leaning in for another longer, lingering kiss, melting my gruffness away. "I think it will be fine," he says when he pulls back, his heavily lashed gaze roaming over my face. "If you do feel jealous, just talk to me, yeah? We'll work through it."

"You make it sound easy," I say.

"It can be."

I nod because he's not wrong. It's just something I have to work on.

"Now," Niko says, patting my chest and taking a step back, "I need to get out of here before I jump you."

"And that'd be a problem why?" I ask gruffly, adjusting the half-chub I've been sporting for the past half-hour, ever since being plastered against Niko's warm back.

"Because I'm trying to be *good*," he replies, his eyes dropping to the motion of my hand at my crotch. He takes a deep breath and blows it out of his mouth, grabbing the box of pottery supplies. "Don't forget to take the bowl out when the timer goes off."

"Right," I say, nodding, trying to catch up.

"And for our next date, you pick, all right? I want the full Dixon treatment," he says, winking at me.

"Wait. *Next* date? Don't you mean our first date?"

Niko stops at the door and puts on his shoes. He grabs the box again and, holding it in one hand, opens the door. "No, I mean next date. This was our second. Next will be our third. And luckily for you, that means I might just put out."

Niko grins as he backs down the hall, giving me a little wave, and I gulp, wondering what I've gotten into this time with Nikolas Adamos.

Somehow, I don't think I'm going to mind it.

Chapter 24

NIKO

"You'll never guess my news," I tell Kipp over my car's Bluetooth speaker.

"Wait, let me try," he says, making me chuckle. He hums aloud. "I know—you found a new favorite cereal?"

"What?" I ask in confusion. "No, that's not even remotely close."

"You snagged yourself a grumpy boyfriend?"

I blink a few times. "Kipp, only you would go from cereal to boyfriend."

"I knew it!" he crows. "Congrats, bro-friend."

I shake my head, glad that Kipp seems to be in much better spirits than he was after Thanksgiving. "Thanks, Kipp."

"So, how'd it happen?"

"I *Ghost*-ed him," I say.

"That...doesn't even make sense. Like, you played hard to get?"

"No," I say, laughing. "Like the movie, *Ghost*."

"Oh, my God," Kipp breathes out in excitement. "You pottery-wooed him."

I laugh loudly. "See, I knew you'd get it."

"That's brilliant, man. I'm happy for you."

"Thanks, Kipp. I'm on my way to meet him right now, in fact." I check my mirrors before changing lanes.

"So why are you on the phone with me?"

I roll my eyes. "Because I wanted to keep you updated?"

"Well, call me again when you have time to dish," he says.

"I'm not giving you sordid details, you horndog."

"*Fine*," he says, sounding exasperated. "Talk later."

Kipp hangs up, and I shake my head, putting my car into park as I arrive at Dixon's apartment. Dixon told me to dress casually and bring a change of clothes—which makes me *very* hopeful that we'll be getting dirty together—so I packed a few things in a small duffle. I grab it and head to the front door. It only takes a minute for Dixon to buzz me up, and not even another minute after that before my tongue is in his mouth.

Truth be told, I'd be happy putting out *before* our third date, but I'm trying to have a modicum of chill about the fact that Dixon agreed to date me in the first place. Yes, he's been...warm maybe isn't the right word, but a lot less chilly to me these past couple weeks. And seeing him smile and laugh on our first non-date date gave me a lot of hope. And the way he leaned into me during our ridiculous pottery non-date date, the way he so easily—eagerly—put himself into my space, was a pretty clear indicator that this *want* was mutual.

But Dixon and I didn't have the most conventional start. We were passively-aggressively at each other's throats when we first met, even though all that tension was because we were teetering on that thin line between love and hate, me doing my best to pull Dixon over and Dixon trying his damndest to stay stubbornly put. We fucked for work even before we knew one another, although it never felt like work for me, not at all like how my scenes with the other performers have felt since then. And only now are we at a point where we've moved from tumultuous to civil to something else entirely.

Most people don't start off their relationships the way we have, and even though I wasn't necessarily looking for anything serious in my life at this point in time, there's no way I'm going to pass up the opportunity to *try* with Dixon.

Because he's different.

He's prickly and grouchy and is full of stealth-sass and a wonderful, dry humor. He's kind, even when he's acting like an ass. He hides behind a mask of stoicism, but when he lets it slip, it's like getting a glimpse into the real Dixon. And finding ways to displace that mask is a mission I've been on since we met, even though I didn't quite realize that's what I was doing at the time. It feels like an accomplishment, each time I get a smile or a laugh or something honest and true. It's like getting hit by a live wire.

And if that's not love, well...it sure is *something*.

But Dixon isn't ready for all that. He's barely accepted that I actually like him, hence the tension lining his frame as I press him against his kitchen counter, the exact location I found him in when I entered his apartment. The tension doesn't last long, though. Within a few seconds, Dixon relaxes, his hands fisting my shirt to hold me close, like I'd think about going anywhere.

Dixon's mouth is minty from his gum, and our tongues tangle, but once his dick takes definite interest in the proceedings, he pulls back with a groan.

"Is that how you always say hello?" he asks.

"Could be." I grin, nipping his lip once more before allowing Dixon to put a little room between us. I can't quite help it when my eyes drop to the nice bulge inside his gym shorts.

"Ready for our third date?" I ask, attempting to distract myself from said bulge.

"*First* date," Dixon amends, raising an eyebrow like he's challenging me to contradict him. Well, he should certainly know I'm always up for a challenge.

"Third," I say confidently. "Where are we going, anyways, with our casual-wear at just past nine in the morning?"

"I thought you might've figured it out by now," Dixon says, a little smirk on his handsome face.

"Well, that's not ominous."

Dixon chuckles, not reassuring me in the least. "For the record," he says, voice softening a little as he takes a step into my space again, bringing a waft of his clean scent with him, "I like to think of this as our first date. Because when I go on a date with you, I want to know it. And I want *you* to know that I know it."

Damn, that sweet man. How can I even argue with that?

"Well, I don't usually put out on first dates," I say with a sullen pout, even though that's categorically false. I just can't seem to help myself when it comes to teasing Dixon.

His eyes darken a little, but he looks at me seriously. "Niko, I don't have expectations when it comes to sex between us. I'm not... That's not why I agreed to this."

"*Maláka*," I whisper-hiss, dropping my forehead onto Dixon's shoulder.

"What's that?" he asks, hands coming to hold me tentatively, like he's unsure whether or not he should.

I lean back so I can see him full-on. "It translates most closely to wanker. But it's like how Americans use 'fuck' to mean so many different things. It can be bad, it can be good, it can be affectionate. I was *affectionately* calling you an asshole for being so goddamn sweet."

"Oh," Dixon says.

"To clarify, I was teasing. I fully intend on putting out," I say, enjoying the clench of Dixon's jaw and the way his fingers spasm against my waist, "but thank you for being such a goddamn gentleman." I step back. "Now we should go before I defile you."

Dixon shakes his head, a little smirk on his face as he grabs his keys. I leave my duffle on the floor inside the door and follow him into the hall as he locks up.

"You make me sound innocent," he mutters.

"Nah. Not innocent, griniári mou. I know better than that."

I revel in the way Dixon's eyes travel the length of my body like he's remembering all of our not-so-innocent moments together. I'm tempted to ask him what, in particular, he's thinking about, but if I do, I have a feeling we'll never make it down the hall. And I'm dying to know what Dixon has planned for us.

"So, this is torture, right? You're getting payback for all those snarky comments I made?"

Dixon shakes his head, but he's chuckling, which makes me grin, despite what we're doing. "It's not torture. Working out releases endorphins. It makes you happier."

He stops his treadmill, and I quickly follow suit, hopping off my machine and trailing Dixon over to a bench press.

"You say that like I'm oblivious to the concept. You *know* I work out, too," I say, lifting my shirt and intentionally flexing my abs. Dixon pauses to admire the view.

"So why are you complaining?" he asks.

"Because I didn't know we'd be working out on our *date*," I answer, lowering my shirt. I'm fully aware I'm pouting, but unlike Dixon, I don't particularly enjoy my regimented workouts.

"Spot me?" Dixon asks, ignoring my sulking.

I nod, taking up position at the head of the bench. When Dixon starts pressing the impressively weighted barbell, I decide I'm a moron. My mouth goes dry, and all my blood rushes south as Dixon's muscles bunch and flex with his movements, his dark skin already glistening thanks to the warmup we did on the treadmills.

This isn't so bad, after all. In fact, it's more like a gift.

When he finishes his reps, he sits up. "Do you want a turn?"

"Uh," I say, coughing. "Nah, what's next?"

Dixon looks at me curiously, but he wipes down the machine and walks over to a rack of dumbbells. I watch as Dixon starts his reps, completely transfixed on his form and wishing he didn't have so many pesky articles of clothing in the way.

"Are you just going to stare at me?" he finally asks when it's clear I'm not making any moves to join him.

"Actually, yes. I've changed my mind. I very much like this torture."

Dixon purses his lips like he's trying not to smile.

"It's okay," I add. "You can bask in the admiration. In fact, I'm positive I'm not the only member of the Dixon fan club."

Dixon's eyes sweep the interior of the gym, and a couple people look away. He snorts.

"Well, you're the only one I care about," he says, his motion faltering like he didn't quite mean to let that slip.

I take a step closer to him, a wide smile on my face. "Is that so?"

He grumbles, "Fuck off," but there's exactly zero venom in the order.

"Oh, I wanna fuck, just not *off*," I assure him.

Dixon looks around again before licking his lips. "I think we're done here," he says, making my smile grow.

"I'm good with that," I tell him.

Dixon cleans up the equipment he was using, and then we make our way to the exit. The cold air slaps my face as we step outside, and I pull my coat tight around me. Dixon zips up his hoodie.

"One more stop," he says.

"Oh, yeah?"

Dixon nods, leading us to a coffee shop just around the corner.

"You're taking me to church?" I ask.

Dixon snorts. "It's coffee."

"Yeah, but that's practically your religion," I point out. "I'm honored."

Dixon looks fondly exasperated as he opens the door and guides me through, his hand a warm presence on my lower back. There's a line in front of the counter, but the barista notices Dixon as soon as he enters the shop. Her gaze pings to me briefly, eyes widening, before she returns to her task, a little smile on her face.

"What's good here?" I ask.

Dixon shrugs a little, which I find curious considering I see him carrying a Hyped coffee cup every morning we're at work together.

"I always get the same thing," he says. "Hazelnut latte."

"You *always* get the same thing? You've never tried anything else?" I ask a little incredulously.

He shrugs again, but he looks self-conscious. I curse internally and squeeze his arm.

"I guess that bodes well for me," I say.

Dixon frowns. "How so?"

"You're loyal," I reply, thankful that Dixon doesn't pull away from my touch. If anything, he leans into my space more as we inch up the line.

"Well, well, well," a voice says, breaking our little bubble. "If it isn't my favorite regular. And he's brought us a present."

Dixon shakes his head. "Back off, Marley. He's my present, not yours," he teases, voice full of mirth behind his growl. And *oh boy*, I'm glad my coat covers my crotch because Dixon getting possessive in that grumpy-bear mode of his is apparently my new horny kryptonite.

Marley grins, the piercings on her face glinting under the overhead lights. "Did you hear that, Jason?" she calls out. "Our Dixon brought a date. And he's smitten."

A young barista sticks his head out from behind the espresso machines, his eyes widening comically below his beanie. "Ho-ly shit," he says slowly, eyes bouncing between us. He clears his throat and mumbles, "It's two of them," before disappearing back behind the machinery.

"Don't mind Jason," Marley says. "He's still learning manners. Speaking of, where are mine? One large hazelnut, and what'll you have, handsome?" she asks, her flirty tone completely harmless.

I glance back up at the board. "How about a peppermint mocha?"

"You got it." She presses a few buttons and swings the card reader our way. Dixon pays before I have a chance to protest. "One hazelnut and one peppermint mocha for the lovebirds,"

Marley calls out to Jason before giving me a little wink. "Have a good day, boys."

"Bye, Marley, you troublemaker," Dixon says, guiding me down the counter.

"That was sweet," I say quietly.

Dixon rolls his eyes.

"Yeah, yeah," I say. "You're not *sweet*."

"Damn right," Dixon replies, except now I know better. He *is* sweet. He just doesn't want anyone to know it.

"One hazelnut and one peppermint mocha," the barista named Jason says a couple minutes later, sliding our drinks over, barely making eye contact.

"Thanks, Jason. Not all heroes wear capes," Dixon says so deadpan it takes me a second to realize he's teasing the guy. Jason shakes his head shyly and walks back behind the machines.

I smile as Dixon leads us over to a small, unoccupied table. "These are some of your people, huh?"

Dixon's eyebrows bounce up as he takes a testing sip of his hot latte. "Yeah. Guess so."

We're quiet as we sip our drinks, looking out the windows at the festive lights and people passing by.

"I liked what you said," I tell him after a minute.

"Which thing?"

"When you implied I'm yours."

"Well, you are, aren't you?" Dixon asks, making me laugh.

"God, it's like... Once you're in it, you're *in it*, aren't you?" I shake my head. "I never would've imagined when we first met that we'd end up here. But I'm glad."

Dixon looks off to the side, and I get the feeling there's something he's not saying.

"What is it?" I prod.

"I don't know how much I have to offer. I brought you here for our date—to the gym and my coffee place—because it's part of me, in a way. It's not much, but I wanted you to see it, for better or worse. I wanted to share it with you. But I know it's nothing special. I'm pretty boring when it comes down to it. There's still time to back out."

His words hit me like a punch to the gut.

"Not a chance," I say vehemently, sliding around the table to sit next to Dixon. I face him, nudging his chin until he gets the hint and looks my way. "You're not boring to me. I don't know where you got that idea, but put it out of your head right now. I know I was teasing you earlier at the gym, calling it torture, but I *liked* this date. I like seeing the real you. I want more of that."

Dixon swallows, and I let his face go. He shakes his head slightly. "I can't promise I'm going to be any good at this. My track record sucks."

"Dixon," I say around a huff of laughter. "Stop trying to talk me out of dating you. It's happening. And for the record, I don't think you should sell yourself so short. You certainly knew how to act like a good boyfriend during our scenes, not that I need you to act with me. I want Dixon, not Dix."

There's a pause, and then quietly, Dixon says, "I don't think I was ever acting with you, Niki."

My heart just about stops.

I cradle Dixon's face, not giving one fuck about PDA and hoping Dixon doesn't either. I'm pretty sure my smile is blinding, but there's no tempering it. "You're already doing better than you think," I tell him.

Dixon doesn't protest in the least when I bring our lips together. It's gentle and chaste, but it feels like an earthquake nonetheless. Like everything is shifting and rearranging into a new order. Like our foundation is settling. Like this is the start of something maybe very good.

When I pull back, it's not far. "Take me home, boyfriend."

I relish in the fact that, this time, those words are real.

Chapter 25
Dixon

When Niko calls me "boyfriend," there's no teasing in his tone. There's no intention to rile me up, at least, not in any way I don't want. There's only affection, and I latch onto it in a way I wouldn't let myself before.

I let myself accept it, and I let myself *want*.

As soon as we're inside my apartment, Niko presses me to the door. I've noticed he's a little more assertive than he was in our scenes, and I have zero issue with that. I like a little back and forth. He doesn't kiss me; he just blocks me in and leans close, the peppermint on his breath tickling my nose.

"Invite me into the shower," he says.

I don't think Niko worked up much of a sweat, considering he was too busy ogling me, but that's beside the point.

"So cocky," I mutter affectionately. "Come shower with me."

Niko grins that big smile that set my heart pounding the first time I met him. I can't believe I ever mistook my reaction as anything other than attraction.

Niko follows as I precede him down the hall, and by the time we're in the bathroom, he's shed all of his clothes. I crank the water on and let my eyes wander over every inch of Niko's exposed skin. He leans against the counter, letting me have my fill as I dispense of my own clothing. His hungry expression matches the one I catch a glimpse of in the mirror as we take each other in, naked for the first time of our own volition. So familiar, yet so new.

For a moment, there's silence apart from the rush of water, and then, all at once, we're on each other.

Our lips crash and our teeth bump together as we stumble under the spray. It rains down my back, hot and heavy, as Niko plasters himself to my front. He grinds against me, his erection hard and needy and slicked from the water rushing between us.

There's no finesse as we rut. We're all gripping hands, tangling tongues, and the hot press of bodies until I'm not sure how much longer I can last.

Niko moves until he has me pinned against the wall, and suddenly, he's the one under the spray. His hair soaks through in seconds, the thick strands falling around his face as he reaches between us and wraps his hand around my shaft.

He hums excitedly. "Jesus, you're sexy."

"You're one to talk, Adonis," I say around a hiss of pleasure.

Niko groans. "Never call me that again. Please."

"All right, princess," I tease. I did always like playing with princesses.

Niko gives me a glare of warning before he drops to his knees in front of me. My gasp is swallowed up by the noise of the shower, but as Niko's lips wrap around the tip of my dick, my resounding groan comes through loud and clear. He sucks me in short, sharp bursts, his tongue a heavy presence on the underside of my cock. Combined with his hand stroking my shaft, I'm taken to the brink much faster than I want.

"Gonna come," I warn Niko.

He takes me to the back of his throat, sucking deeply, and my fingers in his hair are the only thing tethering me as I spill inside the snug heat of his mouth.

Once I'm too sensitive, I pull Niko up. "Dick or ass?" I ask, dropping down in front of him.

Niko groans, looking down at me with fire in his molten-brown eyes. "*Fuck*. Uh, ass," he decides, spinning around and bracing himself against the shower wall.

I lean forward, palming his cheeks apart to reveal his pretty little hole. At the first lap of my tongue, Niko jolts. Then he presses back, widening his stance and dropping his head to the tile.

He's a litany of curses as I eat him out, my tongue working its way deep into his body as my hand strokes his slippery dick.

"Dixon," he groans, his body tensing without warning and his hole fluttering as he coats the shower tile in his cum.

He turns around then, dislodging my relaxed grip on his softening dick, and drops down to a crouch in front of me, grabbing my face and kissing me with feeling, not caring one bit about his taste on my tongue.

It's fire, and it's Niko. And it's hitting me, truly hitting me, that he's *mine*.

"I can't believe I hated you," I breathe out, a hair's breadth from his lips.

Niko grins in response, squeezing the back of my neck affectionately before standing up and holding out his hand. He pulls me upright, and since the steam in the shower is stifling, I turn the temperature down a touch before grabbing the soap. Niko and I don't talk as we wash off the sweat and efforts of our mutual orgasms, but every once in a while, Niko beams at me like he's seeing something worthy of putting that smile on his face, and it makes me believe maybe he is.

It's not even noon, but Niko and I flop onto my bed once we're dried off, me in clean gym shorts and him in a pair of black briefs. He still looks like a goddamn Greek god on my linens, but at least his dick is covered. Otherwise, I'm not sure I'd be able to keep myself off him.

As it is, I know we should talk. One of the things my exes agreed on was my *unavailability*. I didn't communicate enough. I didn't share enough. I didn't have emotions and feelings.

Not that that's true. I did. I do. But apparently, I wasn't skilled enough at showing it. I don't want to repeat my past mistakes, and I want to make sure Niko and I are on the same page about *us*.

"You called me your boyfriend," I start off by saying. Not my most eloquent lead-in, but it does the trick.

Niko huffs a laugh. "Yes, I did."

"Is that what we are?"

"I'd like it to be. Would that freak you out? Is it too soon?"

"No," I say, shaking my head slightly.

Niko is lying in front of me, both of us on our sides, curled toward one another. I'm up on my elbow, but Niko is relaxed into the pillow like a sleepy cat. His leg is pressed against mine, and his fingers are drawing lazy circles on the back of my hand.

"I don't think it's too soon," I add. "I just think we should clarify what 'boyfriends' means."

Niko smiles. "To me, it means dating."

"Agreed."

"And lots of fucking," he adds with a mischievous tilt of his lips.

"Not opposed," I say, eyes sweeping over the line of Niko's neck, down to the gentle swell of his chest and his flat, brown nipples, before I lift my gaze back to his face.

"And exclusivity. Apart from our jobs," Niko proposes.

I nod. "Agreed. And..." I falter, a little nervous about putting voice to what I *really* want.

"What is it?" Niko asks gently.

"I want this to mean something," I say. "I want to really try, Niki. I don't want... I don't want you to be another one of my failed relationships."

Niko's face does something complicated. There's a hint of a grin, a slight shake of his head, and then a softening as he scoots up against me. I wrap my arm around him instantly, tugging his broad form close.

"I want this to mean something, too. It already does."

"I just... If I'm doing something wrong, tell me, all right? Give me a chance to fix it. I couldn't stand the idea of you disappearing on me, too."

"Is that what happened last time?" he asks gently, his fingers skating over my scalp.

I exhale a heavy breath. "Most times," I admit. "I'm not good at talking about shit. Regina, my most recent ex, mentioned it. But then she just *left*. I felt like I never got a chance to fix myself."

"Dixon," Niko says softly. "You don't need fixing. I don't think that's a fair assumption to apply to yourself."

"Just..." I shake my head. "Tell me if I do something wrong," I plead.

The idea of Niko looking at me like my exes have, saying *we're through*, is almost too much to bear. It's like this vacuous hole inside my gut, threatening to collapse and take me with it.

"How about I *ask* you to talk to me if I'm concerned about something," Niko says, running his fingers along my jaw and under my chin, squeezing me there.

I realize my arm is like a steel band, my fingers digging into Niko's back, and I force myself to relax and nod, accepting Niko's words, hoping like hell I can break free from the loop of my past mistakes.

Niko gives me one more squeeze before he leans forward, pecking my lips. It's not enough, and when he rolls away again, I follow, blanketing his body. He grins up at me, hooking his arms over my shoulders. I kiss him harder, longer, until he's moaning, his cock hardening against my own a mere hour after our shared orgasms in the shower.

Niko nudges me until I back up, and I allow him to flip our positions until he's the one on top. He nudges my legs apart and settles there, hovering over me for a moment, hips connected.

"What do you want?" he asks me. "What do you like?"

"You," I answer on instinct, liking the way Niko's breath hitches. "I like anything that involves you."

Niko's lips twitch, but he shakes his head. "Smooth and all, but I'm serious. I want to know what you want, Dixon. Your desires outside of porn. Your kinks."

"Well, I hate to disappoint you," I say, a little surlier than intended, "but I'm pretty boring and vanilla in bed. I don't want games. I don't need power. I just like sex."

"Hey," Niko says seriously. "There is nothing wrong with vanilla. And you, Dixon, have never, not *once*, been boring in bed. That fucking word again." He shakes his head a little. "Throw it out of your vocabulary, okay? I hate it."

I fight my smile, but Niko's words help settle the restlessness in me.

"I'm good with *just sex*," he says, lowering his head and running his lips across my pecs lightly, just a feather of a touch.

"I like you when it comes to sex, too, you know. It's always been different with you. Better."

He licks over one of my nipples before tugging it gently with his teeth, and I let out a shaky breath, immensely relieved it wasn't just me feeling that connection. Feeling like things with Niko were different.

"Yeah," I mutter breathily as Niko's chin bumps against my erection. He takes it between his lips, circling his tongue around my crown, making my heart race when his eyes latch onto my face with an intensity entirely unique to Niko. A fire that makes me believe he'll fight for me. For us. "Definitely better."

"Oh, my God," Alex says, popping into my vision like a sprite on speed.

My head reels back on instinct. "Jesus. What the hell is your problem?"

"What *was* that?" he asks, circling his finger over my mouth.

"My face?"

"Oh, no. Definitely not *your* face. Not the grumpy bear I know. That was Happy Bear. Or maybe Dopey Bear," Alex says like he's giving it serious consideration.

Christ.

"I was just smiling," I mutter, pushing past the man into the break room.

"Oh, Dixon. Sweet Dixie-poo. You don't *just smile*. Tell me what's up," he demands, stepping in my way again before I can reach for a water.

I glance behind me, and when I see the room is empty, I begrudgingly admit, "I might be seeing someone."

It's not that I'm hiding the fact that it's Niko; I just think Alex would appreciate a little more dramatic flair. Or, maybe, if I'm being honest, I'd enjoy torturing him for a short while.

Niko and I agreed we weren't going to stay a secret. In fact, we met with Jerome this morning to disclose our relationship. For a minute, based on our boss's stunned silence, I was afraid we'd broken him. But then he gave us an awkward congratulations, and that was that.

I haven't told anyone else the news, and as far as I know, neither has Niko. Alex will be the first. After I have my fun.

The blonde nymph of a man looks up at me, his bright eyes blinking slowly. Much to my surprise, he frowns. "Is it Melissa?"

I tilt my head, confused. "Didn't you *want* me to date Melissa?"

"Yes?" At my prolonged stare, Alex huffs. "Okay, *no*. I did not want you to date Melissa. I just wanted you to see what you were missing."

"What I was missing?" I ask. "I'm not getting it."

I slide around Alex and grab a water, uncapping it as I make my way over to a couch. Niko should be wrapping up his scene soon, and then we'll head home together. Or, rather, we'll head back to my place.

Alex follows me over to the couch, sitting daintily next to me, even as his face is screwed up in consternation. "You said yourself there were no sparks with Melissa. I thought it would be the push you needed to see the freakin' wildfire that's been right in front of your eyes for the past two months! But *clearly*, I underestimated your stubbornness."

I hide my grin, understanding dawning as I realize he's talking about Niko.

"Adamos?" I question, infusing his last name with as much indignation as I can manage.

"Yes, Nikolas *fucking* Adamos," Alex says, huffing out the words. "My God, I'm not the only one shipping you two, you know. You have a whole fan base."

I can't help but chuckle, and Alex peers at me closely. "Wha—"

He's cut off when the door opens and Niko, the man of the hour, strolls into the room, a broad smile on his face. Ah well, it was fun while it lasted.

Niko walks right over to me, his hair dew damp from his shower, glistening slightly and making him look pleasantly tousled. He doesn't stop his sure-footed strides until he's right in my space, settling over my lap and kissing me without a care in the world. My hands clasp the back of his ass, holding him tight.

I hear Alex sputtering next to us, but while Niko's lips are connected to mine, there's only him.

When Niko pulls back, he says, "Hey, boyfriend."

I grin. "Hi."

"You dick," Alex says with feeling, swatting my arm.

Niko laughs, not even bothering to come to my aid. I simply shrug as Niko disentangles himself from my lap, tugging me to my feet after him.

"Alex," I say. "I think you know Nikolas fucking Adamos, my boyfriend."

"Pleasure," Niko says, holding out his hand.

Alex swats it away. "You guys are the worst. A best friend would have *led* with that, Dixon. You big, contrary oaf."

"Hey," Niko grumbles, looking at me affectionately. "That's my boyfriend you're talking about."

"You're going to use that word all the time now, aren't you?" I mutter in faux-exasperation.

Niko grins. "You bet your ass."

"You two are adorable. Ugh! I hate you. See you tomorrow," Alex calls out as Niko tugs me toward the door. I chuckle, and that damn smile of mine fixes itself right back onto my face.

In fact, I'm on a high all day. While Niko and I grab dinner, taking it back to my place, where we eat while Niko regales me with the details of his scene with Trevor. While Niko and I digest our food, sprawled on the couch watching basketball. Even when we discuss tomorrow and the fact that Niko will have to stay at his own place because he's babysitting Calliope.

And most definitely as we lie in bed, a little sweaty and a lot sated from our tussle in the sheets.

It's then, once the sun is long gone and we're getting ready to sleep, that Niko asks me, "Would you come home with me for Christmas?"

I look over. Niko's face is inches from my own on the pillow, his hair in complete disarray and spread every which way over the pillowcase and his own forehead. I swipe a bit away from his face, letting my fingers linger over his smooth skin.

"With your family?" I ask.

He nods. "Too much?"

That smile resurfaces. "No, it's not too much."

"Is that a yes?" he asks.

"Yes."

Niko grins, making me feel momentarily weightless, and after brushing my lips in a butterfly kiss, he rolls over, reaching for something on the ground. When he resurfaces, there's a book in his hand. He resettles and flips it open while I stare.

"I'm sorry... First the family, and now this? Did we skip right to marriage?" I ask.

Niko looks over at me, amused. "What?"

"You're reading a book in bed. Like we didn't start dating two minutes ago. Like we've been together for years and share the same socks from the same sock drawer, and you have idiosyncrasies like only rotating the toothbrush counter-clockwise when you brush your teeth, and I say things like 'Goddamn kids these days,' and then *bam*, dentures."

Niko closes his book, setting it on his chest and shaking his head affectionately. "Cheeky. You're so fucking cheeky, griniári mou. I *like* reading. You should try it."

"Is that another mystery?" I ask.

He nods. "They're my favorite. I like trying to solve them. Kind of like puzzles." He looks over at me. "Kind of like you."

His words draw me up short.

"And have you? Solved me, I mean?"

I'm not sure what answer I want him to give. I'm a little terrified of someone seeing my entire picture, and yet I yearn for it all the same. I want someone—want *Niki*—to know my every truth. To choose me because of it.

Niko smiles, a sweet thing that makes his brown eyes twinkle. "I'm getting closer. You've been giving me more pieces every day."

I swallow around the heavy lump in my throat. I want to keep giving him pieces.

"All right, then," I say. "Show me what's so great about mysteries."

"Yeah?" Niko asks excitedly.

I nod, and Niko settles against my side, opening up the book. He starts reading, the timbre of his voice ebbing and flowing with the words, and I get caught in it. In this man at my side.

In the sound of him, the feel, the smell. The comfort. The way he makes my gut sizzle.

It's fireworks.

And it's hope.

Chapter 26
Niko

"There's no way it's the butler!" I say, looking fleetingly at Dixon before returning my eyes to the road. "That's too obvious."

"That's what they want you to think," he says, like he knows all about it. "They're trying to throw you off the scent by making it seem too obvious, so you assume it *has* to be someone else."

"No way. It's definitely the chef. That guy is sketchy AF."

"Francisco?" Dixon asks with an incredulous gasp. "He seems so sweet."

"Exactly."

Dixon grumbles some more about *who done it* in the new mystery we're reading together—our second—as I pull up to the house I share with Cass. We're driving to my mamá's today for Christmas and agreed it made the most sense to carpool. Seeing as I stayed at Dixon's last night, like I do a couple times a week, we drove together to pick up Cass and Calliope.

I offered Kipp a ride, too, but he said maybe it would be best for him to drive separately, just in case my "beast of a boyfriend," his words, doesn't like him. I told him Dixon won't be a problem, but he doesn't seem to believe me. I guess I understand. Dixon can look intimidating if you don't know him, not that he ever tries to.

Dixon hops out of the vehicle as Cass comes through the front door. He opens the back of the car for her, and she hustles a baby Calli into the car seat.

"Thanks, Dixon. It's crisp out here," Cass says, pulling her daughter's straps tight. When she shuts the door, she swoops in to give Dixon a hug.

The first time Dixon stayed with me here instead of us spending the night at his place, Cass gave him a warm welcome, hug included. He seemed thrown, but the second time, he didn't hesitate to hug my sister back. Just like that, Cass adopted Dixon into the family, and just like that, Dixon adopted Cass and Calli into his inner circle. My grumpy bear really is a softy underneath it all.

"Good to see you," my sister says after releasing Dixon.

"You, too," he responds in kind, even though it's only been three days since he was last here. Once they're inside the car, I crank the heat for a minute.

"You ready for this?" Cass asks. "You're about to be descended upon by vultures."

"That's no way to talk about your fellow sisters, Cass," I admonish with a tsk.

"Pft," she says. "You know it's the truth."

"They're well-intending vultures," I assure Dixon.

With somewhat wide eyes, he says, "Good to know. Not at all concerning."

Cass laughs from the backseat, and I wish I could reach around and give her a smack. Dixon says he's excited to meet the family, but I can tell he's still nervous. And now that the topic has been brought up again, he's sitting a little more stiffly, his jaw tight as he chews his gum.

"There'll be baklavá," I remind him.

He looks over at me, his mouth tipping into a smile and his shoulders losing a little of their tension. "Thank you for making it."

"Told you I would, anytime you asked."

Cass *awws* from the back.

"They do know I'm coming, right?" Dixon asks.

"Of course," I assure him.

"Everyone is *very* excited to meet you," Cass says. "Just be your charming self and you'll have nothing to worry about."

"Oh, fudge off, Cassandra," Dixon grumbles without any heat, ever-conscious of masking his swear words when Calliope is present. Cass's wide, amused eyes meet mine in the mirror. "First, you tell me they're vultures. Now you say to be *charming*, and I'll be fine. Well, thank you very much. No pressure. They'll be picking my bones. *Charming*. Like that's a thing I am."

Cass titters from the back while I hasten to reassure my boyfriend. "You are charming, actually." I can feel the weight of his disbelieving stare on the side of my head. "You are! When you want to be."

"Like when we first met, and I swept you off your feet," he deadpans.

"Exactly," I reply with a grin.

Dixon shakes his head, but he seems more relaxed than a minute ago, and for that, I'm grateful. It doesn't last long.

When we pull up to Mamá's sizable house an hour later, he's hard as a rock. And not in the fun way. I turn off the car and, as Cass grabs Calli out of her seat, I squeeze his stiff shoulder in support.

"It's going to be more than fine," I remind him.

"Yeah," he says, sounding unconvinced.

We all walk side by side up to the door, and as we step inside, Cass and I both call out, "Ya." *'Hey.'*

Half a dozen yas are shouted back, and before the door has even shut behind us, Elina and Ioanna, the troublemakers, come rushing up.

"The boyfriend is here!" Elina shouts for the rest of the family.

"Jesus, you're even bigger in person," Ioanna puts in, looking up at Dixon.

"Real nice, you two. Very polite," I reply, shaking my head. "Dixon, this is the middle child, Elina. And that one is the evil twin, Ioanna."

"Nice to meet you both," Dixon says before he's unceremoniously tugged toward the kitchen by Ioanna, who starts dishing all the gossip from the morning. Like how Sofia messed up the tzatzíki by adding fennel instead of dill, and how Kipp dropped a carton of eggs and had to go buy more.

Elina follows close behind, and all the while, I watch their retreating forms. "It's like they don't even care I'm here."

Cass snorts, nudging me as she passes. "You're old news, brother," she teases, following our siblings into the kitchen.

When I round the corner myself, I have to stop for a second. Dixon is surrounded on all sides by Adamos women, towering easily over all of them. Mamá is squeezing his arm, telling him how happy she is that he could come. Ioanna and Sofia are whispering amongst themselves, but their smiles are kind. Elina is nodding along to something Dixon is telling our mamá. And Cass, baby Calli in her arms, is standing at Dixon's side, lending her support as Dixon goes up against the loving vultures.

And Dixon, well... He looks *happy*.

Unlike Kipp, who's sitting off to the side, the table between him and the rest of the fam like a barrier.

"Ya," I say quietly, sliding into a seat next to him and bumping his shoulder with mine.

"Hey," he replies quietly, watching Dixon.

"What's up?" I ask. "Everything okay?"

"Yeah, sure."

I give him another nudge. "Dixon isn't going to hate you, I promise."

"How do you know?" he asks, finally meeting my gaze.

"What did I say before?"

Kipp slumps a little. "That you wouldn't be with someone who didn't accept me or our past."

"That's right. So buck the fuck up, bro-friend. This sad sack routine is just...sad," I tell him, grateful when I earn a little smile. "It'll be all right."

"Okay," he says.

I catch Dixon's eye from across the room. The sun is streaming into the window behind him, bathing the terracotta and blue hues of the kitchen in a sort of hazy glow reminiscent of home. Of Greece. Like water and the rocky cliffside and where they meet. And for a moment, I can see exactly how Dixon would fit there.

As family. As home.

Dixon smiles—well, his lip twitches in the faintest up-turn—and I know he's okay. That he's not being picked apart by my flocking family. That maybe everything *is* more than fine, after all. I give him a little smile back.

I know we'll have to help cook soon, but I stay with Kipp until the initial Dixon interrogation is over. Just as Elina goes back to stirring something in a big pot and Mamá starts to roll and shape the melomakárona, traditional Greek Christmas honey cookies, Dixon comes over.

"Hey," he says, sitting next to me and, much to my surprise, pulling me in for a chaste kiss.

Dixon has turned out to be much more affectionate in public than I ever thought he would be. And maybe that was a stupid assumption on my part, to think he'd be more reserved because of his somewhat stoic nature, but I couldn't be happier to have pegged him wrong in that regard. I love the casual displays of affection: the touches, little kisses, a hand on the arm, fingers through the hair. It makes me feel seen. Appreciated.

And I can tell Dixon isn't kissing me to stake his claim in front of Kipp. Honestly, that's not his style. There's nothing lascivious about the kiss, nothing possessive. It's just affection, plain and simple.

Not that I expected Dixon to act like a caveman. Jealousy has not been an issue for us. I know it's only been a few weeks since we started dating *officially,* and our relationship is practically still in its infancy, but much to my relief—and Dixon's—work has continued without any hard feelings from either of us. There's us, and then there's the job. And they're entirely separate things.

"Hi," I reply, squeezing Dixon's arm after he breaks our short kiss.

Dixon turns his attention to Kipp next, his shoulders curled slightly, like he's trying to make himself smaller, less threatening. I almost laugh. My big, cranky, sweet Dixon.

He holds out his hand. "You must be Kipp."

"That's me," Kipp replies, a nervous little smile on his face as he shakes Dixon's hand.

"Niki tells me you're the reason he got into porn," Dixon says, sitting back.

Kipp's eyebrows fly upwards before he turns slowly my way. "*Niki?*"

"Oh, damn it," I mutter.

And just like that, Kipp thaws. "Oh, this is precious. Dixon, buddy, you've just given me a gift," he croons.

Dixon chuckles. "Glad to be of service." I roll my eyes, but Dixon pipes back up. "I wanted to say thank you."

"To me?" Kipp asks incredulously. "What for?"

"For putting Niko into my orbit," Dixon says plainly, like those words haven't just pierced to the very heart of me. *Fuck*, this man.

Kipp's eyes flick to mine briefly, creased with warmth and filled with a million unspoken words, before he settles his gaze back onto Dixon. "Pulled you in like a brilliant, shining star, did he?"

Dixon scoffs. "More like a black hole. Tried my hardest, but I couldn't escape."

Kipp laughs. "Sounds about right."

"Christ. Thanks, you two," I groan.

Dixon squeezes the back of my neck.

"Paidiá," Mamá says. '*Children.*' She waves us over. "There is food to be made. Come."

The three of us get out of our seats and help prepare Christmas dinner. The kitchen is filled with the sounds of laughter, the smells of honey and cinnamon, garlic and oregano, and even the occasional song. My eyes keep finding Dixon throughout the day, and his find mine, and every time, there's a smile and the promise of more.

When we sit down to an early dinner, my sisters can't help but pepper Dixon with more inane questions. He doesn't seem perturbed and answers them with good grace, and I appreciate that everyone is including him.

Until Ioanna opens her mouth. "So, Dixon. We heard you used to hate our Niko. What changed?"

"Ioanna," I chide.

Dixon squeezes my hand. "It's okay. I didn't hate him, not really. I just didn't want to like him, and, as my friend Mat pointed out to me, I overcompensated."

"What does that mean?" Sofia asks quietly.

Dixon glances at me, a flicker of tenderness in his eyes. "He was like...this force of nature. He had the power to throw my life into complete disarray. To knock down my walls." I blink at him in surprise. "And I'd been playing it safe, clinging to old habits for so long without even realizing it. So when he came along, all unruly wild hair and those smart, sharp eyes, I think I figured my best chance at withstanding the storm was to throw it off course."

Oh, God.

"That is so sweet, paidí mou," Mamá says, making my heart clench at her casual, but intentional, use of *my child*.

I squeeze Dixon's hand hard, and he gives me a smile.

Conversation moves on to more neutral territory after Dixon's sweet confession, and when dinner is over, treats are passed out. Dixon grabs several pieces of baklavá, much to my satisfaction, and we take seats in the living room in front of the decorated tree that's full of colorful Christmas lights and a whole host of hodgepodge ornaments we've collected or made over the years. None of it matches or looks picture perfect, but it's a story of family.

We take turns passing out presents, and Dixon looks especially nervous about his gifts for my family, which he insisted on buying. I helped him with ideas, but the final choices were his. An assortment of bath bombs for Cass, a new messenger bag for Elina, a colorful scarf for Ioanna, a leather journal for Sofia, and a new shawl for Mamá. When he gives Kipp his gift, he makes sure to tell him to open it in private, since it contains a rather personal photo of Alex, who gladly volunteered his services. I have no doubt Kipp will love it.

As for his gift to me, the collection of mysteries is a complete surprise, and a very welcome one.

I got Dixon something a little cheesy: a grumpy-looking bear ornament. His voice catches when he thanks me for it, but it's the gift from all of us that has his eyes looking suspiciously moist. Not just the hideous sweater that mismatches with the rest of ours, but the fact that we gather together in front of the tree to take a picture. This year's family Christmas photo.

Dixon told me he's never taken one before, and knowing how much the idea of celebrating holidays with family means to him, it was important to me to make sure he was included. I wanted to give him new memories to hold. And I needed him to know that this is his family now if he wants it. It doesn't matter that we've only been together a short while, and it doesn't matter that maybe it's too fast to be thinking that way.

I haven't been serious about much in my life, but I'm serious about Dixon.

I want him for keeps.

As Dixon thanks Mamá yet again for including him today, Kipp catches my eye. He gives me a little wink from across the room, the reindeer on his sweater flashing its bright red nose on and off. I wink back, feeling settled and warm. Not just from the hot cider in my hand or the extra sweater layered on over my clothes. Not from the smell of cinnamon still hanging in the air or the fire flickering in the corner, despite it being over forty degrees today.

It's Dixon, the man I've fallen for, being with me this year. It's the way he energizes me inside and how he cares so deeply under that sarcastic front of his. It's how he went out of his way to learn about my family, these people I love, and how he seems to revel in the loudness and chaos that is my life.

It's the way he tells me exactly how he feels through his words and his actions. I don't care what his exes thought; Dixon isn't unavailable. He may not vocalize every feeling that flashes through his mind, and he may not volunteer his innermost thoughts without a little prompting, but that doesn't make him cold. It just means he's cautious. And I get that. No one, apart from his friends, has been willing to stick around. To make the effort.

I am.

And I plan to make sure he knows that. I'll keep showing him and telling him. I may not have my life all figured out yet. I don't know how long I'll do porn and whether or not I'll go back to my old management consulting job at some point or find another avenue to explore. I don't know how much longer I'll live with Cass, especially since Carlos will be returning next summer, and he's mentioned making this tour his last. And I don't know if I'll ever leave the desert because even though I don't love it here, it's where family is, and that means more to me than where my feet are planted.

But when I look at the future, I see Dixon. All those other choices, I want them to include this man because he's mine.

And even if he doesn't know it yet, I'm his.

Chapter 27
Dixon

I wasn't sure how today would go. I thought it might be a little awkward or that Niko's family would be welcoming but politely distant.

I didn't expect the tornado that is the Adamos household, even though Niko himself warned me. They sucked me into their very center, into the calm of their storm, accepting me, including me, setting me at ease.

I certainly didn't expect today to bring me to tears. Luckily, I was able to excuse myself to the bathroom before they hit.

I wipe away the final drops of moisture, clearing the cleansing tracks from my cheeks. Somehow, I found the very thing I'd been longing for. Not just the family, not just Christmas in this household full of laughter and love, but *Niko*. I don't understand it, how the things I feel for him can eclipse all of my other relationships in such a short period of time. It doesn't make sense. But I've accepted that the sort of chaos Niko brings to my life is a whirlwind I'll gladly let myself get pulled into time and time again.

I wash my hands before leaving the bathroom, and when I don't immediately spot Niko, I seek him out. I find him on the back porch, bundled in a coat, a mug in his hands.

He snorts when I approach, his eyes sweeping over the ridiculous lit-up Christmas light sweater the Adamoses gifted me.

"You can take that off now, you know," he says.

"Nah, I'm good."

Niko's lips curl up behind his mug, and he takes a sip. "Your secret is safe with me."

"What secret is that?" I ask, joining Niko at the deck railing, leaning against the side of his body.

He presses against me, too. "That you're just a softy inside." When I simply grunt, Niko raises his eyebrows. "Not going to deny it this time?"

"I admit I have a soft spot for you."

Niko's smile widens, and he leans in to kiss me. His lips are cold, but he tastes like warm cider. I wrap my arms around him to keep him close, and he hums happily. When our lips part, I look into his eyes, the brown lit by the multicolored sparkling lights along the roof above us, making his irises flash with a kaleidoscope of colors.

"You're not who I thought you were," I admit.

He laughs loudly. "No shit."

"You don't have to be so cheeky about it," I grumble.

Niko squeezes me closer, grinning softly. "You like me cheeky. Admit it, griniári mou."

"I do," I agree with a sigh. "I like it a lot. I like *you*. You can gloat now."

He hums. "I told you I wouldn't do that."

I blow out a puff of air, and it swirls in front of me like white smoke. "Thank you. For today. For being relentless."

"I've never had someone thank me for *that* before, but you're welcome," he says, running his hand over my shoulder to the side of my neck. His fingers are cold, like his lips, but I don't mind.

"What does that mean?" I ask him. "That name you call me?"

Niko grins. "I wondered when you'd ask."

My eye roll is immediate. "You could've just told me," I reply, even though I understand why he didn't. He was waiting for me to come around. "To be honest, I wasn't sure I wanted to know. I assume you've been calling me an asshole all this time."

Niko chuckles. "No, not at all. It means 'my grump.'"

I wrinkle my nose. "Well, that's not much better."

Niko rubs the skin at my neck before circling my waist again, tugging me firmly against his body. "I'm going to tell you something, and you're not going to freak out," he says.

"Oh, I'm not?" I wing up an eyebrow.

"You *are* grumpy, but I like it. I like all the pieces of you, Dixon, and I call you 'my grump' because you are. It's not an insult. It's a compliment. And I want you to know I accept you. Just as you are."

"*Christ*," I mutter, dropping my lips against Niko's temple. "You've been calling me that for a long time."

"Yes," he says simply.

"Even back then." Back when I was behaving like an asshole.

"Yes."

He's liked me this whole time, even at my worst.

"There you guys are," a soft voice calls from the doorway, interrupting us. I look over, and Cassandra's face crumples in apology. "I'm really sorry to intrude, but Calliope is starting to get fussy."

"Of course," Niko says, smudging a kiss across my cheek before pulling back and grabbing my hand. "It's getting late. Let's go."

After a round of hugs and goodbyes and promises to visit, the four of us head back to the car. I offer for Cassandra to sit up front, but she chooses the back to calm Calliope if needed.

The entire drive home, I can't help but sneak glances at Niko's striking profile, framed by the dark night sky. His lips and strong nose. The way his curls catch the light from passing streetlamps. Even those long lashes of his. When he catches me staring, the corner of his mouth turns up, and he grabs my hand, holding it between us. That's where it stays for the rest of the drive.

Niko drops me off at home first, getting out of the car to give me a goodnight kiss before he and his sister head back to their house. Even after he's gone, I'm left feeling suffused with warmth. I expect my mood to crash once I'm inside my empty apartment, but it doesn't happen. I see a sweater Niko left draped over my couch and his coffee cup on the counter. I see the small Christmas tree he insisted we put up, outfitted with soft, white lights. And the warped approximation of a bowl that we made together when he wooed me, the ugly, wonderful gray mass sitting front and center on the coffee table. I see a few of his books lining my shelves and, in the bathroom, the extra toothbrush next to my own. It makes me feel like he's here, even when he's not. It makes me feel a lot less alone.

I'm just slipping into bed when my phone rings. I expect it to be Niko giving me one last goodnight, but it's not. It's Malibu calling.

I pick up immediately, my gut swooping in concern. "Mal?"

"Hey, Dixon," he says, his voice quiet and a little flat.

"What's wrong?"

"Uh. I need help," he says tentatively.

"Of course," I say, hopping out of bed and slipping on a pair of jeans. "Anything. What is it?"

"Can I come over?"

"Yeah. Absolutely. Can you get here or do you need a ride?"

"I'm nearby. I'll be there in five minutes," he says.

"Okay, I'll buzz you up."

I finish getting dressed and check my fridge while I wait for Malibu to arrive, grateful I still have some of the tea he likes. When my buzzer sounds, I let Malibu inside, and two minutes later, he's walking down the hall toward me. I open the door wide, and he trudges in, his shoulders slumped, a duffle hanging from one arm and another dragging behind him.

"Are you hungry?" I ask.

"Nah," he says, dropping everything by the door and walking into the living room.

I swing by the kitchen to grab the tea I poured, and then I join Malibu. He's flopped back against the couch, his head tipped and eyes closed, although I can tell he's not sleeping.

I slide the glass in front of him on the coffee table. "Here."

Malibu opens his eyes and looks over at me before noticing the tea. He picks it up and takes a slow sip. "Thanks, Dixon." His voice is quiet, almost defeated.

"What's going on?" I prompt.

"I got evicted."

My first instinct is to ask *why*, but I realize that's probably not the most sensitive response. Malibu doesn't need an interrogation right now. He needs a friend.

"You can stay here," I say. It's a no-brainer.

His fingers tighten around the drink in his hands, and he can't seem to bring himself to look at me. "I really didn't want to ask, but I'm out of options."

"You didn't ask," I tell him. "I offered."

"*Fuck*," he says, so quietly I almost don't hear it.

"Are *you* okay, Mal? Housing situation aside."

He sighs. "I don't know. Things have gotten so out of hand. I feel like I can't catch up."

I sit on that for a moment. "I'm not going to lie, I'm not the best at giving advice. Mat has told me I'd make a shit therapist." Malibu chuckles at that. "But I can listen, if you want to talk about it."

He drinks some more of his tea before curling back against the couch and nodding over at me. "You remember me telling you about my mom?"

I think back. "Yeah. Wasn't very nice, wanted you to do conversion therapy when she found out you were gay?"

"That about sums it up," he says a little morosely. "She has dementia. It started a couple years ago."

"Mal, I'm sorry," I say quietly, knowing that can't be easy for him. I understand how conflicting emotions can be when it comes to crap parents. How we can cling desperately to the good memories, even though they're clouded, warped because of the bad. How, as Niko said, our feelings for someone don't simply disappear over time, even if the person disappointed us. Even if they're gone.

Malibu nods. "She doesn't have anyone else. I'm all that's left, and I've been paying for her care."

"Oh, Mal."

"It's just too much," he says in despair. "It ate through my savings so fast. And Jerome already has me maxed out on the schedule, so I can't do more scenes. I sold just about everything I could. And then I started..." He stops to clear his throat. "I started escorting, but please don't tell Jerome. He'd freak out."

"I..." It takes me a moment to process everything. I think Jerome would probably be understanding, not that he'd *like* it. But our exclusivity clause only refers to filming independently or with other studios. And technically, escorting doesn't fall under that purview. "I won't say anything," I finally settle on because it's an easy promise to keep.

"Thank you," Malibu breathes out.

"I'm sorry you've been dealing with this, Mal," I reiterate. "Your mother—"

Mal shakes his head, closing his eyes tight as if he's in pain. He's clearly not ready to talk about her, and I get that.

"The escorting," I hedge, piecing other things together a little. "Is that where the bruising came from?"

Malibu pierces me with the stubborn set of his eyes. "It was *fine*. Don't freak out about it, okay? The guy offered me an extra *two grand* to choke me a little."

"Jesus," I hiss out, rubbing my face.

"He didn't hurt me, not really," Malibu says. "It was just a little bruising."

I shake my head but let it drop, at least for now. "The night at the club? You never drink like that."

Malibu sighs, looking regretful. "I just wanted to forget. For one night, I didn't want to worry about the fact that I was about to hit rock bottom. I know it was stupid and irresponsible, but I wanted stupid over fear. Just for one night."

"Mal," I say lightly, squeezing his shoulder to get his attention. "You can stay here however long you need to, okay? You don't have to worry about that part. The rest, we'll figure out."

"We?" he challenges, although there's a little smile on his lips.

"Yes. I happen to know a business major," I respond, referring to my boyfriend.

My words startle me into realizing not *once* did I think about consulting with Niko before offering up my home to Malibu. *Shit.* I push that aside for the time being because there are other matters to attend to.

"Right now, where are you at? How bad is it?"

"If I don't have to worry about rent and I live off ramen for a while, I'll make do," he says. "I've been getting better escort gigs. Higher-paying ones."

I nod, my mind spinning. "Okay then. You'll live here, and you won't be eating ramen. You'll eat whatever is in the kitchen, and you won't complain about me putting it there. You can't keep up our lifestyle eating noodles and Snickers bars."

Malibu's eyes widen. "You noticed the Snickers?"

I snort. "I noticed the Snickers."

"Nuts are good protein," he says, his lips immediately drawing together to stop his laugh.

"I won't even touch that one," I grumble.

"Dixon," he says seriously. "*Thank you.* I'll repay you when I can."

"You can repay me by being safe and taking care of yourself, Mal. I was really worried. *Am* still worried, if I'm being honest," I tell him.

"I know," he says softly. "Thank you for caring."

I nod. "Thank you for calling. Let me show you to your room."

I take a few minutes to reintroduce Malibu to the guest room and the rest of the apartment, even though he's been here before, and then he retreats with his bags. I pull out my phone, making a checklist of the things I need to get for his stay, as well as a reminder to grab more groceries tomorrow.

And then, only once I'm confident I've done everything I can tonight and that Malibu is resting comfortably in bed, do I let myself acknowledge that I fucked up.

Because I didn't even ask my boyfriend before inviting another man into my life.

I didn't talk to him. I didn't ask for his opinion. I made this big decision all on my own. In a way, it's like I'm repeating my previous mistakes. Not being open, not being communicative.

I know I have to let Niko know what I did, but not tonight. Not when he's asleep in his own bed miles away. It'll have to wait, and hopefully, I can come up with some way for him to forgive me between now and then.

Chapter 28

NIKO

For the second day in a row, Dixon has evaded me. He didn't text me back once on Sunday, and even though we were both on the schedule today, he booked it home before I arrived. He always waits around for me.

Something is definitely going on, and I'm about to find out.

I knock on Dixon's door, grateful for the lady exiting the building who recognized me and let me in, and I wait. Twenty seconds later, the door opens, and Dixon's face goes from surprised to wary.

"Uh, hey," he says.

"Hey? That's all I get?" I ask, inviting myself in. I stop in the living room when I notice someone else's bright red shoes kicked off near the coffee table.

"That's *definitely* not what it looks like," he says.

I set the plastic bags I brought down and turn around, raising my brows. "I assume not," I say because even though I know those shoes aren't mine or his, I also know Dixon isn't a cheater. What I don't know is why he looks so guilty.

"I can explain," Dixon says.

"Please do. I want to know what's going on because you ghosted me, and not in the sexy way."

"Shit," Dixon mutters. "Okay, so..." He pauses to grab my hand, pulling me to the couch. "Malibu got evicted from his apartment, and I invited him to live here for a while."

"Okay," I say slowly because Dixon looks pretty tortured over this news. "Is he all right, otherwise?"

"I mean, not exactly, but I think he will be."

"That's good, then," I say, squeezing his hand.

Dixon rubs his face. "But, I mean, I fucked up. I didn't even *ask* you first, and I should've. This is exactly the sort of thing Regina complained about. I'm so sorry, Niki."

"Woah, let's back it up. First, I'm not Regina," I say. "So let's leave that baggage at the door. This, *us*, is between just you and me, okay?" Dixon nods hesitantly, and I go on. "Second, from what you just told me, I gathered two pieces of information. First, that you're a damn good friend. And second, that you care enough about me that you're this upset over your perceived error."

"I..." Dixon flounders, like he has no clue how to respond.

"Dixon," I say, scooting close enough to get my hands on him. "Why would it bother me that you invited Malibu to stay here? I'm glad he has somewhere safe to be."

"Because I didn't run it by you first?" he guesses, frowning.

I shrug. "Dixon, you're mine, but I don't own you. And technically, this is your place. I don't live here. I just like being a frequent flyer."

He looks lost, eyes wide and blinking. "Niki, this is so goddamn different than every other relationship I've been in."

"Did you think I was going to drop you over this?" I ask softly.

"It'd crossed my mind," he responds.

Oh, Dixon.

I wrap my arms around his broad shoulders, rubbing the tension from his back. "Let's write our own rules, okay? Forget the 'boring' crap and forget that 'unavailable' shit. Just be you. Trust in that guy. Because I trust him, and I like him a whole lot, just the way he is. And I'm not jumping ship at the earliest opportunity."

"Yeah, okay," Dixon breathes out, his body melting as he nuzzles into my neck.

I smooth my palms over his shoulder blades and wonder if Dixon realizes exactly how much he gives away without even trying.

"Are you hungry? I brought food."

Dixon doesn't remove his face from my neck, but he asks incredulously, "You brought dinner, even though I was being an ass?"

"I brought dinner for me and my boyfriend, regardless of how he was acting because I knew something wasn't okay."

Dixon releases a shaky breath against my skin, hot and damp, before pressing a kiss there. "Can it wait?"

"Sure," I say with a grin as Dixon sucks gently against my neck, not hard enough to bruise—because neither of us wants an excuse to visit Raylin—but enough to feel claimed.

"Then c'mon," he says, the warmth of his mouth abruptly gone as Dixon hauls me upright and starts leading me toward his room.

"Aye, aye, Captain," I tease.

Dixon raises one eyebrow at me over his shoulder. "You'd look hot in a sailor outfit."

That has me laughing. "Think Jerome has one?"

"I know he does," he says, kicking the door shut behind us. "Goes to about mid-thigh."

"Hot," I reply, gasping as Dixon practically tosses me onto the bed.

He quickly rids me of my clothes, and then he follows, and before I know it, Dixon's face is buried between my legs.

"My God," I pant out, riding his face and that wicked tongue. "Get up here before I come. I want you to fuck me."

Dixon obliges, scaling my body. I tug him close, the pair of us frotting together for a moment as we kiss. My hands are all over Dixon's ass, appreciating that bubble butt of his, when I slide down his crease without really thinking about what I'm doing. As my finger grazes Dixon's hole, he gasps breathily. I test the motion again, and when a moan leaves his mouth, I pull back.

"You like this?" I ask.

"Yes," he says simply.

"I..." I pause, a little shocked. "Just touching or more? It's fine either way; I like what we do. But you said you don't bottom, so I'm trying to get an idea of what it is you *do* like."

"I don't bottom for work," he says slowly, watching me intently.

I rein in my surprise at the qualifier. "But you *do* bottom?"

"I would for you."

"*Damn*, okay. Let me just wrap my head around that for a moment," I reply, running my hands over Dixon's back as he chuckles lightly. Neither of us are rutting anymore, but we're both still hard.

"Take your time," he mumbles, sliding his fingers across my cock lazily. My hands spasm against his shoulders.

"Have you bottomed before?" I ask.

"A long time ago," he answers. "With my first boyfriend."

"The one you were caught with?"

Dixon nods.

"Can I ask why you don't bottom in porn?"

"I guess I wanted to save something that was just for me," he says, looking contemplative. "That probably sounds stupid."

"Hey, no way. I get that," I tell him. "It sounds ridiculously Neanderthal to admit, but I kind of like that I'd get a piece of you none of the others do." And it's true; I do. The idea that Dixon would share that with me? It makes me feel like...I'm important enough to be his exception. It makes me wonder if there's a way for me to reciprocate. "Is there anything you want me to save just for you?"

"You already do," he says, tracing the corner of my eyelid with his finger. "That look in your eye. That's just for me."

My breath hitches. *This man.*

Shaking my head, I push Dixon onto his back. "You sweet talker, you. New plan." I inch lower. "I'm going to take you apart with my mouth and my fingers because I am *dying* to become acquainted with your prostate and hear you scream my name."

"Pretty sure of yourself, aren't you?" Dixon goads.

"Oh, baby, it's on."

I do make Dixon scream my name with two of my fingers in his ass and his dick lodged down my throat. And yeah, I feel pretty damn proud of myself. But that only lasts until five minutes later, when Dixon is returning the favor.

I guess there are no losers in competitive sex.

"Okay, but this is our first New Year's together," I call out from the kitchen, grabbing a water after my vigorous midday *workout* with Dixon—in lieu of going to the gym, as the man so smartly rationalized. Definitely sounded like a fair trade to me, the only downside being the fact that I'm now dehydrated.

"I don't see how that means we should wear matching sequined shirts. Do I seem like a *sequin* guy to you?" he calls back.

I finish gulping my water before stepping out of the kitchen. "It's festive," I say, coming up short when I spot two figures standing near the front door. I yelp, covering my junk with my nearly empty water bottle.

"Hawthorne, cover your precious, virgin eyes," the man I immediately recognize as Dixon's friend Mateo—aka Silver—says. He holds one hand over his boyfriend's face.

Hawthorne, who looks every bit a rugged cowboy, hat included, rolls his eyes behind Mateo's splayed fingers. "Oh, please."

Mateo grins at me. "Honey, that water bottle isn't covering a thing."

"Dixon?" I call out. "We have company."

"The fuck?" he shouts back.

When Dixon emerges from his bedroom, gym shorts protecting his modesty, he tilts his head comically before crossing his arms and coming to a stop in front of me.

"A little warning would've been nice," he grumbles.

Mateo clutches his heart. "Oh, how I've missed you, too, dear friend."

Dixon sighs heavily, but when Mateo bounds up to him, he crushes the slighter man in a fierce hug. "Emergency key?" he asks, and Mateo nods. Dixon shakes his head, but his voice is fond when he says, "Fuck. It's good to see you, Mat."

"You, too, baby bear," Mateo says warmly, squeezing Dixon with all his might. Dixon, I notice, doesn't seem to be in any hurry to let go. "I also got to see quite a lot of that boyfriend of yours."

"Jesus Christ," Dixon grumbles, finally pushing Mateo away. Mateo laughs as Hawthorne walks up, he and Dixon shaking hands.

I slip away, grabbing shorts and a t-shirt before returning to the living room, where everyone is seated.

"The legendary Adonis," Mateo chirps as soon as I take a seat next to Dixon.

"In the flesh."

Dixon groans, but Mateo grins mischievously. "Come on, Dixon, it was the perfect introduction. It's like a reversal of how you met Hawthorne."

"Right, when you two were having phone sex *on this couch*," he grumps.

"Oh, I bet he was a dick about that," I say to Mateo.

Mateo laughs. "He *was*. You know him so well."

I shoot Dixon a grin, to which he looks affectionately exasperated. "It's nice to finally meet you two," I say.

"Likewise," Hawthorne says politely.

"Not that I don't love your shining company, Mat dearest, my little banana nut muffin, but why are you here?" Dixon asks.

"I wanted to check on you. And on Malibu," he answers.

Dixon's face softens. "I think he'll be fine. Niko is actually helping him with a financial plan."

"That's good," Mateo says, smiling softly. "And you?"

Dixon sighs. "You need me to say it? Fine, you win. You were right."

Mateo tilts his head. "About?"

Dixon grabs my hand, tugging me onto his lap and wrapping his arms around me. "I wanted to hate Niko because I knew he was different from the start. It scared me. I'd never had such an intense reaction to someone before, and it was easier to rationalize it away as animosity than admit to what it was."

My insides liquify as Mateo chuckles. "Dixon. I never actually said that. I suspected you were attracted to him, and yes, I encouraged you to take a risk in your love life. But I think, maybe, you inferred more from my words than what was there based on your own undiscovered feelings at the time."

Dixon pauses before he huffs. "Smartass."

"Never claimed to be otherwise," Mateo says lightly, sitting forward, eyes intent. "You're not going to want to hear this, Dixon, but I'm saying it anyway. I'm proud of you. You've taken a big step."

"Christ, Mat," Dixon mutters, shaking his head.

"Accept my love," Mateo retorts, a sly gleam overtaking his face. "Now what was this I heard about sequins?"

I bark out a laugh, rubbing Dixon's arm as the man sighs impatiently. "They're for tonight. The whole crew is meeting at Sublime. I assume you two will join us?"

Mateo claps his hands together once before leaning back to whisper something to Hawthorne, who blushes. "Wouldn't miss it," he says with a grin. "I can't wait to see the old gang again."

"They're gonna lose their shit," Dixon mutters.

"As they should," Mateo declares. "It's always nice to see old friends."

Dixon huffs at Mateo's pointed glare, but then he opens his arm wide. "All right. C'mon, then. Get in here."

Mateo lets out what can best be described as a *squee* before bounding over to the couch and crashing into Dixon's side, one arm around his friend and the other around me. "Hawthorne," he says sharply.

Hawthorne shakes his head, but there's a smile on his face as he gets out of his seat and comes over, bending down to join the fray.

Mateo sighs happily. "That's the stuff."

I crane my neck to catch a glimpse of Dixon, and although I'm sure he'd deny it with his last breath, his eyes look suspiciously moist. My chest warms, and I lean more of my weight against my boyfriend, smiling when he smudges a kiss against my cheek.

"So," Mateo says, not pulling back, "about those sequins."

Dixon would *not* wear the sequins after all, but he looks just as hot in his bright pink button-down. The man knows how to work a dress shirt, what can I say?

Sublime looks like a glittery wonderland when we step inside the club, with twinkling lights overhead and a large disco ball on a pole, ready to descend at midnight. There's a DJ off to the side of the dance floor mixing popular and traditional songs together, and the blend of dance and nostalgia is perfect for the occasion.

But the noise of the music has nothing on the surprised cheer that goes up when we reach the top of the stairs to the VIP lounge and the Elite 8 crew catches wind of Mateo. Alex positively shrieks, but much to my surprise, he runs straight for Hawthorne, giving the larger man an unruly hug. Hawthorne pats Alex's back, looking bemused.

Mateo has a massive grin on his face as he accepts a few pats on his own back, as well as several hugs, but before long, he politely disentangles himself and weaves through the crowd toward Malibu. When he finally reaches the blonde man, it's like the pair of them melt, embracing one another softly. I can't help but smile as the two talk quietly, Mateo running his hand over Malibu's hair and kissing his cheek as Malibu nods, eyes glistening under the multicolored lights of the club.

I'm so caught up in the happy reunion, I don't notice Dixon until he's wrapping his arm around me from behind. I turn my head, seeking a kiss, and he obliges, his lips pressing gently against my own, leaving behind a hint of gin and cranberry.

"What's that?" I ask, turning in his hold.

He hands me his drink. "New Year's cocktail special."

I take a sip and hum around the undiluted flavors of pine and tart cranberry. "Tastes like the holidays."

"Reminds me of you," he says.

"Yeah?" I ask with a little smile, honored to hold that association in Dixon's mind. I know how much this time of year means to him. How magical he finds it, as he once told me.

"Yeah," he replies quietly, his eyes casing my face and hair. He reaches up, brushing some of the strands behind my ear.

My phone buzzes in my pocket, and, reluctantly, I extract myself from my boyfriend. "One sec," I say, "that might be Kipp."

I check the screen, and sure enough, my friend's name flashes across the top. I jog off toward the stairs, and when I reach the bottom, Kipp is there waiting, held back by security.

"He's with me," I tell the guy, speaking loudly over the music. He nods, letting a wide-eyed Kipp past the VIP rope. I wave my friend forward. "C'mon."

Kipp follows me up the stairs, his blue eyes sweeping the balcony, a look of absolute wonder on his face. "This is amazing," he whisper-shouts, practically vibrating. "I can't believe I'm here. Thank you so much, Nik. Thank you, thank you."

"No problem," I say with a grin. "Why don't I introduce you to—"

"Is this the friend that got my picture?" a flirtatious voice calls out, its blonde owner bounding up not a moment later.

I huff out a laugh. "One and the same."

Alex grins, looping his arm through Kipp's. "Come with me, sugar. Let me show you a good time."

"Oh my God, oh my God, oh my God," Kipp chants, not sparing me a single parting glance as Alex leads his fanboy further into the fray. I grin at their backsides, shaking my head.

"I have a feeling you'll be getting a gift basket soon enough," Dixon says, walking up.

I latch back onto my boyfriend. "Knowing Kipp, it'll probably be filled with dildos. Any word from Marley and Jason?"

While I invited Kipp tonight, Dixon extended invites to his Hyped friends. Marley accepted easily, whereas Jason stammered a bit before nodding and disappearing into the back of the coffee shop.

"Marley texted that they're down below," he says, tugging me close and dipping his lips against my ear. "Come dance with me, Niki?"

My heart skips a beat, happy and electric inside my chest. "Show me your moves, baby."

Dixon leads me, hand in hand, down to the dance floor, and after a quick search, we find his favorite baristas in the crowd. I barely recognize Jason without his beanie, but he nods shyly when Dixon says hello. Marley, on the other hand, gives him a hug on tiptoes.

Once greetings have been exchanged, we claim a space nearby, and true to his word, Dixon shows me his moves. And damn, does the man know how to move. Pressed against his body song after song, sharing kisses, exchanging heated looks and tender ones, I can't imagine a better night than this right here.

New Year's, to me, has always felt special. There's something about the promise of a fresh year that makes me feel hopeful. It's like wishing on a star or making a bucket list. It's looking forward and deciding what you want your future to be. And this year, I know exactly what I want for once. It's this man holding me tight. I want him with me always. And based on the way Dixon can't seem to let go of me for even a moment, I sense he's feeling the same.

As I look around the room, I notice most of the Elite 8 crew have joined us on the main level. Mateo and Hawthorne are snuggled up close. Alex is entertaining a gleeful Kipp. Marco is dancing beside Nathaniel, who's dressed in a black button-down for once instead of his usual argyle. Even surrounded by countless bodies, my eyes easily find each and every one of the men and women who've welcomed me into their found family, including Malibu, who's slow-dancing with Emil.

But when a cheer goes up, my gaze settles forward, and I lock onto the one man whose acceptance has meant the most. Center stage, the ball starts to drop, and a hush falls over the crowd. Everyone stops. Everyone stares. But I only have eyes for Dixon. And when the glittering orb reaches the bottom, signaling the dawn of a new era, Dixon and I meet in the middle, our lips drawn together on instinct. A mutual wish. A shared resolution.

It's almost deafening, the yells and the whistling of the crowd as the calendar year rolls over, and when we part, confetti streams down and decorates the air between us like fireworks. But through it all, Dixon watches me, love shining in his eyes. Even though we haven't said it yet, it's there. I can see it, and I can feel it.

I'll give him the words before dawn.

"I hope next New Year's is just like this one," Dixon says, leaning in close and brushing a piece of confetti off my nose.

"It will be," I assure him over the noise, pressing my cheek against his and breathing in his minty, fresh scent, stronger now than the lingering notes of the cocktail. "I'm not going anywhere. Ever."

"Is that your way of telling me you're my happy ending?" he asks, voice wistful and tender.

I smile against his skin. "No, griniári mou. This is only our beginning."

Epilogue
Dixon

Four Years Later

Do you believe in love at first sight?

Neither did I.

Shows what I know.

The breeze is gentle as I wait at the edge of the short, coppery-colored ledge of rocks that lead down into the Aegean Sea. I look behind me on instinct, like somehow I just *know* he's almost here.

And like a linen-swathed gift, there he is. Niko fucking Adamos, strutting up like he's on a goddamn catwalk, even though we're the only two people here on this private beachfront at the resort we're staying at in Greece. His long hair is pulled back, but a few tendrils escape, crossing his face in the breeze. His clothes billow away from his body, the light fabric looking ethereal in the low, evening light.

Goddamn Greek god, and he's all mine.

"Took you long enough," I grouse.

Niko rolls his eyes, gripping my chin to claim a kiss before he sidles up next to me and looks out over the deep, blue-green waters.

"My apologies, your highness."

"Why do you always walk like that?" I tease. "You're such a fucking peacock."

"My *God*," Niko says, laughing. "That's just the way I walk."

"It's ridiculous. You're too goddamn sexy."

"Is that right?" he asks, angling toward me. He brushes his hand down his own chest, the ring on his finger glinting in the light. "After all these years, I still got it?"

"I don't know why I put up with you," I reply, even as my eyes follow the seductive trail of Niko's fingers as they dip lightly into his waistband.

"It's because you love me."

"I suppose you're right," I concede.

Niko laughs. "I'm always right, husband."

I hum, watching the golden glow of sunlight diminish over the gently rolling waves down below us. The water crashes lightly against the shoreline, a continuous swell and ebb of static.

"Last night here," Niko muses, mimicking my own thoughts. I'm not quite ready for our vacation to be over.

"Back to the grind," I agree.

"Literally," Niko says with a snort. "Get it? Because of the amount of grinding involved?"

"Yes, I understood perfectly," I say as Niko's chuckle rolls over me like the sound of the waves. "And maybe for you. Not for me anymore."

"Once a porn star, always a porn star."

I suppose that's true. Even though, as of earlier this year, I'm not filming anymore. But my videos will always be out there. Niko and I did end up doing another two "seasons," as Jerome called them, of our boyfriend arc. Fans ate it up. We also filmed plenty of single scenes together, which were a lot of fun, like our own little world of roleplay. Even though I enjoyed being able to work alongside Niko, it was simply my time to move on from the porn industry.

Luckily, that transition proved easier than expected. It just so happened that the manager of the gym I frequented was looking to expand their personal training services. After talking it over and getting the appropriate certifications, he hired me onto his staff. I've had a steady business of clients ever since, including several cast and crew members from Elite 8.

Niko, however, still works at the studio. He's not sure how much longer he'll perform, but his fans adore him. I can't blame them. I adore him, too. Although I'd never be caught dead saying so in those particular words.

"Do you remember that one time," Niko says, laughing before he's even finished his sentence, "during one of our last scenes together, how pissed off Jerome got?"

"Yeah," I reply with a chuckle, switching into my Jerome impression. "*For fuck's sake, you two, get rid of the goddamn heart eyes. You're not in love within these walls! You're strangers fucking in the storage closet of a seedy club. One of you probably has herpes. Quit the cutesy shit. This isn't happily ever after!*"

He was wrong about that last part, but I didn't dare tell him so.

Niko wipes his eye, his smile a mile wide. "What can I say? It was our anniversary. I was feeling sentimental."

"I like you sentimental," I admit.

"Don't let anyone back home hear you say that. You might lose your grumpy bear reputation."

"You're a pain in my ass," I grumble halfheartedly.

"Sometimes," he says with a wink.

I roll my eyes. "I like it here. But I also like home."

Home is still my apartment. Only now, it's *our* apartment. Niko moved in the summer after our first New Year's together, shortly after Cassandra's husband Carlos returned home. And Malibu, well, he moved out long ago.

It's still the same place as it was before, but now it has Niko. And *that's* why it's home.

"Yeah. I like home, too," he agrees softly, tucking against my side, our arms around one another as we watch the pinks and oranges of the sunset filter into the night sky, illuminating the surface of the water below like a hazy dream.

"Griniári mou," Niko whispers fondly into the breeze, as if he's thanking the endless horizon in front of us for bringing him me, *his grump*. As if *he's* the lucky one, when I know, for a fact, that's me.

To have found this whirlwind of a man who loves me just the way I am, who's endlessly patient and resoundingly happy. Whose family brought me into the fold like I'd been there all along. This man who challenges me, who pushes me when I need it, but who knows exactly when to back off and is equally adept at handling me with care. He's beautiful and he's funny and he makes me happy every single day.

I'm definitely the lucky one. I know that.

Nevertheless, I reply in kind, whispering my own benediction into the salty air. A quiet thank you. A gentle reminder of what I've gained.

"Agápi mou," I say. '*My love.*'

The End

About the Author

Information about Emmy Sanders and her complete list of works can be found on her website. Subscribe to her newsletter, join her Facebook reader group, Emmy's Enclave, and connect via email or social media:

www.emmysanders.com

Find online:
www.facebook.com/emmysandersmm
www.instagram.com/emmysandersmm